By Steven W. Horn

Sam Dawson Mystery Series

YESTERDAY CALLING

NO GOOD DEED

WHEN THEY WERE YOUNG

WHEN GOOD MEN DIE

THE PUMPKIN EATER

Also by Steven W. Horn

ANOTHER MAN'S LIFE

YESTERDAY CALLING

YESTERDAY CALLING

A Sam Dawson Mystery

STEVEN W. HORN

GPP GRANITE
PEAK PRESS Cheyenne

Cheyenne, Wyoming
www.granitepeakpress.com

GRANITE
PEAK PRESS
Granite Peak Press
www.granitepeakpress.com

This book is a work of fiction. Names, characters, places, businesses, corporations, organizations, and incidents either are products of the author's imagination or are used fictitiously without any intent to describe their actual conduct. Any resemblance to actual events or locales or persons, living or dead, is entirely coincidental.

First printing 2022

ISBN: 978-0-9991248-4-0
LCCN: 2022930957

ATTENTION CORPORATIONS, UNIVERSITIES, COLLEGES, AND PROFESSIONAL ORGANIZATIONS: Quantity discounts are available on bulk purchases of this book for educational purposes. Special books or book excerpts can also be created to fit specific needs. For information, please contact Granite Peak Press, P.O. Box 2597, Cheyenne, WY 82003, or email: info@granitepeakpress.com.

Printed in the United States of America
10 9 8 7 6 5 4 3 2 1

For those who read and share—
Book Clubs

CHAPTER 1

September 2011

Hello," Sam said, slightly out of breath, pressing the cool receiver to his sweaty ear. He swallowed the mouthful of potato chips he had grabbed on the way in and swept the salt from the corners of his mouth.

"Is this Sam Dawson?" The man's voice was distant and weak.

"Ye-es." Sam drew out the vowel impatiently. He paid the phone company extra every month for an unlisted number. Still, he received unwanted solicitations. This one was interrupting his plans. Anticipating a hard winter, Sam had been pushing to finish splitting the jag of wood he had unloaded the day before. The *Farmer's Almanac* warned of below-average temperatures and above-average snowfall for 2011, and September had borne that out with early fall colors.

He glanced at the kitchen clock. It was just past 11:30, almost time for lunch. *Wrong again,* he thought as beads of sweat slid down his face. Sam sighed. He tilted his ball cap back on his head and dragged a dirty sleeve across his forehead. The caller did not speak. "Hello?" Sam repeated.

"This is Hank Thompson."

Sam waited. He had to remind himself to breathe. It was his turn. He stalled. "Who?" he lied. He knew exactly who he was. Sam had never spoken to the man but he had waited a lifetime for this call.

"Hank Thompson," the man repeated softly, then cleared his throat.

Sam's mind raced. He was tempted to tell him he must have the wrong number, hang up, pull the phone from the wall, and cut the line. Instead, he inhaled deeply and said, "Yes?" He was surprised by the weakness in his own voice. It was an acknowledgment of the past, an admission of guilt.

"Val died on Tuesday."

Sam did not respond. He waited. What could he say? What was he supposed to say? Grief would come to him later. So would all the things he should have said.

"I thought you should know."

Sam still could not find the words. He closed his eyes and inhaled slowly.

Hank Thompson hung up the phone with a gentle click, then silence. Valentina Thompson was dead.

CHAPTER 2

June 1979

When Sam was fifteen, his father had taken him to the Social Security office to apply for the number that the world would use to identify him, track his every movement, and collect his contribution to society. He had done the same for Sam's sister five years earlier. The following year she disappeared. His father never laughed or smiled again.

After Sam's sixteenth birthday, he joined the adult population, got a job, paid taxes, and ran on life's treadmill. His father considered an allowance akin to welfare and believed it would result in dependency. Sam had argued to no avail that childhood was a form of social dependency and necessitated financial support. His father insisted work, like Wonder Bread, would build strong bodies, and frugality would build strong minds. Sam delivered newspapers, cut lawns, and caddied for his spending money.

Sam was only interested in three things: fishing, cars, and girls—not necessarily in that order. Fish were easy and free for the taking. Plenty of them packed the streams in and around Boulder, Colorado, where he grew up. This summer, his plans included hooking a big brown trout that lived in Boulder Creek below the 28th Street Bridge. He also had his eye on a '63 Mercury Comet convertible at Dealin' Bob's Used Cars out on Baseline Road. Sam and the car were the same age.

Cars, however, were strictly dependent on cash, of which he had little. The girls were everywhere—and totally unavailable. He was not sure why he was attracted. He determined it was curiosity. They were just different. He avoided them. Still, there was an attraction.

The Left Hand Lodge and Restaurant was within biking distance and they needed a busboy that summer. Black dress slacks, white shirt, black bow tie, and a starched white linen jacket transformed Sam the Boy into Sam the Well-Dressed Nerd, a dweeb with a pimple and an Adam's apple that caused his bow tie to twitch when he talked. The waitresses wore shiny brown dresses trimmed in white, and linen tiaras pinned to the top of their heads. For some reason, the Fair Labor Standards Act exempted food service people from the minimum wage of $2.90. The waitresses were dependent on tips. The busboy was dependent on the waitresses to supplement his meager $2.00 per hour. They each grudgingly gave him a dollar at the end of their shifts. Three waitresses meant three bucks. Sam figured he would have enough to buy the Comet by the time he applied for Social Security.

Valentina Thompson, the hostess, was a black-haired beauty with big dark eyes that took Sam's breath away and caused him to stutter and say things that made no sense. She wore tasteful tight-fitting evening dresses with dipping necklines, and high heels that accentuated her perfect rear end when she walked seductively toward a table, the oversized menus clutched to her propped-up bosom. Her thick Russian accent was straight out of a James Bond movie. When she leaned in and whispered to set up a table for six or to clean table number three, her breath on his cheek would cause Sam's heart to race. She was twenty-one, married, mother of one, and perfect. He was sixteen, gangly, inarticulate, and dumbfounded when around her. Not to mention he rode a bicycle to work, for crying out loud. He was the opposite of cool. At his age, the five years that separated them was analogous to a geological epoch. She was a woman, an adult, and to be avoided if he was to be saved from his stupidity.

One particularly slow evening, Sam was in the kitchen folding the linen napkins that came back flat and stiff from the laundry. Valentina, without asking, positioned herself across the stainless steel table and began helping him. Her satiny hair, glistening like the coat of a well-groomed thoroughbred, shielded one eye when she leaned forward. He could not help looking down the front of her dress as she repeatedly reached across the table to secure another napkin. "So you're Russian, huh?" he heard his stupid self ask.

She looked at him curiously and smiled. "I am half Russian and half German."

"Which half is Russian?" Sam said seriously.

She smiled broadly with luscious red lips, winked at him, and said, "The good half."

Small talk was not his game. She was to be avoided.

CHAPTER 3
September 2011

The early fall air was crisp. Sam sat out on the deck watching the day's light slowly slip away. His bloodhound, L2, sat next to the porch swing. He gently kneaded her large, soft ear. A strand of drool trickled from the corner of her mouth to the floor. The aspen leaves were glowing as though phosphorescent, while the pines discreetly faded into the background of night.

"A penny for your thoughts," Sidney said as she joined her father on the swing, a mug of tea cupped in her hands. Her hearing aids squealed when she swept a wayward strand of jet-black hair away from the temples of her heavy eyeglasses.

Sam smiled and continued to stare toward the aspen grove. "I was thinking about an old cigar box, King Edward Imperial, which I had for years. It was filled with useless little treasures I'd saved when I was young. The box still had the faint odor of cigars. There were a couple of lead soldiers—one holding a bazooka on his shoulder and another carrying the American flag. There was a polished agate or two, some Monopoly money, a broken compass, a collection of rabies tags from long-dead dogs, a two-dollar bill, poker chips, a Zippo lighter that didn't work, and a love letter from a woman I knew before I met your mother."

"I didn't know men kept things like love letters," Sidney said, smiling at her father.

Sam shook his head slowly and grinned. "I wasn't a man then. I was just a boy in transition. I hid the cigar box in the attic of the garage. It was my secret. I never told anyone about it. Not the guys, not my mother, no one, until now." He looked into the forest twilight. "I should have thrown the letter away. I'd read it so many times, I had it memorized. Years later, I found the cigar box right where I had stashed it." Sam paused and took a deep breath, then a long exhale. "Of course, I always knew exactly where it was. Scarcely a day had gone by back then and even now, that I had not thought about that letter…and her."

"Pretty mushy, huh?"

Sam chuckled and smiled broadly, deepening the creases at the corners of his eyes. "No. Not a single 'I love you' in the entire thing. It was a tender declaration of loss of innocence and stolen youth, both hers and mine. More than anything else it was an expression of what could have been. Lost dreams, I guess." He paused to remember. "It was beautifully written and scared the living bejesus out of me."

Sidney furrowed her brow as she looked at her father. "Why?"

Sam had a way of rubbing his chin when deep in thought. The roughness of his beard stubble scraped audibly against his calloused fingers while Sidney waited. "Life's full of decisions. Sometimes we make good decisions, sometimes bad ones. Did you ever wonder how different your life would have turned out if you had made some other choice way back when? Chose the road less traveled? Think of the little choices that could have changed your life entirely. Make the wrong one and end up unhappy or in prison. Make the right one and end up unhappy or in prison. Life's a crapshoot. We can't control outcomes. As Yogi Berra said, 'The future ain't what it used to be.'"

"Well, I for one am glad you made the decisions you did. Otherwise I wouldn't be here."

Sam nodded. "I read the letter one more time after your mother and I were married, then ceremoniously burned it. It would have been hard to explain. Tonight though, I wish I had it to read just one more time, to sit and remember."

"Why tonight?" Sidney asked softly.

"Because, she died on Tuesday," he said without looking at her.

CHAPTER 4
October 2011

The state of Wyoming has a hundred and sixty cemeteries, give or take. Texas has fifty thousand. Sam believed he had just discovered a cornucopia of financial opportunities that could keep a photographer like him fully employed for the remainder of his unfulfilled life. Earlier, he had published four large-format coffee-table pictorials of lost or obscure cemeteries, but the royalties did not even cover his monthly utilities. His calendars and greeting cards of scenic alpine imagery no longer paid the bills. He needed a fresh approach and new financial backing.

Sam preferred the quiet solitude of graveyards and the still-life quality of weathered tombstones. Who better to photograph, catalog, and record the historically important reminders of the past than him? He had worked diligently on a grant proposal to the Wyoming Department of State Parks and Cultural Resources, only to find out they funded local government—city and county—projects exclusively. He turned to the Wyoming State Historical Society and made the pitch that cemeteries were one of the most valuable historic resources in the state. Making the past accessible to the future seemed to be the Society's mission, even though their grants were typically small and would not even cover the operating expenses of such a large project. He stressed that the state's historical record needed a photographic catalog of Wyoming's cemeteries, which were being threatened by urban development, uncontrolled vegetation, uncompassionate cattle, vandalism, and neglect. He did not mention the limited market for a book that consolidated all the state's cemeteries—county by county, city by city—between two covers. It would be essential for Sam to retain all rights to the publications. The deadline for proposals was looming. Grants for the upcoming year would be made midwinter.

Texas was more receptive and seemed better prepared to fund such an undertaking. The downside, of course, was that it would take years to complete and would require him to be gone for long periods of time. That did not sit well with Sam. With a law degree from the University of Wyoming, Sidney was the current breadwinner of the family. Her legal consulting business continued to grow. But the progressively degenerative effects of Usher syndrome were slowly robbing her of sight and sound. She could no longer drive at night. And she was troubled by the prospect of someday having to turn down clients or add staff to her one-person office. Though she refused to be defined by her genetic disorder, Sam preferred to stay as close to home as possible.

"It's for you, Pop," Sidney yelled from her office, the former guest bedroom.

Sam picked up the extension in his study. "Hello?"

"The day she died it was incredibly quiet," Hank Thompson said calmly, continuing the conversation from the week before, as though the days and nights had blended into a single afternoon. "Funny what you think about when you suddenly realize you'll never speak to a person again."

Sam said nothing. He listened.

"Did you let the dog out? Don't forget to take out the trash. How many times do I have to ask you to turn off the light in the pantry?" Hank Thompson paused for what seemed an eternity. "The quiet never stops. My ears ring from the absence of her voice. At this point I'd accept anything—a complaint, a nag, a clearing of her throat. Do you have any idea how wasted language is, Mr. Dawson? Words are like raindrops on a tin roof. They just mean it's raining."

Sam closed his eyes to better concentrate on the soft, faltering voice a hundred miles to the south in Boulder, Colorado. Was the man waiting for a response? What was he supposed to say? What could he say?

Again, without a word of goodbye, Hank Thompson hung up the phone.

CHAPTER 5

July 1979

The Left Hand Lodge and Restaurant sprawled over several acres in northwest Boulder. Two rows of tidy log cabins with green-shingled roofs amid giant blue spruce and ponderosa pine gave the motel a mountain chateau ambiance, when in fact, it was surrounded by semiarid foothills. A spectacular view of the flatirons—the reddish triangular hogback that jutted upward at the base of the mountains to the south, added to the illusion. A turquoise swimming pool completed the picture-postcard appearance of the 1950s-era tourist attraction. Sam was offered the job of groundskeeper, pool man, handyman, and parking lot sweeper during the day to supplement his nighttime busboy duties. He bought the Mercury.

There was no overtime, no benefits, and he had to punch the clock for lunch and breaks. His hardened body glistened in the sun and tanned up like the Coppertone girl. He would punch out at 4:00 p.m., shower in the tiny dressing room for the waitresses, change into his evening garb, and punch back in at 5:00 p.m. The restaurant closed at 10:00. Sam would then strip the tables and reset them for breakfast, vacuum the carpeted dining rooms, and mop the lunch-counter floor. Seldom did he finish before 11:00. Twelve-hour workdays were the norm. On a slow night, Valentina would close one of the dining rooms so

Sam could set it up and vacuum early. She often stayed until he was finished, busying herself by tabulating receipts, counting money, folding napkins, and sorting silverware. She would remove her high heels and tie her hair back in a ponytail while humming cheerfully. Sam kept a furtive eye on her. He could not help it. He believed she was the most beautiful woman in the world. Most likely a Russian spy trained to kill. She was to be avoided.

On a hot July night after locking up, Sam raced downstairs to the dressing room to gather his work clothes and shed his dorky busboy uniform. He was eager to jump into the Comet, put the top down, and drag Pearl Street once before heading home. The shower was running. The stall was separated from the dressing room and lockers, where the waitresses kept their uniforms, by a threadbare shower curtain that was partially open. Valentina's dress and undergarments were draped over the bench in front of Sam's locker. He glanced toward the shower and saw flesh-colored movement through the two-inch gap where the curtain failed to meet the wall. Sam froze. He could not breathe. He could not swallow. He backed slowly away and quietly took two stairs at a time in an exaggerated upward climb to the landing, then out the door to the parking lot. She was to be avoided.

CHAPTER 6

October 2011

A gunshot echoed across the canyon. The large-bore rifle sound carried on the October wind above the rustling aspen, their golden leaves raining to the ground. Big-game season had opened. The national forest that surrounded Sam's property, normally quiet, was punctuated by an occasional round fired at a nervous deer or elk. Sam was nervous too, since it was his favorite time of the year for taking nature photos and wetting a line in the many streams and beaver ponds that surrounded his land. His isolated mountain home provided the ideal backdrop for his fly-fishing obsession. Recently, he had come to realize that fishing was the excuse he needed to bathe in the solitude and grandeur of nature. He loved Wyoming.

Sidney's horse, Daisy, had raised her head and pointed her ears toward the unnatural sound coming from the forest. Sam eyed both his daughter and her horse through the open barn door as he worked at the log pile across the driveway, filling the log carrier for the night's fire. He smiled with pride at the sight of his brilliant daughter, who moved with the confident grace of an athlete. It was a beautiful fall day—bright blue skies with billowy white clouds. He almost forgot about the winter that would begin in earnest in another month.

Sam would drive to Laramie after lunch to meet with the Department of Communication and Journalism head at the

University of Wyoming. He and Sidney had argued for the past several days over his reluctance to accept another temporary instructor position to teach Introduction to Photography. The professor he had filled in for almost four years earlier now had prostate cancer and was scheduled for surgery, chemotherapy, and irradiation at the start of spring semester. Sam had found teaching incredibly frustrating. The art form of photography and its mechanics came in a distant fourth behind grades, sex, and their annoying smart phones, which they thought were cameras.

Sidney had not-so-tactfully reminded him of all his recent failures, his troublesome relationships, his lack of focus, and his inability to finish a project. His excuses were weak and she had quickly dismissed them. Sam argued that a low-paying, non-benefited, temporary teaching job, which would not even cover his monthly health insurance premium, was not the answer to either his career or his financial woes. Sam worried the theme of their arguments had become repetitive. He was active and fit, but pushing fifty nonetheless. He wondered if there might be some validity to her assertion that he seemed lost in space, that his midlife crisis had turned into a permanent state of affairs, and that he needed professional help, perhaps grief counseling. He had been unable to move on after Annie's death. She was the love of his life, the woman who inspired him. She had saved Sidney's life but had died doing so. He could not help feeling responsible. Photography had been his total preoccupation. His published pictorials of lost and forgotten cemeteries and scenic alpine imagery had both satisfied his creative needs and provided a modest living for him and his daughter. After Annie died, his creativity drained from him like ooze from rotting flesh. Nothing motivated him.

The phone rang as Sam struggled through the door with the log carrier. He quickly picked it up, hoping it was the department secretary calling to say his meeting with the department head was cancelled. "This is Sam Dawson," he said as if he were running a business.

"Before she died, she told me she wasn't sorry she had made me cry," Hank Thompson said. "She wasn't sorry for telling me about you and how she felt. She said her memories of you had made her happy in an otherwise unhappy life and she had no regrets about it."

Sam closed his eyes and nodded his head toward the floor. He had hoped these troubling phone calls were over with. It had been several weeks since the last one.

"She didn't care about all the years I had worshipped her, provided for her, cared for her when she became ill." He paused as if he needed to recover from the pain of disclosure. "Funny how you think you know someone, the person you spent your life with. Then one day they remove the mask of the beautiful person you loved and you discover that underneath is this horribly disfigured monster that reaches down your throat, pulls out your heart, and hands it to you."

Sam did not like the tone or the direction of this conversation. "Mr. Thompson, what is it you want from me?"

"I want you dead, of course. I want you to join her in hell." With that, Hank Thompson hung up.

Shaken to the point of trembling, Sam slowly carried the firewood to the living room. Halfway there, his feet crunched shards of broken glass littering the floor.

CHAPTER 7

August 1979

The restaurant at the Left Hand Lodge closed early on Sunday evenings. At 7:00 p.m. Valentina would place the closed sign on the door and pleasantly turn away disappointed customers who could not comprehend the meaning of the word. Sam's vacuum sweeper, an upright Hoover that sucked noisily at around seventy decibels, could usually drive the slow eaters out the door by 8:00. In the summer months, enough daylight remained that, if he hurried, he could join his friends, Woody and Chip, outside the ice cream shop downtown. There, the popular guys would smoke and exchange boisterous stories that always fell into one of three categories: how smart they were, how tough they were, and, of course, their sexual conquests. The most popular guys could lie convincingly and spin a yarn that embodied all three concepts while ogling and making lewd comments to the girls who frequented the store.

Sam was not considered a popular guy. Rather, he was a congenial bystander, an audience member who could laugh on cue and nod approvingly at the outrageous assaults on credibility and acceptable human behavior. Tall for a sixteen-year-old, almost lanky, Sam could immediately disarm an aggressor or befriend a stranger with his contagious smile. But he had no yarns to spin with his friends, thought cigarettes disgusting, kept his honor roll status to himself, and believed fighting was best confined to the organized sports of football and wrestling. His sexual conquests were restricted to a few somewhat frightening and totally embarrassing dreams. Sam knew girls were to be avoided. Still he was curious.

The August night was sticky, rare for Boulder's elevation. The day's heat seemed trapped just aboveground as Sam exited the restaurant and locked the back door behind him. He was always the last to leave. The smell of chlorine reminded him that in a few hours he would be cleaning the pool, changing the filters, and adding the foul-smelling chemical to the reservoir in the pump house, thus beginning another day of work. He wondered if this was his future—eat, sleep, and work. He would ask the guys at the ice cream shop, though he suspected they did not know the answer. He imagined they would someday graduate from root beer floats to Coors Light and be telling the same stories in the bar at the bowling alley.

Sam rounded the pump house and headed for the parking lot. A splash from the pool startled him. Cautiously, he slipped back into the shadow of the restaurant and peeked around the corner toward the pool. All the lights were off. The soft moonlight reflected from the uneven surface of the water as Valentina glided along silently at the deep end of the pool, her ponytail trailing behind. Her clothes were piled neatly on a lounge chair near the diving board. She was naked.

Sam could feel his heart pounding at the back of his throat, his eardrums keeping cadence. The water was dark. He could imagine what was just below the surface. Aside from an occasional dirty magazine shared with Woody and Chip, he had never seen a naked woman, a live one anyway. His body trembled and his breath came in spasms, not from some perverse Peeping Tom gratification, he realized. Rather, it was from fear. This woman scared him half to death and he was unsure why. He was certain of one thing, however. She was to be avoided.

Sam backed away slowly and made a hasty retreat toward the parking lot, where he hoped he would be able to catch his breath. "Holy crap," he managed to whisper as he slid behind the wheel of the Comet. *Wait until the guys hear about this.* With a little embellishment, he finally had a story to tell his friends at the ice cream shop. For years afterward, he wondered why he never told anyone.

CHAPTER 8
October 2011

"Crazy bastards hopped up on booze and testosterone, out wandering around in the woods shootin' at anything that moves," Sheriff Harrison O'Malley said as he probed the tiny hole in the log wall next to the fireplace. "Looks like thirty caliber, maybe two-seventy. I can dig it out if you want, Sam. It's gonna leave a big messy hole in your living room wall." Standing back, the sheriff hunched down and squinted across the room toward the French doors leading to the deck. "I'd say it came from the ridge on the other side of the valley." He grinned. "I believe that's Albany County," he said, pointing across the valley. "That's out of my jurisdiction."

Sam rolled his eyes. "Everything is out of your jurisdiction. I thought you represented the law and weren't encumbered by political boundaries." Sam knew the answer. His friend had been elected repeatedly by the people of Laramie County, the most populous county in the least populous state. Nestled in the southeast corner of the tenth largest state by area, the sheriff oversaw nearly two hundred employees centered in Cheyenne, the state's capital.

"It's complicated," said the sheriff with a wink. "You're lucky it only took out the one pane."

"I'm lucky that Sidney was in the barn mucking out Daisy's stall. I can't tell you what I would have done if she had been injured, or worse. She'll be twenty-eight in a couple of weeks and I've kind of gotten used to having her around." Sam smiled at his daughter, then turned back toward the sheriff. "Look, if I'd been in the house, a foot or two to the right, it would have splattered my brains all over the room," he said, his voice rising with irritation.

"You and I both know you don't have enough brains to make that kind of a mess," the sheriff said, smiling. The ends of his handlebar mustache exaggerated his look of amusement. He liked Sam Dawson. A seemingly mismatched relationship born of disaster nearly four years earlier had evolved into a friendship that always included put-downs and barbs.

"Amen to that," Sidney said as she handed a mug of coffee to the sheriff. "You want your muffin heated, Harrison?"

"No thanks, Sid. I'll take it cold." He pulled a chair out from the kitchen table, removed his Stetson, and sat down. "Any reason to think this wasn't just an accident? Any threatening letters or phone calls?" he asked, looking at Sam.

"Just the usual."

"You owe money to anybody?"

"Everybody."

"Been sniffin' around anybody's wife?"

"Not for several days." Sam walked to the French doors and looked across the valley. The sheriff's question had struck a nerve. The last call he received from Hank Thompson, while disturbing, was not explicitly threatening.

"What about her?" the sheriff said and nodded toward L2, the puddle of flesh and fur on the deck. "Did she respond to the gunshot?"

Sam sniffed and shook his head. "Her hearing is shot." A ground squirrel scampered across the deck, its tail held high as if it had just captured L2's flag. L2's head came up and she stared at the retreating rodent, pondering the energy required to pursue it. She lay back down, stretched her legs to the side, spread her toes, and yawned. Sam loved his bloodhound, his constant companion and successor to Elle, his first bloodhound. She smelled bad, drooled, and passed noxious gas that would turn a zombie away. "If it doesn't involve food or a belly rub, she couldn't care less."

The sheriff sipped his coffee. "Look, Sam. What do you want me to do about this?"

"How about you call the Forest Service and get them to create some kind of a 'no hunting' buffer around my place?"

"It's public land. It would take the feds years and a bunch of town hall–type meetings before they could make a decision. You don't know what red tape is."

"What about Game and Fish?"

"Same sort of a deal, Sam. You live on an inholding surrounded by national forest. You don't have your property fenced or posted. Even if I found the person who shot out your window, I couldn't charge them with anything that would stick. Reckless endangerment is a possibility. What do you think, Sid?"

"That whole concept is pretty loosey-goosey. You'd have to prove the accused's behavior was careless in a way that endangered the rights or safety of the public. That'd be tough to apply to someone hunting way out in the forest. If they shot at a deer standing in the middle of a grade school playground during recess, you might have a case."

Sheriff O'Malley beamed. "I love this girl, Sam. I wish she would come work for me."

"You can't afford her." Sam paused, then said, "Hell, I can't afford her either. She eats like a horse, never fills up the gas tank on the truck, and leaves the lights on during the day. She's my legal beagle, and you can't have her."

The sheriff smiled and shook his head. "Without her, Sam, you'd be my best customer at the county jail. Say, is there any chance I could get you to donate a book or two for the silent auction at our annual Sheriffs' Association meeting? We're meeting up in Casper this year."

"Sure. I'd like to tell you I need the deduction. Something from nothing is still nothing, however. Pick a couple from the shelf before you leave and I'll sign them," he said, gesturing toward the floor-to-ceiling bookshelves lining the west wall of the living room.

"Working on anything interesting?" Sheriff O'Malley asked.

"What's interesting to me and what's interesting to potential publishers or funders are two different things. Sidney wants me to take another temporary teaching job at the university. I'd rather crawl through ground glass and drink purple porpoise pus."

"That reminds me...my counterpart over in Laramie was asking about you last week. It seems that sometime way back, the university or the city—I'm not sure which, moved some smaller cemeteries to create Greenhill Cemetery on the outskirts of town. Of course, Greenhill is now almost in the center of the University of Wyoming campus. Anyway, long story short, the city and university did a piss-poor—excuse my French—job of moving bodies and simply built over the top of some of the graves. Apparently one of the cemeteries was where Merica Hall or Knight Hall now stands. There is so much superstructure and infrastructure in and around them that ground penetrating radar is useless. The sheriff wanted to know if I thought you might be able to find the graves."

"I've published several books on lost cemeteries, and now everyone thinks I have some sort of magic wand I can wave and out pops dead people. What'd you tell him?"

"I told him I'd talk to you."

"Is there money involved?"

"I doubt it. Lots of personal satisfaction, I'll bet."

"I could use some of that." Sam smiled. "Why are they trying to find this lost cemetery?"

The sheriff looked down and twisted the end of his moustache between his thumb and forefinger. "I don't know. I suspect it has something to do with all the stories about things that go bump in the night."

"I've heard some of those rumors," Sidney chimed in. "Merica Hall started out as a women's dormitory and is said to be haunted. I've been in it a couple of times and it's cold, dark, and spooky. I think the university uses it mostly for storage since they can't seem to keep people in it. I wouldn't wander around in there at night."

"Well, I'm not about to go wandering around there day or night," Sam said with a note of finality. "In case you haven't noticed, dowsing for graves is viewed suspiciously by most educated people. What credibility I have left, I need to preserve. As far as ghosts are concerned, I'm not buying it."

"Even after what Annie went through?" Sidney asked softly. She was hesitant to bring up the frightening experiences her deceased friend, her father's soul mate, had encountered in the isolated ranch house they had called Horse Creek Creepy.

Sam shot her a serious look. He seldom spoke of Annie. It was too painful, their love cut short by a serial killer. "Who knows what Annie really saw or heard? She had a terminal brain tumor that most likely accounted for a lot of it. Look, I believe in inexplicable phenomena, not ghosts. The answer is no."

"One thing for sure," Sheriff O'Malley said, standing and putting on his cowboy hat, "it wasn't a ghost that fired that bullet into your living room." He smiled at Sam. "If it happens again and you're still alive, give me a call."

"I knew I could count on you for sage advice."

The sheriff thanked Sidney for her hospitality before Sam walked him to his pickup truck. The sun felt good on Sam's shoulders in the crisp fall morning. The aspen had shed most of their leaves, which rustled like wrapping paper with every step.

"Sam, I've been in this business for most of my life, and often I've found that it's what people don't tell me that is most important." He gave Sam that broad O'Malley smile, made broader by his upturned moustache and a quick wink. "Drop by when you feel like talking."

Sam watched the sheriff's pickup disappear down the long driveway, aspen leaves fluttering from the ground in its wake. Familiar pangs of guilt washed coldly over him, displacing the sun's warmth, betraying secrets too uncomfortable to share.

CHAPTER 9

September 1979

Tommie Tucker was Sam's first true girlfriend. He'd had boyhood crushes on a couple of neighborhood girls, even kissed the one who owned the wiener dog that lived across the alley. It was Tommie, however, who stole his heart at the beginning of his junior year in high school.

She was a sophomore, as pure and innocent as a child bride. They were a pair as they fumbled through the complexities of a romantic relationship. Her given name was Thomasina, after a cat from a movie of the same name that came out the year before Tommie was born. She did not particularly care for cats—or the vulgar feline nickname some boys tried to assign her that referred to her genitals. A bit of a tomboy, Tommie was not to be trifled with. Feminine, almost sexy, one minute, she could become aggressively masculine when offended. Sam liked her a lot. He believed she was the prettiest girl in school, and he enjoyed the added bonus of her somewhat rough-and-tumble approach to teasing—he never had to defend her. When she became a cheerleader, Sam feared she would rush onto the wrestling mat if he found himself bested by an opponent. They were inseparable. Their relationship was not clingy or mushy; rather, it was a best-of-friends bond. Woody and Chip accused him of being pussy-whipped and always referred to her as Cat

Girl, which they embellished with meow sounds. Sam knew they were jealous.

At the time, Sam believed he and Tommie would always be together. He played to her soft side and held her hand at homecoming dances and proms. She easily accommodated his manly pursuits, learning to fly-fish and ride a dirt bike, even though she preferred to cast a worm and bobber or ride a horse. He enjoyed how her naïveté matched his inexperience and how they awkwardly approached adulthood together. He liked how she smelled.

Sam was unsure if such a thing as women's intuition really existed. He learned they often saw things differently than guys did. They picked up on subtle mannerisms—especially from other women, that totally escaped most men. The day Sam and Tommie ran into Valentina at Waldenbooks demonstrated this phenomenon in spades. Before his eyes, Thomasina turned into the Cat Girl, her claws exposed. Sam finally understood the meaning of the word "catty." He was not sure what had happened, but that evening Tommie allowed him to explore some of the forbidden regions he had only dreamed of. Woody's and Chip's rude inquiries about Sam and Tommie's physical relationship went unanswered after that. As for Valentina, she seemed more seductively alluring than before. She frequently spoke to Sam entirely in Russian, sometimes in German, all the while smiling enticingly with an occasional wink. She was to be avoided.

CHAPTER 10
January 2012

Y ou know, her dying wasn't easy." Thompson's voice on
the phone was matter-of-fact.

"Mr. Thompson?" Sam asked with both surprise and
caution in his voice.

"It was a long process. 'Unpleasant' is too kind a word.
Funny what you remember after they are gone."

"Doctor Thompson, how did you get this number?" Sam's
surprise had taken a quick turn toward anger. He looked out
the window at Prexy's Pasture below, where the university
president had grazed his horse in the late nineteenth century.
The view of campus from Arts and Sciences was expansive.
Few students hustled along the web of cement pathways that
coursed through the pasture, mostly graduate students who
were too involved, and too scared, to leave their projects during
Christmas break. Sam had been unpacking his lecture materials
from a cardboard file box—the same lecture notes from four
years earlier, when he accepted his first temporary teaching
position at the University of Wyoming.

"When I was young, I knew nothing about nonexistence,
about being nothing. The sick and the old just vanished. One
day they were here and the next they were not. We simply went
about our busy and insignificant existence with little thought
about lives lost. You don't think about it much until someone

close to you, someone you loved, dies horribly. In most cases
it's a long, slow process that fills your nostrils with the stench of
death, your ears with the rattling phlegm-filled hacks and gasps
of drowning, and your eyes with the ugly uncensored spectacle
of bodily decay."

"Doctor Thompson, this is my place of employment.
You can't—"

"It takes the death of someone close to you to make you
realize who you've become. Mortality is a distant concept. It's
who you are now that is the true awakening. You discover you're
only remotely related to the person you once were." His voice
was soft and calm. "Who are you now, Mr. Dawson? Who have
you become?" Thompson hung up.

Sam stood looking at the floor—black squares and white
squares of linoleum placed in a symmetrical pattern, a giant
chessboard that seemed out of place in a building dating back
to the mid-1930s. *Legitimate questions*, he thought. He did not
have time to be disturbed by them—legitimate or not, yet he
was haunted by them. *Who am I now?*

Sam knew of Hank Thompson only from what Valentina
had told him. A scared sixteen-year-old kid did not pay attention to details, especially when a beautiful woman was pressed
against him in the front seat of a 1963 Comet convertible. She
had said Thompson was older than her. Eight years seemed
to stick in his mind. He slowly did the math. He would be
sixty-one or sixty-two now, Sam figured.

She said he was an assistant professor of modern languages
at the University of Colorado in Boulder. He taught Russian.
He had landed a small grant having to do with the influence of

the German language on Russian and the resulting dialect of the Volga Germans. She first met him in the Volgograd oblast on a dark and snowy February morning. He had left his hotel for his daily constitutional, a jog through the unplowed streets of the former Stalingrad. "He had the entire city to himself since the Russians find it difficult to smoke and jog at the same time and do not run," she said with a laugh. People on the street eyed him suspiciously, as if he were being chased by the authorities. Bundled in dark coats under fur hats, they had to stand in line, waiting their turn at military-looking water buffalo trailers that dispensed their morning ration of milk. Most were elderly women—"babushkas" she called them, with their headscarves tied under their chins. They looked like pudgy Russian nesting dolls. Val was the exception—a tall, slender teenager at the end of the line who said *"Mahekeh,"* under her breath as Hank Thompson passed by. He slid to a stop on the ice-covered path that had been trampled over the sidewalk. "Who are you calling a dummy?" he said to her in Russian.

Looking surprised, she said, *"E'meriken?"*

"Da. You speak English?"

"Jes," she said confidently with a slightly embarrassed smile.

Val explained that most young Russians could speak rudimentary English since it was taught in the state-run school system. She said she unnerved him by maintaining direct eye contact and challenging the concept of, and justification for, jogging. He, in turn, questioned the sanity of standing in line in freezing temperatures to obtain and drink the drippings from the underside of a cow. They chided each other every morning for nearly a week before she politely asked him to dinner with her family.

She said her father was an old-school Communist who had fought in Afghanistan. His father, her grandfather, had survived the battle for Stalingrad and still treated his German daughter-in-law as an indentured servant. Her mother had worked on a collective farm, and her stories had convinced Valentina that a career in agriculture was her key to prosperity. The family was curious about their American dinner guest. They seemed interested solely in impressing him with statements of Russian superiority. No one seemed to notice Thompson's fascination with the seventeen-year-old Valentina.

Val said that, a year later, Dr. Hank Thompson was back in Russia, this time a couple hundred miles to the north in Engles, the de facto capital of the Volga German Republic—or at least it was prior to 1941, when the Russians purged the city after the German invasion. Just across the Volga River was Saratov, home to the Saratov State Agrarian University, where she was studying dairy science. He later confided in Valentina that it had been no coincidence when she found him standing in line behind her at a coffee kiosk near campus on a cool summer morning. Four months later she was pregnant, married, and living in a one-bedroom apartment in Boulder, Colorado, United States of America. She was eighteen years old.

CHAPTER 11
January 2012

Spring semester started with an exceptionally cold and snowy Tuesday right after Martin Luther King Day. The interstate shut down just after lunch. Sam suspected the usual—semis scattered across the summit between Cheyenne and Laramie to the east, and Elk Mountain between Laramie and Rawlins to the west, either wrecked or stuck. Winds gusting to sixty miles per hour seemed to ensure a long delay in reopening the only road between Laramie and Sam's home in the Pole Mountain area of the Medicine Bow National Forest, twenty-five miles west of Cheyenne. He called Sidney.

"That line is busy," the mechanical, yet pleasant, voice proclaimed, then offered to keep trying for an extra fee. After several attempts, Sam assumed the lines were down. Heavy spring snows, combined with Wyoming's wind, took a toll on both lines and poles. Landlines were still the better alternative, given the lack of cell service in mountainous rural areas. Corded phones worked even in power outages, unlike cordless phones that need electricity. He tried her cell phone anyway.

"Dad!" she shouted into the crackling phone before the eerie silence of being disconnected forced him to hang up and dial again. The line was busy. He hit redial. "Dad!"

"Sid. Are you okay?"

"Dad!"

"Sid. Can you hear me?"

"Dad, there's somebody—"

Sam could feel the hairs on his arms stiffen. "Sid, are you there?" He pushed the disconnect button in the phone's cradle and tried again. After five rings she picked up.

"Hi!"

"Sid, who's—"

"This is Sidney. Sorry I can't come to the phone right now. Please leave your name and number and I'll get right back to you—"

Sam hung up and frantically redialed again. The line was busy. This time he pushed some buttons.

"O'Malley," the sheriff said curtly.

"Harrison, it's Sam Dawson." Sam was suddenly thankful the sheriff had given him the number of his direct line.

"Howdy, Sam. What's—"

"It's Sidney. I think she's in trouble. The lines are down, cell service is intermittent, and I'm stuck in Laramie. I think there's somebody there."

"Who's there, Sam?"

"I don't know. It didn't sound good. Can you get to her?"

"I'm on it, Sam. I've got a man at the highway gate up at the state park. I'll dispatch him now."

"Call the patrol and tell them to let me through on Interstate 80. I'll be in the Willys," Sam said, referring to his 1953 Willys station wagon, a Jeep that was the first SUV. He had painstakingly restored the relic. The Willys made him smile when he drove it and had never failed to deliver him to a remote stream or little-known string of beaver ponds.

"Done, although those boys will have the final say."

⋆⟞◉⟝⋆

The tiny wiper blades on the Willys lurched randomly. Sam rolled down his window and snapped the driver's side–blade against the windshield to remove the ice. The highway patrolman held onto his hat, his head tipped downward as he struggled toward the Willys. The flashing red lights on the candy-striped pole across the highway framed a sign that said, "Road Closed."

"I called dispatch and they confirmed the sheriff's request," the patrolman said, still holding on to his Smokey Bear hat. "My captain up at the summit says he doesn't have the manpower to come dig your ass out if you get into trouble. He strongly advises against it, but—"

The word "but" was all Sam needed. He released the clutch pedal and the '53 spun its wheels and slid sideways past the patrolman's cruiser. He glanced at the flip phone Sidney had purchased for him. He knew there would be no service in the canyon leading up to the summit even on a good day. Semi-tractor-trailer rigs with drivers who should have known better littered the steep roadway that snaked through the canyon. Sam had locked in the hubs on the Willys before he left Laramie. In four-wheel high he sailed past the stranded trucks, some jackknifed across two of the three lanes. He left the Interstate at the summit and turned onto Happy Jack Road. It was unplowed. The Willys burst through the scattered drifts across the original road between Cheyenne and Laramie, named for a woodcutter who sang to the mules that pulled his wagon. Sam knew the road, but visibility was so limited that he was forced to use the reflector posts to guide him toward the center of the highway. The Forest Service road held hints of tire tracks in the areas protected from the wind. Just past the turnoff where Sam's driveway intersected the Forest Service road, he found a sheriff's department pickup truck, nose-down in the borrow pit. Sam dared not stop for fear he would lose momentum. The Willys plowed like a battleship through stormy seas before it slid to a halt near Daisy's corral.

"Sidney," he yelled as he burst into the mudroom off the kitchen. Startled, L2 scrambled to her feet, her toenails scraping loudly on the floor.

"In here, Pop," Sidney called as Sam rounded the corner into the kitchen. A kerosene lamp glowed from the center of the kitchen table, where she and a young man in uniform sat holding mugs of tea. The officer jumped to his feet.

"Are you all right?" Sam said hurriedly, ignoring the sheriff's deputy. "Who was here?"

"I don't know," Sidney said, shaking her head. "When I went outside to throw a flake of hay to Daisy, I saw a man standing in the timber about thirty or forty yards from the loafing shed. It was snowing so hard, I couldn't make out any details. I called to him and he just stood there staring at me. A gust of wind swirled snow through the trees. When it cleared, he was gone. That's when I got scared. You called shortly after that."

"Did you lock the doors? Did you get the gun? Did you—"

"Dad, this is Nick."

Sam eyed the handsome deputy as if he were sizing him up for trouble—tall, perhaps six-two, well-proportioned, with dark hair and a face right out of a magazine ad for a men's razor. Sam's eyes shifted to his daughter. She too was looking at the young man and smiling demurely. She slid her heavy glasses up the bridge of her nose. "Sam Dawson," Sam said, stepping forward and offering his hand.

"It's a pleasure to meet you, sir. The sheriff speaks highly of you."

"You're new to the department?"

"Yes, sir."

"Ex-military?"

"Yes, sir."

"Call me Sam."

"Yes, sir."

Sam looked at Sidney, who seemed transfixed by the deputy. He looked back at Nick and studied him for a moment. "What are your intentions concerning my daughter, young man?"

"Dad!" Sidney yelled. "That's not funny." She pinned her father with an angry stare. "Please excuse my exceptionally rude father," she said to Nick.

The deputy sheriff smiled at Sam. "My intentions are honorable, sir."

"They better be, because you're stuck here for a while," Sam said, smiling back.

"You are so weird." Sidney shook her head and pursed her lips.

Outside, the storm raged on.

CHAPTER 12
January 2012

We had a revocable trust rather than a simple will, mostly because we wanted to avoid probate," Hank Thompson said as if he and Sam had been having a lengthy conversation.

Sam squinted at the clock above the kitchen sink. It was five after four in the morning. The pine floor was cold against his bare feet. He had to pee. "Listen to me, Thompson—"

"Our lawyer told us to handwrite directives to accompany the will that would instruct the trustee to award certain personal items—things that had sentimental value, to specific individuals. He said that would eliminate any disputes that might arise over the disposition of such items that represented the life of the deceased—memorabilia really, things worthy of being remembered."

"Stay away from me, Thompson. Stay away from my family. I'll get a restraining—"

"I had asked you who you are, Mr. Dawson, who you have become. Unless you know the answer, how can you bequeath a legacy? It took her death to make me realize who I am and that material things are truly unimportant. You can't own the things I wish to leave for my survivors—a scarlet sunrise, the smell of freshly mowed grass on a summer's evening, the sound of gentle rain on a windowpane, or the warm touch of my wife's hand on my face."

Sam was glad he had picked up the cordless phone from his study. The wall phone, his hedge against spotty cell phone service and power outages, would have tethered him to the kitchen. He took it into the hall bathroom and clutched it between his shoulder and ear as he fumbled with the drawstring on his pajama bottoms. "Uh-huh. That's all very poetic, Mr. Thompson, but—"

"She left you something, Mr. Dawson."

Sam's urination was cut short, stopping midstream. His mind raced for potential responses and found none.

"It's uncontestable. It's a legal document. As trustee I'm bound to carry out her wishes. My authority or power of attorney ended when she died. So did my medical power of attorney. The decisions are no longer mine. They are the state's, Mr. Dawson. You are an heir. You have rights under this legal process. The law is a bit fuzzy, however, when delineating the time period for disposition of the inheritance. I had six months to notify you that you were named as a beneficiary. Consider yourself notified. I'll deliver your inheritance to you someday when you least expect it." Thompson hung up.

Sam stared at the phone in disbelief. The fact that it was working and the light was on in the bathroom told him the power had been restored sometime during the night. He listened intently for sounds of the wind before flushing the toilet. It was deathly quiet outside. When he opened the door, he was startled to see Sidney standing on the other side, a blanket wrapped around her shoulders.

"Is everything all right, Pop?"

"Everything is fine, sweetie. Go back to bed."

"Who keeps calling here at all hours of the day and night?" She adjusted her glasses and one of her hearing aids.

"Is there a problem, sir?" Nick stepped from the shadows of the living room, where he had been sleeping on the couch. His white T-shirt and socks seemed to gather all the light escaping from the bathroom.

"Call me Sam." A hint of annoyance had entered Sam's voice.

"Yes, sir."

Sam shook his head and exhaled with a huff. "Sid, break out the tortillas. As long as everybody is up, I feel the need for the house special, my green chili breakfast burrito." The phone rang again before he could place it in its stand.

"Have you got my deputy?" the sheriff said nonchalantly.

"I do," Sam said, nodding his head.

"Christ, Sam, why can't you live someplace civilized? We've been worried sick. I'll call off the dogs."

"I'll give him back as soon as I feed him and pull his truck out of the ditch."

"I'd appreciate it. My best to Sidney."

"Will do." Sam pushed the off button. "The sheriff sends his best to you, Sid. Nick, I think you're in big trouble."

"Yes, sir."

"Let's go, people. The sun will be up in a couple of hours. Sidney, put the coffee on while I get dressed," Sam barked.

Sidney did not budge. Instead, she stood firm, glaring at her father through the tops of her lenses, her chin tucked, waiting for an answer about the unexplained caller.

Sam silently mouthed the word "later," before turning and retreating into his bedroom. With the door closed, he stood facing the wall. His breathing was labored as he transcended the decades. He remembered.

CHAPTER 13
May 1980

The future seemed to hold unlimited promise in the spring of 1980. Sam had turned seventeen in February and he considered himself an adult. Graduation was still a year away, yet on occasion he found himself thinking about the prospective offerings that lay ahead. The world really was his cherry, ripe for the picking. His anticipation of the future sometimes felt like guilt when so much of the present needed his attention. But spring dominated. It was awash with new beginnings. He daydreamed of the prom, a twelve-foot pole vault, a bamboo fly rod, a blue-and-white Toyota Land Cruiser for sale at Dealin' Bob's, and of course, Tommie. He thought they would always be together. He envisioned her at his side in all future scenarios. After all, they were a couple, almost a mated pair. He worried about that too. If Woody and Chip knew he was still a virgin, they would laugh him out of school. Then there was the college thing. Four more years after high school to get through before he could settle in as a professional fly fisherman, a log home in the forest, a yellow lab on the front porch, and Tommie. He thought it only mildly troubling that he had never asked her about her future. Sam just assumed she would be next to him. Lately, he began to have visions of her in a black-and-white habit, standing outside a nunnery waving goodbye to him, her vow of chastity intact.

Valentina continued to haunt him day and night, both in person and in his dreams. He gave her a wide berth while discreetly studying her perfect form out of the corner of his eye. She was an apparition, a phantom that shimmered and twinkled in his mind. Her deep and throaty accent ran down his spine like a soothing electrical current. When she winked and smiled at him from across a room, he would tremble and forget what he was doing or where he was going. Her eyes sparkled like stars on a moonless night. Even her dark hair reflected the most muted light. It shone with the lustrous intensity of a supermodel's, like the ones on the covers of fashion magazines. She was to be avoided. Sam was good at that. It required constant vigilance. Then, on a particularly cool May evening after work, he let his guard down as he approached his car in the dark employee parking lot.

"Saaam," she said with her characteristic short vowel.

Startled, he clumsily spun around to find her standing half in the shadow of a large blue spruce. "What?" he said much too loudly.

"I dropped car key on way to car and cannot find it."

"I have a flashlight." Sam nervously hurried toward his car.

"Never mind, I already look. Give me ride home. I have spare key there."

Sam's mind raced and he stuttered. "Y-you could call your husband from the restaurant."

"Not home. He went to meeting in Pennsylvania."

"Don't you have a babysitter or something?"

"He is at sitter down street. She has no car. Sam, you give me ride, jes?"

"Yeah, sure." He swallowed the lump in his throat. "Hop in."

Normally a cautious driver, Sam, for unknown reasons, raced through all four gears, slamming the four-speed Hurst into place and popping the clutch to make the tires squeal. Valentina's head jogged back and forth as she braced herself against the dashboard. "I can get rubber in all four gears," he said proudly.

"Rubber? You don't need rubber," she said seductively.

Sam's throat stuck shut. When he tried to speak, he squeaked, like air being released from a pinched balloon. He switched on the radio. Billy Joel was happily singing "It's Still Rock and Roll to Me." He turned up the volume. "Where do you live?" he shouted.

Valentina switched off the radio. "You know where. I see you go by. You try to see in window, yes?"

"No," he protested. He was starting to panic. Sam had driven by her house numerous times, hoping to catch a glimpse of her through a window. He cast a quick look in her direction. His eyes pulled downward at the sight of her exposed thighs. Earlier, he had noted how short her black cocktail dress was. Seated in a relaxed fashion, her legs partially spread, he could see the tops of her dark nylons and the snaps that held them up. She was wearing a girdle or garter belt or some such thing, just like he had seen in the Sears catalog. None of the girls at school wore such a contraption. Pantyhose with panties underneath seemed to be the norm. At least that was what Woody told him, and Chip had agreed. Tommie wore pants. Sam's hands began to sweat. "I sometimes come this way on my way to school."

"School is in other direction," she shot back.

He thought pensively for a long moment. "I believe you are right. I'm not very good with directions. I get turned around once in a while. So which house is yours?" he said, slowing up.

Valentina ignored his weak denial. "Just pull in driveway."

Dutifully, he obeyed and came to an abrupt stop in front of the small, detached, single-car garage that was popular in the 1940s when this section of Boulder was developed. Tiny brick houses with sharp angles and pointy roofs lined both sides of the street, many nestled behind huge spruce trees and squared-off hedges. "I'll wait here."

"No, you come in," she ordered. "There has been Peeping John in neighborhood."

Sam ignored her malapropism. "Um, if I see him, I'll honk the horn." He was rather pleased with his response.

"Saaam, do not argue. You hurry, please. It is late."

Sam dutifully complied. He was too frightened to object. He said nothing when she pulled what appeared to be car keys from her purse and unlocked the front door. She switched on the lights and closed the door behind him.

"Wait here. I change clothes," she said, then turned away from him, stopped, and lifted her silky hair from the back of her neck. "You unzip."

"What?"

"I cannot reach. You unzip."

"No," he said without thinking. He wanted to run, but his feet were stuck to the floor. He had seen this movie.

"Saaam," she said forcefully. The short vowel made it sound like "some." "Unzip, please."

His hands shook as he fumbled with the tiny zipper at the back of her dress. He could smell her perfume. He could feel the warmth of her skin on his fingertips as he slid the zipper down until it stopped at the small of her back. Valentina twisted her shoulders and the tiny black dress dropped to the floor. Her bra, garter belt, and panties were a matched set of black lace.

"Are you trying to seduce me, Mrs. Robinson?" he said, his voice much too high and with a slight quiver.

Stepping from her dress, she turned toward him. Her large dark eyes searched his face for only a moment before she leaned into him and kissed him fully, passionately on the lips. Then suddenly, unexpectedly, she began to cry. She sobbed spasmodically and covered her face with her hands. Awkwardly, Sam put his arms around her and held her to his chest. He would later reflect that it seemed the proper thing to do, given the circumstances. His heart pounded wildly and his entire body began to tremble. Sam could not get enough oxygen. He thought he should say something. He had no idea what. Instead, he just stood there, his knees shaking, holding the most beautiful woman in the world, who just happened to be almost naked, and patting her back like she was an Afghan hound.

Valentina gently pushed back from Sam's embrace. She did not make eye contact with him. Her head bowed toward the floor, she wrapped her arms around her perfect breasts. "You go now."

"Don't you want a ride?"

She shook her head and repeated, "You go now," this time a little more forcefully.

Dazed, Sam drove slowly toward home as he relived the passionate kiss and the warmth of her body pressed to his. *She's a married woman*, he thought over and over. *This is bad. This is very bad. She has a kid. She has a husband. What about Tommie? She'd be crushed. Should I tell Woody and Chip? It was just a kiss, for crying out loud. Why do I feel so guilty?* Conflicted as he was, one thing was certain. She was to be avoided.

CHAPTER 14
February 2012

Spring semester is a misnomer in Wyoming. January and February are cold and windy. March and April are the big snow months, and it does not stop snowing until June, after the students have gone home. The short days of winter were depressing. Sam hated driving home from campus every evening in the dark, the forest black and foreboding beyond the beam of his headlights.

The first time he taught Introduction to Photography, he had been excited to share his experience and passion with students. He was soon reminded how much they did not care. At the same time, he knew their apathy was the result of his failure to motivate them. He was using the same course syllabus, lecture notes, PowerPoint presentations, and assignments he had used four years earlier. Although varied, the quizzes and exams were essentially identical. If they did not care, he did not care. He went through the motions. No one seemed interested in f-stops, depth of field, or shutter speeds. Their phones did not even have shutters. Rather, they had a preprogrammed sound effect that imitated a shutter opening and closing. Sam worried their phones had become an extension of their bodies and minds. It led them and they followed, as if an invisible tether were attached from their devices to the rings in their noses. He would turn forty-nine next week and wondered if his contempt was caused by the generation gap, or if students had really changed that much since he was in college.

Interstate 80, the only road leading east from Laramie, had closed before Sam finished preparing the lecture materials for his next class. Angry that he had lost track of time and misjudged the intensity of the latest February snowstorm, he popped another powdered doughnut into his mouth. The vending machine in the basement had offered him few choices for a well-balanced meal. Sidney had already scolded him for not paying attention to the storm warnings. She would save him some of the squash soufflé she had prepared for dinner.

Sam looked at the large Seth Thomas clock above his office door. It was almost midnight and he was tired. The tiny office had no room for a couch or even a comfortable chair. He stepped to the single window that looked out over Prexy's Pasture. The campus was dark except for the overhead lighting along the sidewalks, which had been installed to make women feel more secure as they made their way back to their dorms and apartments during the evening hours. Snow angled down through the narrow bands of light beneath the security lamps like confetti shot from cannons. The lights in his office flickered once, then a second time, before going off completely. His computer let out a sigh as it powered down and undoubtedly lost the lecture material he had failed to save. Emergency generators quickly restored electricity solely to the laboratories with refrigerators, freezers, and controlled environments. He was out of luck. Sam craned his neck to look between the towering blue spruce trees toward the streets of Laramie. The entire town seemed to be blacked out. "Great," he whispered, his breath fogging the window.

He was about to step away when he saw a faint light through the churning snow and storm-tossed trees outside of Merica Hall. Sam strained to see it again. It briefly reappeared, flickering as though it might be a candle or kerosene lamp. The light traveled along the fourth floor—the top floor, the one with all the dormers. It came and went as if someone was carrying a lamp down a hallway. "Who the—"

The phone on his desk rang with the intensity of a fire engine's horn. Sam spun around, startled. The landline was obviously unaffected by the power outage. It rang a second time before he picked up the receiver and responded with a weak "Hello?"

"She has been gone five months today," Hank Thompson said, as if under oath to tell the truth.

Sam looked up at the clock. It was 12:01. He said nothing.

"She missed autumn. It was her favorite. She enjoyed the crisp mornings and sunny afternoons when the leaves were on the ground. She was always homesick in the fall. You know, her family never forgave her for marrying me. They never wrote. They never called. They're mostly dead now. You know, Mr. Dawson, it's hard to give up your family. We've all done it. It's inevitable. It doesn't make it any easier. It's even more difficult when you find out that your sadness has been wasted, that you've grieved for something that never existed."

"Doctor Thompson—"

"I've not visited her grave. Five months, and not once have I gone to stand over her. What's the point? It's all gone bad.

I've lost my family in more ways than you realize, Mr. Dawson. You know, I think of you. I think of you a lot. In her final days when I washed her once perfect body with warm water, soaped her ghostly white skin drawn over her bones like papier-mâché, and cleaned her private parts that made her sob from helplessness, I thought of you. I thought of you panting and sweating over her, of her clinging to your shoulders. I thought of the deception, the years of lust and lies, the ruined lives. Betrayal, Mr. Dawson, is the ultimate insult. Do you have any idea what you have done, the lives you have ruined? And for what? A moment's gratification?"

Sam sensed the threat that had crept into the disturbed man's voice. "Listen to me, Thompson—"

"She's gone now. Five months and I have not visited her grave. It's winter, a time for reflection. There is no forgiveness. There is no redemption, no salvation." He paused. "Only vengeance, Mr. Dawson, vengeance is the balm to soothe this wound." The line went dead.

Sam listened as wind-driven snow ticked against the windowpane.

CHAPTER 15
February 2012

The new university president was a little guy whose voice reminded Sam of Ross Perot, the failed 1992 candidate for U.S. president. An unapologetic autocrat, he stripped the deans of their power, took away their donors, and centralized position control. He politely thumbed his nose at the governor, legislature, and constituency groups, even going so far as to orchestrate a political coup of the alumni association. He cultured support from key members of the board of trustees and set about micromanaging everything at the university from tree trimming to changing the school colors. Sam would listen sympathetically to the threatened faculty while secretly admitting the little guy was truly a change agent. Napoleonic in his attitude toward the teaching staff, he buffered himself with layers of vice presidents to carry out his authoritarian policies. The provost had been replaced with a VP for Academic Affairs. Sam had no idea what the difference was. He knew, however, it could not be good that he had been summoned to his office.

"Have a seat, Dawson," the VP said, his back to Sam as he read from a sheet of paper.

Sam dutifully complied.

"You're as temporary and unprotected as they come, Dawson. Since we are only one-deep in photography over in Communication, I'm going to give you the benefit of the doubt and not fire you today. Heaven forbid someone in your department would have to pick up your teaching load."

Sam immediately pinched his chin between his thumb and forefinger, squinted, and said, "I don't understand."

"Allow me to make you understand," the VP said, turning to look at Sam over the rim of his half-frame glasses. "You are not one of us. You'll never be one of us. So I'll talk slowly in order that you grasp the concept. I normally would not respond to an anonymous letter of complaint. However, given the topic of sexual misconduct and the university's zero tolerance policy on matters of this nature, I have no choice."

"Excuse me?" Sam said. Surprise was evident in his voice.

"I have here a letter"—the VP held the letter slightly above his head exhibiting it as if it were evidence in a murder trial—"from a very angry parent who claims you have made unwanted sexual advances toward their daughter both verbally and physically."

"Who? That's not true."

"Anonymous, and I don't care. The accusation has been made and, like I said, we have a zero tolerance policy. The parent has threatened legal proceedings against you and the university. I've already talked with our attorneys. You're a temporary instructor and will not be represented by the university. You should retain legal counsel. From an academic standpoint, I am the law. I have called your dean, who in turn has called your department head. Your entire department will participate in sexual harassment sensitivity training, and you, Mr. Dawson, will report to the associate vice president for Human Resources, who will direct you to counselors in the

Harassment and Discrimination Prevention Training center for one-on-one therapy sessions. Am I clear?"

"But I didn't—"

"Again, I don't care." The VP smiled. "Good day, Mr. Dawson."

The VP's administrative assistant shot Sam an accusatory glare as he exited the outer office in a confused stupor. Dripping with embarrassment, he decided not to return to his office, where he was soon to be regarded as a pariah. Instead, he passed by HR on his way to the Willys. Over and over, he replayed varying scenarios of his conversation with the VP in which he astutely defended himself and brilliantly won the arguments against him. He had just passed Walmart on east Grand Avenue when he realized he had a class to teach in thirty minutes. He thought about calling the department secretary and canceling. He thought about calling the department head and resigning. *Who needs this kind of crap?* Both actions would proclaim guilt. He thought about writing an anonymous letter to the university president claiming the VP for Academic Affairs tried to extort oral sex from him in exchange for dropping the sexual misconduct charges. *That would serve the pompous bastard well.* Sam turned the Willys around and headed back to campus. *Guilty until proven innocent*, he thought. *The court of public opinion is now in session.* Sam mentally scanned the faces of female students in his class. *Who would do such a thing?*

Hurriedly, Sam unlocked his office door. The phone was ringing. "Hello."

"I would imagine you've already heard from Academic Affairs," Hank Thompson said casually. "First there is grief.

Then there is anger. Lastly, there is revenge. I'm afraid we are entering the last stage of the mourning process. Good luck, Mr. Dawson." Thompson hung up the phone.

CHAPTER 16

August 1980

Cemeteries fascinated Sam's adolescent mind. During lunch hour, it was a place to hide out with Woody and Chip, who smoked cigarettes like 1940s movie stars while guessing the bra size of female classmates. After football games on Friday nights, Columbia Cemetery was a protected place to sneak a can of beer while reliving the most brutal plays of the game and guessing the cup size of cheerleaders' breasts. They never mentioned Tommie when Sam was with them. They knew better. Tommie was thin. "Athletic" was the term Sam used. It was apparent the guys made fun of her behind his back. Sam endured comments like, "Anything more than a handful is wasted—right, Sam?" when they were discussing breasts, or "The meat is most tender closest to the bone—right, Sam?" when commenting on girls' bodies, which seemed to enter most conversations. He did not care what they thought about Tommie's body. He liked her a lot, maybe even loved her. How could he not love a girl whose panties had tiny cartoon characters on them? She smelled good too. Sam was pretty sure she could kick their butts if she had a mind to.

Sam never brought Tommie to Columbia Cemetery at night for fear of being found and harassed by Woody and Chip. Instead, he would park at Green Mountain Cemetery and fog up the windows with unconsummated passion. Sometimes they would walk among the graves while holding hands, and silently speculate about the lives of the deceased. They showed reverence, unlike Woody and Chip, who would grind out a Marlboro on a headstone or relieve themselves while standing over a grave. Sam especially liked the quiet of a cemetery. Even on windy nights when tree branches hummed and leaves clattered, a soothing silence prevailed over the hallowed ground. There was no future when standing in a cemetery at night, only the past. The confusing array of challenges facing a teenager trying to make sense of the world vanished between the graves as if sucked into the ground rather than dispersed into the air. For Sam it was absolution, a cleansing of bad thoughts and impossible choices. Tomorrow did not exist. How could it?

The summer of Sam's seventeenth year was especially perplexing. A huge mountain in Washington State blew up and covered Boulder in gray ash for days. The Ayatollah Khomeini seemed to have President Carter over a barrel when it came to negotiating the release of American hostages. The Soviet Union invaded Afghanistan and, for reasons unclear to Sam, the U.S. would boycott the Moscow Summer Olympics because of it. An old film actor from California won the Republican nomination for president, and Sam seemed to be the only guy in school who did not like the movie, *The Empire Strikes Back*. He had successfully avoided Valentina, who seemed pleasantly distant when around him. She was cordial yet guarded.

The night clerk from the motel office—a hard-looking, middle-aged woman named Doris, poked her head into the dining room just as Sam was wrapping up the cord to the

Hoover. "Sam, Valentina Thompson just called. She said no one answered the phone in the restaurant."

"I've been vacuuming and wouldn't have heard it ring," Sam said defensively.

"Well, she said she left her purse below the cash register and wants you to drop it off on your way home."

"I-I can't," he stammered while standing frozen over the vacuum cleaner. "I'm meeting a friend in Lyons," he lied.

The night clerk glanced at the clock behind the lunch counter. It was after eleven. Lyons was in the opposite direction from Boulder and at least a dozen miles away. "I'm just the messenger. Do you have her number?"

"No," he shot back quickly.

"I'll call her back and tell her she's S.O.L. and that you're a weenie who told her to take a flying leap at a rolling doughnut."

"What?"

"Christ, Sam. Take the woman her purse. Who knows, you might get lucky."

"What?" Sam said with a wince.

"It's just down the road. Ain't no traffic this time of night. Drive by and toss it in her yard, you little chickenshit."

"All right, all right, I'll take it," Sam said wide-eyed. He feared that Doris might put him in a headlock if he disagreed.

On the way into Boulder, he rehearsed the purse handoff as if he were in an Olympic relay, passing the baton to the runner on the final leg of the race. He did not see Valentina as he came to a stop in front of her driveway. The passenger door to the Comet suddenly opened and Valentina quickly slipped into the seat. "Drive," she commanded, rolling the *r*, before Sam could protest. She was still wearing the tight-fitting, low-cut, black dress from work.

"Where?"

"Jus drive."

"I have your purse," he managed a minute later.

"Turn here." She pointed to the main entrance of Columbia Cemetery.

"The cemetery?"

"Do not argue. Jus turn."

Dutifully, Sam turned into the dark cemetery and drove slowly down the narrow single-lane paths with squared corners until Valentina told him to stop.

Before he could respond, she reached over to the steering column and turned off the ignition. Leaning over him farther, she pushed in the headlight switch, then quickly found his lips and kissed him passionately while falling back and pulling him toward her. When he tried to talk, she pressed her lips even harder on his and probed his mouth with her tongue. She yanked her dress upward and wrapped her legs around him. "Val, I don't think—"

She smothered his mouth with hers, moaned, and pressed almost painfully against him. Sam was scared, almost overcome with fear. Or maybe it was guilt. He was not sure. "This isn't right," he managed to say before she again clamped down on his mouth. "Val, this is wrong. You're—" He managed to squeak "married" a few moments later.

She tried to shush him, and then breathed warmly into his ear. He thought he might faint. He pulled away abruptly, his head bulging the fabric of the convertible's top, then scrambled over her while opening the passenger door. He stumbled awkwardly from the car as he tried to swallow the lump in his throat. The cool night air felt good against his clammy skin.

"Is that a potato in your pocket?" Chip said, leaning against a tall monolithic gravestone. A faint orange glow bobbed up and down from the cigarette between his lips. "Or are you just glad to see me?"

Sam froze in terror. His mind raced.

"Christ, Dawson, quit dry-humping and get back in there and finish the job," Woody said with a giggle. "Maybe Tommie needs a relief pitcher to close."

"Put me in, Coach," Chip offered.

"You morons take one step closer and I'll mop up this cemetery with your sorry butts," Sam threatened.

Both Woody and Chip laughed and shook their heads. "Ooh, shakin'," Woody said.

"Come on," Chip said to Woody. "Let's leave Lover Boy and Cat Girl alone."

"Don't do anything I wouldn't do," Woody called to Sam.

Someone meowed as they faded into the dark.

Sam gripped the steering wheel tightly and stared straight ahead during the short trip back to Valentina's house. She cried again.

CHAPTER 17

February 2012

"Let me get this straight," Sidney said as she turned from the kitchen sink to face her father. She dried her hands with a dish towel. "The person who keeps calling here at all hours is the husband of a now-deceased woman who he claims was infatuated with you some thirty years ago, and now he has incriminated you as a sexual predator and the university is going to fire you if you don't get counseling."

"That's about it," Sam said. He squeezed his chin. "The whole department has to attend sexual harassment sensitivity training. I'm screwed thirteen ways from Sunday. There's no way out that doesn't make me look guilty. We'll have to move to another state."

"Not so fast, Pop. I'm thinking." She pushed her glasses up the bridge of her nose with her index finger and stared at nothing for what seemed like an eternity. Finally, she turned toward Sam and said, "I'll start packing in the morning."

Sam placed his hands behind his neck, fingers interlaced. He sighed.

"Look," Sidney said, "the burden of proof is on the university. The VP has not taken any formal administrative action that would be considered punitive. He's just covering his butt in case this thing goes nuclear. Institutions are generally slow to react and almost always viewed as being insensitive. He's trying to get ahead of the curve. However, singling you out for counseling or using your name publicly sets him up for defamation—libel if he puts it in writing, slander if it's an oral statement. You then have to prove harm. It's a lot of attention toward an unattractive subject. Generally, there are no winners in cases like this. Wrestle with a pig and you're going to get dirty. What about going to the source? There's your defamation case right there. If you can prove his letter is libelous, then your case goes away. Except, of course, for the stigma of being accused of a sex crime. No winners here, Pop."

"I can't believe this is happening. This guy is a real nutjob."

"Can you prove he's the author of the poison-pen letter?" Sidney pushed her hair behind her ears and fiddled with her hearing aids.

"It was typewritten. There's probably some forensic method of determining whose typewriter or printer it came from. The fact that it was an anonymous letter is what galls me."

"Has this guy made any other threats?"

"Just that he wants me dead?"

"That seems a little harsh," Sidney said, her eyes wide. "Tell me more about his wife. Why is this guy so angry?"

Sam rubbed his chin and thought for a long moment. "Today she would be called a stalker. I was just a kid, sixteen, when it started. She was twenty-one. Today, five years means nothing. To a teenage kid it was a generation."

"She was an adult and you were a child, by legal definition," Sidney interrupted.

"Yeah, well you don't think about those things at the time. Take Crazy Larry, for instance, my college roommate. He dated a high school girl. Your mother and I used to double-date with them. We chided him about robbing the cradle. He never considered he was doing anything illegal. A year after he graduated college, she graduated from high school, and Larry promptly married her. They had two kids and were happy as clams. Go figure. Anyway…what was I saying?"

"Your stalker?"

"Right. We worked together at the Left Hand Lodge and Restaurant. I quit after a couple of years because she was bugging me all the time. But it didn't stop. She sent me letters, kept calling, at home, at work."

"Was this the cigar box letter woman?"

"Yes."

"How long did this go on?"

"It pretty much stopped after your mom and I were married. When I worked for the governor, I would occasionally get cards or letters of congratulation when she saw me on TV or read my name in the paper. She even showed up at a book signing once. She left before I finished my talk. Her behavior always seemed a bit impulsive and erratic."

Sidney hung up the dish towel slowly. "Why did you keep her letter hidden in a cigar box?"

Sam shrugged his shoulders and gave a weary exhale. "I don't know. I've thought about it. Maybe it was a reminder of a more carefree time, of youthful innocence. It was flattering to have such a letter. I'm not sure there is a way to explain it. I destroyed it sometime after your mom and I were married."

"Did you love her?"

Sam seemed momentarily caught off guard by his daughter's question. "I don't know," he said, looking down at the floor. "She was drop-dead gorgeous and had a thing for me. She was obviously unhappy in her marriage. She was the forbidden fruit in that utopian garden that surrounded a teenage boy. She scared me half to death. How would I explain her to my parents? Later on I worried how I would explain her to my wife...your mother. How would I explain her to her husband?" He paused and smiled. "How would I explain her to my daughter?"

"There's nothing to explain, Pop. You did nothing wrong. She put a guilt trip on you by turning her illegal and immoral behavior into your problem. The sad thing is that even after all these years, even after she's dead, she has succeeded in making her problem your problem. Did you explain any of this to the VP?"

"He wouldn't let me speak. Besides, I don't think the 'jealous husband' excuse would have helped my case any."

"Well, he's about to hear from your attorney. He either drops this or we'll take him to court. The university always gets weak in the knees when threatened with litigation. This is Wyoming, for crying out loud. We're all related. The chief counsel for the university is a former classmate who hit on me all through law school. Did I mention the fact that he was married?" Sidney said with a smile. "Not to worry, Pop. I'll call him in the morning."

Sam did not respond. There was a distant look in his eyes as he worked his chin between his thumb and forefinger.

Sidney stared at him for a moment, then added, "All right, I'll do it pro bono."

He did not hear her.

CHAPTER 18
March 2012

March came in like a schizophrenic lion. An occasional warm-and-sunny day was followed by two feet of snow, and enough wind to halt the migration of greenies from Denver as they pushed northward like a plague of locusts. Finals week and graduation were within reach. Sam was counting the days. All was quiet on the western front. Sidney had worked her legal magic on the university's chief counsel and the entire issue of sexual misconduct had been dropped. Sam's department head viewed Sam warily and rarely spoke to him. The vice president for Academic Affairs was suspiciously silent. Sam just wanted to finish the semester and withdraw into the solitude of his forest home. He had heard nothing more from Hank Thompson, who Sam hoped had given up his misguided pursuit of vengeance. Sidney seemed almost giddy over her new relationship with Nick. There had been dinner dates and movies and a fair amount of loitering in Sam's living room. Sidney was happy, and Nick was starting to grow on Sam even though he still insisted on calling him "sir." Catkins were forming on the aspen trees, and the sides of mule deer does were swollen with the promise of new beginnings. It was Sunday morning, bright and sunny. Sam was grading the photo essays his students had turned in on Friday, when Hank Thompson called.

"I sat with her day and night for months," he said. As usual, the conversation sounded as if it had been going on for some time. "I held her hand. I fed her." Sam listened as Thompson took a deep breath. "It's impossible for you to understand such closeness, Mr. Dawson." Sam was growing weary of people telling him what he did not understand. "The grass needed mowing. The mail was piled up next to the door. Dishes were stacked in the sink. Nothing else mattered. I was with her constantly. I got up to take a shower and when I came back, she was dead." He paused. "She died alone, Mr. Dawson. Do you have any idea of the guilt I felt for not being there? Do you think she did it on purpose?" He waited for Sam to respond. Sam said nothing. He was tempted to hang up. "Was it one final act of defiance after a life of treachery? Why would she do that? Maybe she was trying to spare me the trauma of watching her take her last breath. Or maybe she didn't want me to hear her whisper your name as she held that last breath. I often wondered who she saw in her silent, intense staring at me. My reflection in those dark eyes of hers seemed distorted. Perhaps it was you she saw and not me." Sam heard a slight chuckle. "Who knows what evil lurks in the hearts of men, Mr. Dawson?"

"The Shadow knows," Sam answered, playing into Thompson's theatrical quote from the famous radio show.

"Yes indeed. Just like the Shadow, I know the face of evil when I see it. It was your face I saw in her dying eyes." He was silent, as if for effect. "I wonder whose face I will see in your dying eyes, Mr. Dawson."

Sam was not sure who hung up first. The only audible click he heard was when he pushed the stop button on the small, handheld tape recorder he had plugged into the phone.

⋆⇒◉⇐⋆

"The threat isn't explicit, Sam," Sheriff O'Malley said, leaning back in his squeaky desk chair. He straightened the ends of his moustache. "He didn't threaten to kill you." He gestured toward Sam's tape recorder. "He simply wondered what he would see in your dying eyes. He could be talking about your dying eyes in a nursing home thirty years from now. As for his first alleged threat five months ago, it's your word against his. Where's Sidney? What'd she tell you?"

"She's down the hall"—Sam said, gesturing over his shoulder—"mooning over your deputy. She thinks it might be criminal harassment. She said he doesn't need to intend to harm me, just make me fear for my safety."

"Did she tell you how unlikely it is you could prove that in court?"

"He calls me at home, calls me at work—"

"Look, Sam, he doesn't even live in this state. I could give the sheriff in Boulder County a call and ask him to investigate. When he gets done laughing, he'll tell me he doesn't have the time or the manpower to look into veiled threats that make people feel unsafe, that he's got real crime to attend to. Even if he did look into it and make an arrest, the prosecuting attorney would have to be convinced to take the case to court, a court whose docket is probably filled for the next six months. Let's say that happens. Are you prepared to testify under oath, in front of a defense attorney who will try to discredit you? You wanna talk about your sex life in front of a bunch of strangers? And if you were to get a conviction, the best you could hope for is a restraining order."

"Wait a second. Why are we talking hypothetically about what they would do in Boulder? The crime was committed here in Wyoming. As a responsible citizen I have come here to the sheriff's office to lodge a complaint. You're my sheriff. Do something."

"Not so fast, small bear," the sheriff said, smiling. "Even if I could be convinced of the jurisdictional requirements, I have all the same arguments against pursuing it. It just ain't gonna happen."

"Can't you just put the fear of God into him?"

"Change your phone number. Or get caller ID. Turn off your voicemail. Just deal with it, Sam, and leave me out of it. You're taking the notion that I'm a public servant to a whole new level."

"Thank you, Sheriff O'Malley. I knew I could count on you," Sam said as he stood up to leave.

"And, Sam, take your daughter with you. I need my deputy back."

CHAPTER 19
December 1982

Sam's mother loved chocolate-covered cherries, but not just any chocolate-covered cherries. They had to be Cella's, the ones in the red box with a picture of a cherry suspended in a thick, sugary sauce oozing from the center of a milk chocolate shell. Each piece was wrapped in gold foil, as they had been since 1864. More expensive chocolate-covered cherries could be found in the fancy candy stores on Pearl Street. However, Mrs. Dawson wanted Cella's. It was a Christmas tradition that had been going on since Sam was in grade school. She always acted surprised and proclaimed them her favorites when she stripped away the holiday wrapping paper. Walgreens drugstore was where Sam would find a shelf filled with the brightly colored boxes.

A cold December wind pushed by him as he entered the store and stamped the snow from his feet. Sam was momentarily stunned by the flash of gaudy Christmas lights and silvery garlands clinging to every available surface. Holiday music played through dime-store speakers. A mechanical, gyrating Santa Claus greeted customers with a belly laugh worthy of the real Saint Nick. The sensory invasion worked. He would buy his mother two boxes of chocolate-covered cherries. She deserved them, having put up with him during his freshman year when he lived at home. Now emancipated, Sam was midway through his sophomore year at the University of Colorado and was no longer nervous about whether he would make it through college. He was more concerned about his relationship with Marcie. While only dating for a short time, she seemed a little too serious for his liking, acting as though they were destined for marriage. She talked about it all the time. He was more interested in the career opportunities his new diploma might offer. The last thing he wanted was to be bogged down by domestic responsibilities, he thought as he stood in front of the neatly stacked boxes in Walgreens. Tommie Tucker was stamping price stickers on boxes of tampons at the end of the aisle.

Sam secretly watched her as he pretended to read the label on the Cella's box. She had cut her hair short and dyed it a streaky blonde. She was taller than he remembered. Her cuteness had been transformed into a more seasoned beauty. She appeared to be a woman now rather than a girl. Sam had not spoken to her in two years, and he was at a complete loss as to what he would say if she should confront him. He had treated her badly his senior year of high school and he regretted it.

They had been an item for more than a year, inseparable. Everyone assumed they would ride off into the future together, still holding hands and smiling happily. They were hometown favorites, homecoming royalty destined for a big-name college, a house in the suburbs, two cars in the driveway, a dog in the backyard, and a couple of kids who looked like miniature versions of themselves. He had thought about writing her a letter in which he tried to explain the inexplicable—how his selfish goals trumped their love for one another. It was more than a high school romance where immature people fumble with mature concepts. If he had not walked away, he would have been forced into adulthood with all its responsibilities, his dreams abandoned. Biology and reason would have collided head-on in the backseat of his Mercury Comet and passion would have been the victor. Sam reasoned they both would eventually be sorry. So one day he walked away. He did not know the words to say to her then and still had no idea how to explain his actions. They were simply too young.

Both families were at a loss. Tommie's mother called Sam's mother. Tommie would not get out of bed, would not go to school. It was rumored she had taken pills. When she finally pulled it together, she lingered in the background, withdrawn and injured. She quit cheerleading and just about everything else, then started dating Paul Weaver, an unlikely outcast with no ambition and no future. Tommie dropped out of high school and disappeared for some time. When she resurfaced, she was married with a kid, a trailer house, and a red Walgreens vest with her name on it. Her shattered dreams, which Sam had never asked about, were gone. The last time he had seen Paul Weaver he was wearing an orange jumpsuit and picking up litter by the side of the road.

Boulder was a small town. Sam feared he would someday run into her and find her waiting tables, checking out groceries, or stocking shelves, an older Tommie Tucker with adult responsibilities and adult disappointments. And here she was. He could walk up to her and say something stupid, like "You look great. Are you happy? How long has it been?" Sam stared at her and remembered the warm summer nights, the softness of her lips, the firmness of her breasts, and the jingle of her lighthearted laugh. He had loved her. He guessed he still did.

Hard-packed snow squeaked loudly under his shoes as Sam hurriedly made his way down the street. Two boxes of Cella's chocolate-covered cherries were tucked under his arm. His mother would act surprised.

CHAPTER 20
April 2012

To tell you the truth, Mr. Dawson, I don't much care whose responsibility it is," the Albany County sheriff said over the phone, his office just down the street from UW in Laramie. Sam was grading his last pop quiz and did not want to be dragged into the controversial issue of finding lost graves. "The university is the big dog in this county, with an annual payroll of nearly a hundred million. When they bark, I jump."

"Have you talked to anyone in the Division of Criminal Investigation?" Sam asked as he circled a score of nine out of a possible twenty points on the quiz.

"They're only interested if there's been a crime committed."

"What about the city police? Greenhill is a city cemetery. They're the ones who supposedly moved the graves."

"Yeah, yeah, we're all working together on this—campus security, city cops, and my office. I've even got the Game and Fish forensic lab on campus looking at the bone that came up in the soil core. They're pretty sure it's human. Now I've got archeologists involved. Look, the university architect is driving me nuts. I'm getting calls from vice presidents I've never heard of, and one pissed-off trustee who happens to be married to my wife's cousin. Bids were solicited and contracts were let. It's all about money, Mr. Dawson. When construction of this parking garage gets delayed and starts running over budget and the governor and legislature begin asking questions, the sh—poop's going to run downhill and stop at my doorstep. All I'm asking is that you take a look and see if you come up with anything."

Sheriff O'Malley had led Sam to believe the issue had to do with things that went bump in the night at Merica Hall. The real issue was the delay of the much-needed multistory parking garage the university had sought funds for in every budget request over the last two decades. They now had the money, but a pinkie-finger bone in a soil sample had brought the entire process to a halt. The Native American student organization was quick to involve both tribes on the Wind River Indian Reservation—the Eastern Shoshone and the Northern Arapaho. They assumed the remains were of ancestral tribe members and were demanding repatriation. The tiny university president with his Ross Perot voice weighed in with an appeasement gesture. He would move *Battle of Two Hearts,* a statue of Chief Washakie on horseback, from in front of the dining center on Grand Avenue to the parking garage entrance on Ivinson Street. Washakie was an Eastern Shoshone chief, so the Northern Arapaho said, "Not so fast." They wanted Arapaho representation on campus and believed that a statue of Chief Left Hand was both appropriate and due them. Sam was reminded of what Henry Kissinger once said when asked why academic debates were so acrimonious. "Because so little is at stake," he responded in a deep German baritone.

⊶═⊙═⊷

The sun was setting behind Elk Mountain, west of Laramie. A red sky, streaked with orange, rose up from the Snowy Range of the Medicine Bow Mountains as if an ancient volcano had erupted. *Sailor's delight*, Sam thought as he made his way toward the site of the proposed parking garage. It had taken him longer than anticipated to grade the quizzes, since each wrong answer demanded a correction in red pencil. He would be glad when the semester was over and he could stop pretending to be patient with his students' lackadaisical behavior. The professor he was filling in for was making remarkable progress in his battle with prostate cancer and planned to return before fall semester. Also, Sam had received an encouraging letter from the state of Texas regarding his proposal to create a photographic catalog of the state's cemeteries. The light at the end of the tunnel had gone from a dim glow in the distance to a beacon of hope. Unfortunately, government moved slowly.

The pace at the university slowed each day at twilight. It was when the faculty and staff had gone home for the evening, and the students were eating and settling in to finish assignments due the next day. The campus seemed almost deserted. Sam pulled his bent welding rods from his belt loop and gazed across the grassy field between Merica Hall and Ivinson Street. Huge blue spruce and cottonwood trees dotted the property with a distinct depression at its center. Sam had read that at one time a pool called Peanut Pond was located there. It had been the site of an annual tug-of-war between incoming freshmen and sophomores and was drained and filled in when mosquitoes became a problem. Concrete and steel would soon replace the trees and flower gardens that had been planted over the reputedly abandoned Laramie cemetery. *This is a no-win proposition,* he suddenly realized, and a chill descended over him. If he found something, the pro-garage faction would have him burned at the stake. If he found nothing, the anti-garage crazies would declare him a fraud. That was why he was stumbling around in semidarkness. He could not risk being seen. He scrunched his shoulders upward and took a quick look around to make sure no one was watching as he raised the brass rods in front of him.

⋅⋅⋙◉⋘⋅⋅

The Willys had a two-speed heater fan that, on high, sounded like a Cessna taxiing onto the runway. "Holy crap," Sam repeated every minute or so as he followed his headlights along the winding road toward his home. By the time he reached the turnoff, he had accepted the only possible solution. Aside from Sidney, he would tell no one.

CHAPTER 21
March 1983

Sam had turned twenty in February. He was ready to finish the semester and become an upperclassman. Marcie was a broken record, her needle stuck in a groove about the future. Her mother's influence on Marcie was evident. They dreamed of domestic bliss where a woman's role was that of a mother and respected debutante, dependent upon her husband's successful career. Marcie never mentioned his journalistic pursuits, a log house in the mountains, or fly-fishing. It made him nervous.

A fake ID, a few beers, perhaps more, with Woody and Chip at the Palomino Club watching sad-looking women dance naked around a pole gave him the courage to drive by Val's house. Twice.

Valentina stood sensuously in the doorway, silhouetted against a yellow living room halo of light, her arm outstretched, the orange glow of a cigarette between her slim fingers. Sam had smelled cigarette smoke on her before. He hated smoking, but believed all Russians smoked. He pulled over. She waved and he waved back awkwardly. He cut the engine. She put her cigarette out on the step, tugged at the legs of her tight-fitting jeans tucked into cowboy boots, pulled the scrunchie from her ponytail, and shook her hair loose. She was wearing an orange Broncos sweatshirt. Her boots scraped on the pavement as she approached the passenger side of the '67 Land Cruiser Sam had traded in the Comet for. The temperature was just above freezing. Valentina hugged herself and stamped her feet.

"Saaam," she purred, leaning on the door, her voice low and inviting. "No see long time."

Sam smiled and looked directly into her huge dark eyes. The years between twenty-five and twenty had melted away. "Is Mr. Thompson home?" he asked, surprising himself with his liquor-induced boldness.

"Why? You come see him not me?" she asked with a frown.

"Yes—I mean no. I was just wondering." She still had a way of quickly painting him into a corner.

"He is in Mother Russia taking 'vantage of young girls, no?" Sam raised his eyebrows.

"Research, so he say."

"Where's your little boy?"

"Sleeping in house. You come see him too?"

Sam smiled and shook his head.

"You smell like beer. You want beer? Come to house. Hurry. Is cold out." She straightened up and stepped back from the vehicle. "Come," she ordered.

Sam scanned the neighborhood. It was dark.

"Come, we talk about old days at Left Hand Restaurant."

He eased unsteadily from the Toyota and quietly pushed the door closed. Valentina stood shivering on the sidewalk halfway to the house. She was gorgeous, the most beautiful woman in the world.

CHAPTER 22
April 2012

A woman who looked like Valentina was bound for misfortune," Hank Thompson said with an air of resignation. Sam glanced at the kitchen clock. It was almost 4:00 a.m., again. His snooze alarm would not go off for another hour. Sidney emerged from the hallway and squinted into the harsh light of the kitchen. Sam covered the mouthpiece with his hand, whispered, "Go back to bed," and smiled. She read his lips, shook her head in disgust, turned, and stepped back into the darkness. L2, who lay on her overstuffed bed in the corner, stretched her legs outward with her toes spread. She never opened her eyes. At twelve years of age, she was more interested in a soft bed than the one-sided machinations of her owner.

"Men were attracted to her," Thompson admitted. "I sometimes wondered if it was a chemical attraction, the way they would swarm around her at a party, follow her at the mall like dogs trailing a bitch in heat. I think it was a combination of things that made her so desirable: the way she moved, her impeccable taste in clothes, her total indifference to those who were attracted to her. I expected her to go astray once in a while. Aside from you, Mr. Dawson, she never did. She just enjoyed being the center of attention, stirring up a little trouble for those who couldn't resist her charm."

Sam could see her in her cotton dress, flaunting her beauty, twirling to music she had turned up while he vacuumed the restaurant floor. She would sing along in Russian with Billy Joel's "It's Still Rock and Roll to Me," pretending to hold the microphone to her lips as she danced, her dress swirling above her perfect thighs, her garter straps exposed, her ample breasts bouncing sensuously. He could see the tiny mole, perhaps a freckle, on her right breast just above her cleavage. Often Sam forced himself to look away for fear of being struck blind. She was a beauty, and she knew how to work her charms on men and boys. He understood exactly what Thompson was talking about. Sam looked at the clock again. He yawned audibly and scratched his head.

"Sorry if I'm boring you, Mr. Dawson. I thought you should know that you weren't the only one who found her irresistible. You were, however, the only one she mentioned in her sleep. The one she dreamed of. And in the end, you were the one she saw when she saw nothing else. She was unashamed, unrepentant. She couldn't have cared less about her family. Finally, when she had lost all that had made her attractive, I asked her how many times she had been unfaithful to me. She held up just one finger, Mr. Dawson, the middle one."

CHAPTER 23
May 1985

Overwhelmed by uncertainty, yet filled with a sense of excitement for the future, Sam jockeyed back and forth between feelings of dread and jubilance. At twenty-two he was a newly minted college graduate with a degree in journalism. Shiny as a new penny, he was the assistant to the assistant editor of the Colorado politics section at the *Rocky Mountain News*, arguably Colorado's largest newspaper. Sam did not have a clue what the Colorado politics section was or what they did. They gave him a camera and told him some travel was involved. It was minimum wage, but he had his foot in the door. It was better than delivering pizza and polishing floors in the student center, his night jobs when he was struggling to finish his degree.

Marcie had surprised him at the end of his sophomore year with the news of her pregnancy. They quietly eloped, releasing a flood of heartbreak from her mother that quickly turned into resentment toward her underachieving gentile son-in-law. Married for the past two years, and working nights while continuing as a full-time student, had been relatively easy compared to being the father of a delightful two-year-old daughter and a husband to Marcie, who spent most of her time shopping for things he could not afford. She easily gave up pursuing her degree in elementary education in favor of the Mrs. Degree that Sam suspected she had sought all along. She reveled in playing the role of a Jewish American Princess, compliments of the trust fund her parents had set up for her. Life was good. Still, he could not shake the sense of being trapped. Expectations and responsibilities seemed to surround him like the walls of a prison cell closing in, threatening to suffocate him. Sam was still unsure if he was ready for this forced transition into adulthood. He was scared.

Summer abruptly turned to fall. Sam gave his job everything. Marcie complained endlessly that he loved his work more than he loved her. He believed she might be right. To say he was conflicted was an understatement. Guilt, combined with ambivalence, resulted in his active avoidance of all things domestic. He wondered what he would have done had Marcie not become pregnant, and what life would have been like with Valentina Thompson. Those musings faded when he met his daughter, Sidney. They stopped completely when he met Annie.

CHAPTER 24
May 2012

I may have told Nick," Sidney said, peeking over the rim of her coffee mug.

"You may have told Nick," Sam repeated, his hands placed squarely on his hips as he loomed over the kitchen table. "Either you did or you didn't. Which is it?"

"Well, I guess I sort of did. I'm pretty sure Nick wouldn't have called the media."

"Somebody did, and you were the only one I told."

"Look at it this way, Pop, it's free publicity for your book on Wyoming's lost cemeteries."

"It's out of print, and the rights are held by my former publisher who just happens to be married to your mother."

"Well then, it's publicity for your new book—the catalog of cemeteries county by county." She fidgeted with her eyeglasses, avoiding Sam's gaze.

"That proposal hasn't been funded yet. That's why I'm teaching Introduction to Photography to a bunch of morons who think their phone is a camera. Look, Sid, my credibility is shot if this is as bad as I think it is. Maybe Nick told one of his buddies in the sheriff's office who told one of his buddies in the Albany County office. You know those guys have their own fraternity: Sigma Alpha Stop or I'll Shoot."

"That's not a fair characterization of our law enforcement professionals and you know it," Sidney said, her hackles raised.

"Somebody called the *Boomerang*," Sam said, referring to the local Laramie newspaper. "I suspect they called the *Branding Iron*, the student newspaper, too. Why else would the VP for Academic Affairs want to see me as soon as I get to campus? I'm sure the president has seen the article. I'll be the only person in Laramie who hasn't."

"Here it is," Sidney said as she tapped the keys on her laptop and leaned over the screen. "Page one, above the fold. Oh my, there's a picture. Here's the caption: 'Award-winning photographer Sam Dawson, noted for finding lost cemeteries, uses divining rods to dowse for hidden graves.'" Sidney looked up at her father. "I thought you said there was no one around when you were there."

"There wasn't."

"You must have overlooked the person with the camera and flash," Sidney said, frowning.

"This is worse than I thought. I'll be lucky if that picture doesn't go out over the wire and get picked up by a major news service."

"How sure are you about the graves?" Sidney leaned back in her chair and pushed her heavy glasses up again.

"Damn sure! There's a lot of other junk down there. Probably water lines, gas lines, buried electrical lines, maybe even the infamous steam tunnels that all somehow missed the small cemetery. It's there all right. I counted eleven graves— two rows of four and one row with three. They're symmetrical, laid out east to west. It's a cemetery for sure. Too big for a family plot. I seriously doubt that it's Native American unless the Army buried them. It probably predates Old Main."

"I read someplace that the Union Pacific Railroad had gifted ten acres to the City of Laramie to be used as a park when the city was first plotted," Sidney said as she tapped her keyboard. "Here it is. Old Main was built in the center of the park. Construction began sometime around the early-to-mid 1880s, when the state was still a territory. Let's see…" She hovered over her computer screen. "Greenhill Cemetery was established in 1881 when several smaller cemeteries that predated Greenhill were taken out of the City of Laramie. It says here that some were never relocated. They were just built over without the bodies being removed."

Sam distractedly rubbed his chin. "Cemeteries in parks were pretty common back then. They may have moved some of the bodies then ran out of time. They probably just transported the gravestones and called it good." He held his arms out, palms up. "So what's the big deal? Dig 'em up, move 'em, and build the stupid garage. Get on with it already. Why crucify me?"

"You're being paranoid, Pop. The university probably wants your help in locating the graves so they can expedite the process."

"That's it. I'm sure you're right," he said facetiously. "They most likely want to thank me publicly and maybe even give me a reward."

Sidney shook her head. "Just hear them out. It'll be all right. I'm sure."

⤙═◉═⤚

The vice president for Academic Affairs, Sam's department head, the university's chief counsel, and a uniformed campus security cop were waiting uncomfortably when Sam was shown into the VP's office. "No need to sit down, Mr. Dawson. This will take only a moment of your time," the VP said, looking up at Sam from behind his desk the way a snake eyes a mouse. "This university is built upon a reputation of strong adherence to ethical and moral principles. From a research standpoint, our mission is to discover the truth, then teach it. Our integrity as an institution of higher learning depends on our ability to foster trust with our many publics."

Sam scanned the room. No one except the VP was looking at him.

"You, Mr. Dawson, have betrayed that trust. The university will not tolerate meaningless incantations and rituals that present this institution as something less than truthful and wholesome. I had hoped that we could tolerate your antics until the end of the semester. However, your latest escapade leaves me no choice. Your employment with this university is terminated, effective immediately. Officer…" He hesitated and strained forward to read the man's nametag on his uniform.

"Cantrell," the officer quickly offered.

"Officer Cantrell will escort you to your office to pick up your personal belongings. He will then walk you to your vehicle. Leave this campus, Mr. Dawson, and don't come back. Good day." He nodded toward Officer Cantrell.

Wait, Sam wanted to yell. *Don't I get a last meal, a cigarette, a blindfold or something?* His eyes darted around the room. Still, no one would look at him. He cleared his throat. No words followed. Officer Cantrell stepped toward him and held his hand out toward the door. Humiliation suddenly engulfed him like a vaporous gas. His heart pounded wildly in his chest.

Sam remembered little of the quick trip to his office to gather his things or the walk to the parking lot where he fumbled with the keys to the Willys. He was past the summit on Happy Jack before the reality of what had happened settled in. It was Wednesday. On Sunday, the *Boomerang*'s giant headline read: "Eleven Bodies Found on UW Campus."

CHAPTER 25
May 2012

"If you are feeling vindicated, Mr. Dawson, don't," Hank Thompson cautioned over the phone. "Nobody cares if you were right. Most people only care if you are wrong. As a society, we're funny that way."

"Give it a rest, Thompson. I'm in no mood for one of your pep talks." Sam stared at his reflection in the framed photograph of the picturesque cemetery in eastern Iowa where Annie was buried. He had not shaved since the morning he was fired. His salt-and-pepper beard stubble added a few years to his appearance.

"In time, people will forget. Someday a well-intentioned alumna with time on her hands will write a book on the history of the University of Wyoming. She'll mention the graves. She won't say who discovered them or the fact that you were fired for doing so. The graves themselves will become an obscure footnote to the history of a university that few people even know exists. I'd be willing to bet that if you polled America, less than a quarter of our populace could even find Wyoming on a map, and less than ten percent would know where the university is located. Obscurity is your future, Mr. Dawson. Even your outdated books will be removed from library shelves, placed in a cardboard box, and the whole lot sold for a dollar at some organizational fundraiser. So much for your legacy and your contribution to the future of society. No matter, Mr. Dawson, for you'll be dead."

"Quit trying to cheer me up, Thompson. And by the way, are you threatening me? Because if you are, you should know there are laws against that."

Thompson snickered. "Are there laws that enforce conjugal faithfulness? Are there laws that protect the sanctity of marriage? Are there laws against the destruction of a family? What about laws that prevent pain and suffering? Don't talk to me about laws, Mr. Dawson. This is the Wild West. There are no laws."

"Stay away from me, Thompson. This is the New West and there are laws. Your harassment has got to stop. I don't know how you got that picture of me. You're obviously following me. You've gotten your pound of flesh for whatever perceived wrong you think I've committed. Now leave me alone."

"I'm looking at her robe hanging on the back of our bedroom door. There's a tissue sticking out of the pocket. Her toothbrush still sits in the holder in the bathroom, the bristles bent and frayed. On the water glass next to the sink is a perfect impression of her lower lip in Christian Dior's 999. You know how she loved red. On the vanity is a bottle of Chanel No. 5, along with her hairbrush. There's gray mixed in with the black. Toward the end she didn't care. Her skin was drained of color—sort of a dull, sallow tone that was cold to the touch. Those eyes, those giant horse eyes black as coal, lost their shine. They still captivated me. Listen to this, Mr. Dawson." Thompson said excitedly.

Sam heard the click of a button being pressed. Valentina's voice suddenly came over the line, cheerfully announcing she couldn't come to the phone and to please leave a message and she would get right back to you. Her voice had not changed. He had not heard it in nearly thirty years, yet he recognized it immediately—smooth and sensual, her Russian accent still pronounced. He saw her vividly in his mind's eye. She was still twenty-five, smiling, and wearing her Broncos sweatshirt and cowboy boots. Sam could smell her heady perfume.

"I play it a dozen times a day," Thompson said softly. "I'm scared that I will wear it out. I honestly don't know what I would do if I couldn't hear her voice anymore."

Sam was silent. He understood the emotion. He had been there himself after Annie died. He wanted to tell Thompson to move on, to get a life, to get help. He wanted to tell him not to worry about losing the sound of her voice, that it would always be with him. Sam could hear clearly all the voices of the people he had been close to in his life. They were etched into his memory as plainly as their faces. "They say time heals all, Mr. Thompson. Please do not call here again. If you persist, I'll be forced to take legal action." This time Sam hung up first.

CHAPTER 26
May 2012

L et me get this straight," Sidney said. She stood in the middle of the kitchen, arms crossed, her chin slightly tucked, and her eyes narrowed in a laser-like glare. "You've been canned from the only paying job you've had in the last two years."

"My contract was up at the end of this month anyway." Sam, seated at the counter, picking at a muffin, attempted to build his case. "Besides, I can't help it if somebody snapped a photo of me dowsing. I took every precaution. I was framed."

"Your checking account is overdrawn, you haven't paid the mortgage, utilities, vehicle registrations, health insurance, or any of the other bills, including food, that are piled on that trash heap you call a desk." She took a step toward her father. "The phone company is threatening to cancel our service, on which my business and our only source of income depends, and you probably think that's a good thing because you're tired of getting calls from the jealous husband of the woman you once had a thing for. And then you have the nerve to tell me, the daughter you're living off of, that I was an accident, an unplanned pregnancy that forced you into a failed marriage that stole your life? Is that pretty much the gist of it?"

"You can't condense history into a few run-on sentences that make me out to be some kind of ogre and you the hapless victim. It's much more complicated than that. Your mother and I were planning on getting married, just not as soon as we did."

Sidney cocked her head. "What kind of marriage did you think you were going to have when you were chasing after Olga…Nadia, or whatever her name was?"

"Valentina," he corrected. "It's complex, Sid. Don't rush to judgment. Your mother and I weren't officially engaged at the time."

"You were about to be."

"That's right, and I took the vows of marriage seriously. Look, it's hard to explain. I was young and confused about the future and—did I mention drunk?"

"That's no excuse."

"Yes, it is. Marriage was a scary thing to a guy just finishing his sophomore year in college. Maybe booze gave me the courage to take one last shot at sexual freedom. It certainly broke down the social inhibitions that normally kept me from making a complete fool of myself. Actually, I don't remember much of anything about that night."

"Were you in love with her?"

"I don't know, maybe. I had thought about her for years. We had worked together when I was in high school. She was married and had a kid. I just sort of put her out of my head. To this day, I'm not sure what happened. It was kind of an alcohol-induced amnesia where you only remember bits and pieces. The important thing to realize is that I came to my senses, accepted adulthood with all its responsibilities, got out the rule book, and played the game according to Hoyle. My reward was you."

"I'm not buying it. You said I was an accident?"

"No, you were planned. We just didn't know it at the time."

"If Mom hadn't been pregnant, would you have married her?"

"Yes," Sam said without hesitation. "Believe it or not, your mom and I, at one time, were very much in love. We were absolutely thrilled at having you pop into our lives. The day you were born was the most magical event of my life. I have lots of regrets, Sid. You're not one of them. Get it out of your head that you were an accident. You were a temporal miscalculation that brought unexpected joy to both your mother and me. Life, as Forrest Gump said, is like a box of chocolates—you never know what you're going to get. We lucked out. We got you." He held out his arms to her.

Sidney had lost her fierceness. Her eyes searched her father's face. She took a deep breath and exhaled it slowly, then shook her head and smiled. "No, I'm not buying it. Nice try though. You can still schmooze with the best of them. Something's not ringing true here. You said you were just finishing your sophomore year in college. I was born on Halloween." Sidney silently counted the months by raising her fingers, starting with her thumb. "Assuming I was full-term, Mom was three months pregnant when the two of you were married."

"You were premature. Didn't we tell you that?"

"Not that premature." She started counting on her fingers again.

"Your mom was a hippie."

"No she wasn't."

"We didn't believe in formal marriage," Sam gushed.

"Your wedding was in May. Oh my God." She looked at Sam in total surprise. "I can't believe I haven't done the math before."

"It was a long time ago, Sid. Months and years sort of blend together."

"Oh…my…God," she repeated slowly. "You were boinking Tatiana when Mom was pregnant with me."

"Valentina," Sam corrected. "Look, it was complex."

"Don't say that again, Pop. There's nothing complex about it. You were cheating on Mom."

"Please don't make this into something it wasn't," Sam said somewhat sternly. "You weren't there."

"Yes, I was." Sidney put her hands on her hips.

"I was twenty." Sam said defensively.

"Quit making excuses. Did Mom know?"

Sam shook his head.

"How long did this go on?"

"It was just the one time. I sobered up pretty fast when I woke up the next morning at her house with a hangover and a sketchy memory. Valentina sort of stalked me at first. She tried to contact me off and on then eventually gave up. The entire time I was married to your mother, I lived under a constant threat of exposure."

"Who else knew about this?"

"Until Hank Thompson called, I didn't think anyone knew. I assume it was some sort of deathbed confession."

"What does he want?"

"Revenge, I guess. He said he wants me to join her in hell. I took that as a threat."

"Do you have any idea of what he must be going through?" Sidney stared intently at her father. "Well I do. It's a bit of a revelation to suddenly find out the person you loved and spent a lifetime with isn't the person you thought they were. You've sullied your reputation as a husband and as a father, Dad. You've betrayed the people who loved you. And to think I believed it wasn't your fault, that you hadn't done anything wrong..." She shook her head slowly. "It was your fault. You weren't the victim; you were the perpetrator."

"I'm sorry to disappoint you, Sid." A note of anger entered his voice. "You thought your father was infallible. Well guess what. I'm not. I've made mistakes my whole life. I'd like to think I've learned from those mistakes. I—"

"This was more than a mistake, Dad. It was an error in judgment, the likes of which can't be dismissed with a weak apology. This was a screwup of gigantic proportions."

"Look, life doesn't come with an instruction manual. Hell, like other members of my gender, my prefrontal cortex didn't mature until I was twenty-five. My assessment of risk was preadolescent at best. I made a freaking mistake. How about cutting me some slack and accepting me for who I am now?"

"Well, that's a problem. I'm not sure I like the person you've become. When you stop making excuses for the past and start accepting responsibility for the mess you've created, we can talk. Until then, I think it best that you reconsider your defense, file your brief, and let the court of family opinion decide your fate." Sidney gave her eyeglasses a push, shot her father a stern look, spun on her heels, and marched from the kitchen and on down the hall.

Sam heard her bedroom door slam. He sighed. He glanced at his fly rod standing in the corner behind the mudroom door. His fishing vest hung on a nail next to it. In spite of patches of late spring snow, a mess of brook trout was the medicine he needed. L2 looked up at him sympathetically from her bed. He patted her leg, grabbed the rod and vest, and opened the door for her. "That's what I like about dogs," he said softly as he followed her out. "They're nonjudgmental."

CHAPTER 27
August 2012

August nights felt pleasantly strange when sitting on the deck. They made up for heat that pierced the treetops and dried the wildflowers that had been nurtured by the monotonous mountain showers of summer afternoons on the shaded north slopes. Snow would arrive in a month. In the pale moonlight, a string of elk slipped silently in single file through the trees across the valley. Sam watched them, cows and calves, as they flowed in a serpentine line through the ponderosa pine and aspen and disappeared over the ridge. He liked sitting on the porch swing he had hung from the huge ponderosa that shot upward through the deck floor like a giant beanstalk. Sam had built the patio around the tree and was proud of the fact that not one live tree on his land had been sacrificed during the construction of the deck or the renovations of the old cow camp bunkhouse. He smiled and nodded approvingly.

The Wyoming State Historical Society had brokered a deal with State Parks and Cultural Resources to fund Sam's proposal of a photographic catalog of the state's cemeteries. Parks would fund the County Commissioners Association, who in turn would contract with Sam to do the work. The stipend was modest but Sam would retain all publication rights. It would take him three years to cover all one-hundred-sixty-one cemeteries within the state's twenty-three counties. He would start in September. While the counties would receive a cost-efficient black-and-white inventory, the fall colors would be essential for book and calendar sales. He had been busy working out a travel schedule that stayed within budget while maximizing the number of cemeteries he could visit in a geographic area. His goal was to spend as few nights away from home as possible. Three nights in the Airstream was his limit. Pulling Bambi over the mountains in winter would be a challenge. There was no end to the excuses he could manufacture for not leaving Sidney alone. He worried about her when he traveled. Her night blindness had progressed to the point where she was unable to drive after sundown, although she refused to admit it. She refused to admit a lot of things, like having an imperfect father. She had warmed to him over the summer while maintaining an aloofness he could not describe. He was sorry he had hurt her.

In the distance, the red blinking light of a passing airplane reminded him how insignificant his concerns were. Everyone in that plane was dealing with their own problems, whether they were flying into them or away from them. The cordless phone lying on the porch swing beside him rang with an annoying series of chirps.

"Death is part of living, Sam. Do you mind if I call you 'Sam'?" Hank Thompson asked politely. "I feel that we've become much closer over the past year."

"What do you want, Thompson? I'm in no mood for—"

"We tend to get all sentimental about death. Some people just seem to dismiss it and move on with their lives. They think of the deceased as an old, ragged piece of furniture or an appliance left behind in a house they once owned—the refrigerator door left open, mouse droppings on scuffed linoleum, stuffing poking out of a tear in the arm of a well-used recliner. They move on. Yet they remember the utility of that old Frigidaire and the comfort of that La-Z-Boy after a hard day. They can still see the scuffs and scrapes and dents on the things they left behind, the things they no longer needed or couldn't take with them. No sense in getting all sentimental about it. Move on. That's what you told me to do, Sam. 'Time heals all.' It's no big deal. Death is just as ordinary as birth. Pack up your life and move on. How's that working for you, Sam?"

"While you're moving on, get some help, you crazy bastard."

"That's what you're for, Sam. You are my therapy. Without you, I'm afraid I couldn't get through this. You're the reason I get up in the morning. You give me hope. I know my grief will subside as life pours from your veins, Sam."

"Are you threatening me again, Hank?"

"Oh, heavens no. I'm merely stating a belief. I'm a very patient man. I can wait. I know that therapy can take a long time. I'm already seeing results. However, Sam, I can't wait forever. I've suddenly come to the conclusion that I'm growing old. You know, I was older than Val." He paused as if reflecting, or maybe waiting for Sam to acknowledge his admission.

Sam said nothing.

"Funny, I don't envision myself as being an old man. I still see myself as a young buck with my life ahead of me, rather than behind me. Mirrors are cruel inventions designed to scare us into accepting reality. I don't know what I was thinking when I took Val as my wife. You don't consider all the things that would degenerate, become flabby and limp with age.

You don't see yourself bald with wattles and age spots, your skin drawn over arthritic joints. You see yourself as a threat to mankind. Oh, the purity of masculinity! I loved her old as I loved her young, perhaps even more so. Don't misunderstand me, Sam. I'm not bitter for losing her. Rather, I'm grateful for having loved her. The memories will not die. I will always hear her voice floating through an open window in the summer, her scent lingering in a room like notes from a violin, her graceful movement as she walked barefoot across the kitchen floor."

Sam exhaled and swallowed hard. He saw Annie, not Valentina. "What do you want from me, Thompson?"

"In due time, Sam, in due time you'll see what I want you to see. You will feel the enormity of my loss and what you have done. There will be a reckoning."

"There you go threatening me again. You know that two can play this game."

"That's the spirit, Sam. Put your big boy pants on and get in the game. You'll enjoy it. I'm all in, Sam. I have nothing more to lose. I'm calling you. Let's see what you've got. Oh, and Sam, don't forget to put that pretty daughter of yours into the pot."

"She's off limits, you crazy piece of—"

Hank Thompson had already hung up.

CHAPTER 28
August 2012

The King Edward Imperial cigar box was where he had left it concealed. In his mind it was not "hidden." The garage attic was filled with mementos of an earlier life, mostly junk to the unassuming eye. Each item, it seemed, held some invisible attachment to a past that tugged on Sam's heartstrings. A cuckoo clock his father had treated with the reverence of a prized possession was packed in newspaper in a dusty FedEx box. It had been off-limits to everyone else in the family. His father would ceremoniously wind the clock precisely at eight o'clock every Sunday morning.

A pair of dusty and battered ice skates, their laces tied together, hung from a rafter nail. He could feel Tommie's quivering arm as he kept her from falling. Sam's overstuffed scrapbook of high school newspaper articles about football games, wrestling matches, and track meets that seemed momentous at the time, but he could no longer remember, had yellowed with age. He could smell the locker rooms and hear the referee's whistle, yet all the contests seemed to meld into nonspecific times and places.

He used his sleeve to wipe the dust from the top of the cigar box then opened the lid slowly as if expecting something to escape. Nothing had changed. The polished agate, a lead soldier carrying the American flag, tattered confederate play money, Scout badges, a ballpoint pen with a woman whose swimsuit disappeared when the pen was turned upside down, and a folded piece of paper all remained in the box, a time capsule from his youth. An empty feeling invaded his chest as he remembered the letter Val had written him. It had always evoked an emotional response. He wished he could read it just once more. But at the time, destroying it had been the right decision. *Water under the bridge.* He inhaled deeply.

Sam carefully unfolded the child's drawing of a bus, sketched in crayon. The top of the bus was yellow, the bottom blue, including the fat tires. Tiny red hearts dotted the windows. The crude printing of a child learning to write titled the drawing "Yellow Blue Bus," scrawled across the bottom half of the page. He turned the paper over and examined it as if he had never done that before. Sam tried to remember the year Val had unceremoniously handed it to him. It was when he was still press secretary, during the governor's first term. The speaker of the House and the president of the Senate had declared political war over the governor's threat to veto the education bill if he did not get his way. The governor was pushing for a property tax initiative designed to keep the state out of the red while he put together his reelection bid. Sam was up against a deadline for a press release that would be the next day's headline, when he looked up to see Valentina standing in the doorway, smiling at him with bright red lips.

"Saaam, you look tired," she said. Her dark eyes flashed mischievously.

Sam quickly calculated the years. "How long's it been, Val…six years?"

"Jes, almost *sieben*," she said, mixing German with her Russian accent. She looked around the room, inspecting, then shook her head. "You know dis is all puppet theater?"

Sam could not help laughing. Val still could easily see through the tangle of political gamesmanship and reduce it to a simple analogy. "Yes, yes it is," he said, smiling broadly. He noted a few creases at the corners of her eyes. Little else had changed. She was strikingly beautiful, impeccably dressed, and still unnerving in her confidence.

"You have little girl, no?"

"Yes. Her name is Sidney. She's in first grade."

"Sam," Bianca, the governor's deputy chief of staff, interrupted over Valentina's shoulder. "The governor needs to see that press release before it goes out, and he's leaving in"—she said, checking her watch—"ten minutes for the airport." She raised her eyebrows and flashed the whites of her eyes at him.

"You'll have it," he said with a note of frustration in his voice.

Without apology, Bianca turned and melded into the swirl of commotion in the governor's outer office.

"I go now," Val said as she reached into her coat pocket and pulled out a sheet of paper folded in half. "Dis is for you," she said, stepping forward and handing it to Sam.

He caught the faint scent of her perfume and could feel his skin tingle. He unfolded the paper and studied the childlike drawing and printed title. He looked up at her, wrinkled his brow, and cocked his head slightly. "Yellow Blue Bus?"

"It is Russian." She locked eyes with Sam for a moment, smiled, turned, and left the room. It was the last time he would speak to her. A few years later, he glanced up from the table at the Tattered Cover where he was signing books, and spotted her standing in line, a copy of his book clutched to her chest. When he looked again, she was gone. That was the last time he saw her. The crayon drawing remained in a drawer until he rediscovered it while cleaning out his desk after resigning from the governor's staff. He called a professor of Russian in the language arts department at the University of Denver, who chuckled at Sam's question. "Roughly translated, it's English for a common Russian expression of endearment *Ya lyublyu vas*. It means 'I love you.'"

CHAPTER 29

September 2012

Hysteria seemed to be the norm in the tight, cordoned-off spaces of the emergency room. "Room" was a misnomer, Sam thought. Curtains on sliding tracks provided little privacy and less comfort. A child cried in cyclical rhythms with an occasional outburst of unintelligible words. Muted voices on the other side of cotton fabric offered reassurance, or calm directives to remain still, sit up, lie back, swallow, can you tell me.... Something made of glass shattered. Loose wheels on everything portable rattled as equipment moved back and forth along the corridor that supplied people and machines to the sick and injured. Tones, rather than alarms, played musically from the wired and plugged devices. An intercom with too many speakers calmly asked people and places to respond to people and places.

"I'm fine, Dad, really. Please don't make the situation worse by embarrassing me with one of your hissy fits."

Sam ignored her and spoke calmly to the attending physician, who looked to be just out of high school. "What do you think?"

The young doctor, his hair in a man bun, pulled the suture high above Sidney's forehead. He adjusted the tension on the stitches that bound the gash just below her hairline. "Hmm," he said, inspecting his work. "I'm thinking twelve hundred, maybe thirteen-fifty—not including hospital charges, radiology, pharmaceuticals, and laboratory tests."

"What?"

"Wait till you see the total after all is said and done. It'll pucker your butt." He tied the final knot, clipped the suture, and tossed the scissors and hemostat into a kidney-shaped pan. The loud clink signaled his accomplishment. "You get to buy those too." He pulled the surgical mask from behind his ears and smiled at Sam. "She'll be fine. The wound is superficial. You know how head wounds are. They're highly vascularized and bleed like a stuck hog. We'll clean her up, dress it, and get you out of here in a jiffy. Give her five hundred milligrams of ibuprofen when you get home. Keep it clean and see your GP within five days to get those stitches out. Or you can come back here and we'll do it. You'll need to take out a second mortgage to pay for it."

"How's Nick?" Sidney interrupted.

"Suspended, pending investigation," the sheriff said as he parted the curtains and dipped into the bay. He held his Stetson against his chest. "A high-speed chase with a civilian ride along? What the hell was he thinking?"

"It wasn't his fault," Sidney protested.

"Yes it was," the sheriff countered immediately. "In addition to my favorite girl getting banged up, I'm down one vehicle and one deputy. I can't afford to lose any of them. And did I mention the bad guy got away?"

"If he's suspended, can I smack him around a little without getting arrested?" Sam asked.

"Be my guest," the sheriff said. "I'd do it myself, except there's something in the rule book about kicking the crap out of employees."

"He was just doing his job. We were sitting in his truck—"

"My truck," the sheriff interjected.

"In the driveway—"

"What were you doing sitting in his truck in our driveway?" Sam protested.

"Talking," she said sternly. She shot a look at her father that said, "Watch your step, buster, I haven't forgiven you for all your screwups." Sidney continued, "We were just talking when he got a call about a disturbance over at Upper North Crow Reservoir. He asked if I wanted to ride along since it was only a few miles away, and I said sure and that I could show him a shortcut across the national forest that would save him half the time. Anyway, when we got to the North Crow road a dark SUV with Colorado tags came speeding toward us. It was all over the road and nearly forced us into the borrow ditch. Nick turned around and started after them. You know how washboard that road is. We were too light in the back end and the truck started to float. Nick hit a deep pothole in front of a cattle guard, blew a tire, and lost control. We slid into the ditch and rolled over. I banged my head on the rearview mirror."

Both Sam and the sheriff stared silently at her. Finally, Sheriff O'Malley cleared his throat and asked, "And how wasn't this his fault? One"—he held up his thumb—"he had an unauthorized civilian in the vehicle. And two"—he added an index finger—"he engaged in a high-speed pursuit under dangerous road conditions and lost control of his vehicle, in spite of all his training, that resulted in a one-vehicle rollover with a civilian—you, sustaining injuries. Am I missing something here?"

"What were you doing sitting in the driveway?" Sam asked again.

"Just talking," the adolescent doctor said without looking up from the clipboard he was writing on.

Everyone turned to look at him.

"An orderly will wheel you to the front door. You're dismissed."

◦→═◑◯═→◦

It was dark when Sam and Sidney arrived home. The Willys's headlights cast an eerie yellow glow on the cabin and outbuildings. The folded white paper, stuck between the door and its jamb, shone brightly in the reflected light.

"Sam," someone had scrawled in cursive. "Sorry I missed you. Maybe next time." At the bottom of the paper Hank Thompson had simply signed "Hank." The P.S. that followed sent a shiver down Sam's spine: "Sidney—Keep it clean and take five hundred milligrams of ibuprofen." Sam spun around and quickly scanned the darkness that oozed from the forest and surrounded the buildings. Slowly, he unfolded the paper. The child's crude drawing and printed title, "Yellow Blue Bus," caused his hands to shake.

CHAPTER 30

September 2012

The world seemed upside down. Sam had not been so confused since Annie's death and Sidney's near-death experience four years earlier, at the hands of a psychopathic serial killer who had successfully wooed his daughter. The simple solution was to eliminate the source of his anger and confusion—to beat Thompson to a bloody pulp before cutting his throat then sticking a revolver in his mouth and blowing his brains out the back of his head. First, he would nip off his fingers with pruning shears. That would prevent him from writing any more intimidating notes. Anyone who threatened his daughter would receive similar treatment. He did not have a revolver or pruning shears—or even a knife that would not require significant sawing. Sam was unprepared to exact revenge or to defend himself and his daughter from Thompson the Lunatic. *By God, that will change*, he thought as he brought the six-pound splitting maul down on the bole of wood standing upright on the stump. Splitting wood had always been his therapy, especially when angry. This time, however, the only noticeable result was a huge pile of split wood. *The best defense is a strong offense.* He repeated the thought again and again. *Two can play this game.*

"Dad, phone," Sidney yelled from the porch. "It's Sheriff O'Malley."

"Sam, before you go off half-cocked, I thought you should know that we were able to run the partial plate Nick got from the vehicle, along with its description. Two teenage boys from Wellington, just down the road in Colorado, with a poached deer in the back of their mom's Tahoe. We've turned it over to Game and Fish."

"Uh-huh," Sam said skeptically.

"It's unrelated to your gentleman caller, Sam. So don't be barkin' up that tree."

Sam had not told the sheriff about the note on his door or the fact that someone had been in his garage attic. He had avoided the embarrassing discussion of his relationship with Val. "Uh-huh," he repeated.

"Have you seen my suspended deputy?"

"Yeah, he's in my living room, drowning his sorrows with my beer. You wanna talk to him?"

"What do you think? Should I make him suffer a little longer?"

"I can't afford it. Plus, it's not fair to Sidney, who's now supporting two unemployed deadbeats."

"Put him on. And Sam—"

"Uh-huh."

"Take a deep breath and stay out of Colorado."

"Nick," Sam yelled across the kitchen.

"Yes, sir."

"The sheriff wants to talk to you, something about a warrant for your arrest."

◆══◐◑══◆

Sam lay in his bed, listening to the wind stroke the giant pine trees that surrounded the house. It was too windy for early September. The mornings were cold—see-your-breath cold, a warning of what was to come. The safety of a warm bed in a solid structure was negated by the sight of his 30-30 standing upright behind the door. He remembered. Innocence replaced by guilt. Guilt replaced by fear. This was not how it was supposed to be. He had made a mistake. Time meant nothing, and it was unfair. When sleep finally came, Sam dreamed he was an old man. He looked the same and felt no different. He explained to the officers that he was seventy-seven and the man on the floor needed killing. The house moaned as the wind continued its assault.

CHAPTER 31

September 2012

"I liked to pretend that we were the perfect family," Hank Thompson said to Sam over the phone. "We stood erect like the steel legs of a water tower, the model family in the model home eating Belgian waffles on a Saturday morning, smell of bacon frying in the kitchen. We were proud to be the all-American family. She didn't mean to mention your name. It was a slip of the tongue. The Norman Rockwell family on the cover of the *Saturday Evening Post* had gathered for breakfast, fresh-squeezed juice in their glasses. It was too late. She couldn't take it back. To me it was like the fat lady who sat next to you in church and passed gas that brought tears to your eyes. There was no escaping the faux pas."

"From what I heard, Thompson, you weren't Ozzie Nelson or Ward Cleaver," Sam said, irritation in his voice.

Thompson ignored him. "She said it was the recipe from the Left Hand Restaurant that she and you liked, something about a dash of vanilla and extra oil. The silence that followed that little announcement was palpable. It was a perfect morning, suddenly ruined by the smell of a fat lady's fart. She realized her mistake. But now that the cat was out of the bag, she couldn't have cared less. She pissed all over Norman Rockwell's painting of the perfect family. She had a habit of ruining a pleasant moment. I never could decide if it was the Russian or the German in her that made her so contemptuous."

"I think it was her sense of humor, Hank. We both know Val never suffered fools and you were the biggest fool of all. You've always been a nutjob. She was poking fun at you and your idealistic view of the all-American family. Unfortunately, you were too humorless to see that."

"There's nothing humorous about infidelity, Sam. It's more than just being unfaithful. The bond between a man and a woman is sacred. Breaking that bond is the worst kind of treachery. I believe that kind of disloyalty is treasonous and punishable by death."

"Whoa, hold that thought, Hank. Are you threatening me again or are you referring to Val?"

"The Lord works in mysterious ways, Sam. I'm not a terribly religious man. I believe that God oversees and directs the affairs of mankind. He has told us what is right and wrong and allows us to make choices. When you defy His word there are repercussions, a price that must be paid."

"I thought God was supposed to be benevolent and forgiving. You're saying He's a vengeful God who whoops up on anyone who disagrees with Him. Who made you His lackey?"

"You're a crude man, Sam. Someday you will have to answer for your irreverence and misdeeds. If the good Lord needs my assistance, I will gladly give it."

"Well, today is a whole new chapter in your book, *How to Be a Crazy Bastard.* Just when I thought you were a conventional lunatic, you toss in the God thing. I had no idea you were a religious zealot too. What can I expect next, Hank, a suicide vest, a car bomb? As God's messenger, what are you going to deliver? I'm kind of hoping for a hand-tossed Meat Lover's pizza. I'll tell you what, if you threaten me or my daughter again, if you come anywhere near us, I'll arrange for a personal meeting between you and your God. Now there's a threat." It was Sam's turn to hang up first.

"You better hope he wasn't recording that call." Sidney had quietly appeared. Her arms were folded across her brown university sweatshirt with gold lettering, hanging halfway to her knees. "If anything happens to that guy, you're the first person the authorities will come to."

"Fire with fire, Sid. Nothing else seems to work with this moron. I'm thinking of driving down there and doing a preemptive strike on his face." Sam worked the stubble on his chin hard.

"Be careful, Pop. I'm not a criminal attorney and you can't afford to hire one." She studied her father. He was lost in thought. "Did you hear what I said?"

"Uh-huh. Meatloaf is fine." *How can I get my hands on Valentina Thompson's health records?* he asked himself.

CHAPTER 32
October 2012

"Thanks for calling Kaiser Permanente. This is Mia. How can I help you today?" The woman's voice sounded young and cheerful. Sam had discovered that the University of Colorado offered four different health plans for their staff and faculty. He took a wild shot that Hank Thompson had gone with Kaiser. It was a little more expensive for both the policy holder and their spouse with a higher deductible and co-pay. However, the plan's benefits looked more attractive. He called customer service.

"Hi, this is Hank Thompson and I have some questions about bills that you folks have sent me regarding my wife, who passed away last year."

"I'm sorry to hear that, Mr. Thompson. Could you tell me who the primary policy holder is…or was?" she added somewhat awkwardly.

"It's me, Henry Thompson."

"Policy number?"

"I'm sorry, I'm traveling and don't have my records in front of me."

"No problem, Mr. Thompson. If you will bear with me for a moment, I'll verify your account information. Home phone?"

Sam recited Thompson's phone number, which had been stored under recent calls on his own phone.

"Thank you for that. Can you verify your home address for me?"

"601 Spruce Street, Boulder, Colorado…" Sam hesitated, unsure of the zip code. The online phone directory had given him the phone number and address without it. He quickly googled Boulder zip codes, downloaded a map, and scanned the color-coded areas.

"Zip code?" Mia asked.

"80302," Sam said confidently as the numbers came up on his screen.

"Thank you," Mia said slowly. "There we go. Thanks for your patience. There is just one last verification question. Can you give me the last four digits of your social security number?"

Sam had anticipated the question. He had researched tax liens, military service, vital statistics, and come up blank. When he checked with the secretary of state's office to see if Hank had borrowed money and offered something as collateral under the Uniform Commercial Code, he struck pay dirt. His SSN was written in large numbers at the top of Sam's notepad. "Eleven-ninety," he said a little too loudly.

"How can I help you, Mr. Thompson?"

"Unfortunately, my wife didn't keep very good health-care records. Would it be possible for you to send me her complete medical records?"

"I'm afraid we only have copies of benefit statements, which show billed charges, plan exclusions, allowed amounts, and benefit exclusions. You would have to contact her primary provider for the actual medical records."

Disappointed and losing patience, Sam sighed. "Toward the end, there were so many doctors involved that I'm a bit confused as to who her primary care physician was."

"My records indicate it was Doctor Muhammad Husain Ali at Baseline Medical Offices, 580 Mohawk Drive in Boulder." She read the phone number to Sam slowly.

When Sam finally reached a real person in medical records at Baseline's offices on Mohawk, he asked in a commanding voice, "To whom am I speaking?"

"This is Marisha," the woman said somewhat unsurely.

"This is Agent Graves with the Federal Bureau of Investigation, Insurance Fraud Division. Before I continue, I am required to ask if you have legal representation."

"For what?"

"A team of agents is on their way to your location with a number of arrest warrants. I can add one more unless you cooperate."

"What are you talking about?"

"Numerous violations under Title IX," Sam said, thinking of women's sports for some reason. "Will you cooperate?"

"Title IX has to do with equal opportunity."

"I'm talking about Title IX under the Uniform Insurance Code. You'll need to hurry, Marisha. I need you to download the complete medical records of Valentina Thompson to my operative in Wyoming." He slowly recited one of Sidney's email addresses. "I can offer you immunity if you use discretion, Marisha. Do you understand what I'm saying?"

"Immunity from what?"

"Obstruction, for starters. The clock is ticking, Marisha."

Sam could hear her tapping her keyboard.

"Valentina Thompson at 601 Spruce Street in Boulder," Marisha said.

"That would be the one. Send it now."

"Yes, sir." There was a slight pause as she typed in the email address. "It's on its way, Agent Graves."

"Thank you, Marisha." Sam looked at his pocket watch. "If I were you, I'd take an early lunch and call in sick for the remainder of the day."

"Yes, sir."

Sam hung up the phone just as Sidney stepped into his study with a puzzled look on her face. "I just received this from Baseline Medical Offices in Boulder," she said, holding up a single sheet of paper. It was a picture of Lucy pulling the football out from under Charlie Brown as he attempted to kick it. Charlie Brown was upside down in midair.

"That went well," he said, frowning. "I was trying to get Valentina Thompson's medical records."

Sidney shook her head, turned, and vanished into the hallway. She returned a few minutes later. "Epithelial carcinoma of the ovary," she said, scanning Valentina Thompson's death certificate. "If you're going to off your wife, ovarian cancer is not a practical murder weapon. You're barking up the wrong tree, Pop."

Sam pinched his chin and stared at the floor.

"You might be able to stick him with a restraining order if you can prove his stalking is somehow endangering you. You better be prepared to answer a lot of potentially embarrassing questions as to why this guy is harassing you."

"Life is full of embarrassing questions, Sid. It's the embarrassing answers that get you into trouble."

"That's why lying was invented," she said, smiling over her shoulder as she left the room.

And that's why God created lawyers, Sam thought. He decided not to respond.

CHAPTER 33
October 2012

The forest seemed on fire. A bright red exploded through the trees on the eastern horizon as dawn pushed darkness to the west. The Willys bounced onto Happy Jack and headed east. "We're in for it now, girl," Sam said to L2, who was glowing auburn sitting on the seat next to him. There were twenty-three cemeteries in Laramie County. He would start in the southeastern corner. He hoped to cover the tiny towns of Carpenter, Hillsdale, Burns, and Pine Bluffs, maybe Albin, in one day and be home before the storm hit. The light was marginal. It would be partly cloudy in the morning, before the clouds stacked up in the afternoon and a uniform gray descended on the area. The aspen in the high country were starting to turn gold. Unfortunately, there were few cemeteries in the mountains where he could use their color for background. An early-season snow would strip the trees of their leaves. He would have to rely on the cottonwoods at lower elevations for his fall shots.

Darcy Kinkaid's lone grave lay in an oxbow of Lodgepole Creek, north of the farming community of Hillsdale. The sun was still low in the east when Sam saw the grove of mature cottonwood trees that surrounded the single-grave cemetery. He had found the map coordinates on a list of Laramie County cemeteries. No public lands existed in this part of the state.

Sam assumed it was private property. There were no postings other than an occasional tire fastened to a fence post with "No Hunting" crudely painted in white on the sidewall. He parked the Willys in front of a wire gate and surveyed the surrounding countryside. It showed no sign of human habitation, present or past. "Leave no trace, girl," he said to L2 as she slipped under the bottom strand of barbed wire. "A couple of quick shots and we're out of here."

Sam wondered how a single grave constituted a cemetery. He had found several lone graves, some marked and some unmarked, during his career of photographing cemeteries. Most were along the many east-west wagon trails that crossed the state. Some were the beginnings of family plots that never developed when homesteaders moved on. Most did not have ornate, carved headstones like Darcy's. The marker had probably been laid many years—perhaps decades, after her burial. The actual grave was probably somewhere else in the vicinity, having been obscured by nature, especially in a floodplain. Darcy had died in 1878 when she was forty-three. Sam calculated she would be one hundred thirty-four years old—give or take a year depending on the month of her birth, if she were still alive.

"How you holding up, Darcy?" he asked as he focused the 50mm lens on his Nikon. "Well, I'm no prize either," he said, suddenly realizing his age. He was now six years older than Darcy had been when she died. "I'll bet you were beautiful, especially when you were young with your whole life ahead of you. We were all beautiful when we were young. All of us new, like that first sunrise, filled with hope and expectations of adventure. Then life happens. Ain't reality a kick in the butt?" L2's head and tail shot upward as she oriented back toward the road. Turning, Sam saw the sheriff's cruiser parked behind the Willys. "Uh-oh, we're in big trouble now, girl. Cripes, five minutes into my crime spree and I'm busted. Let me do the talking." Halfway back to the Willys, L2 broke into her version of a run, tail waving back and forth as she scooted under the fence to greet the deputy.

"Hey, Mr. Dawson," Nick called out as Sam approached.

"Nick," Sam acknowledged with a sigh of relief. "Call me Sam," he repeated from habit. "What the heck are you doing out here? Did somebody call and turn me in? I just got here."

"No, sir. I was on patrol and saw your Jeep. I just stopped to say hello."

Sam studied him curiously. It occurred to him that he had never had the opportunity to speak with Nick alone. Sidney had always been present. He was suddenly at a loss for what to say. "I haven't seen you around since the accident. I was wondering what happened to you."

"Sheriff O'Malley reassigned me to Laramie County's version of Siberia. It's where deputies go when they screw up."

"Is this permanent?"

"No, sir. I'm filling in for the deputy who lives in Pine Bluffs, east of here. He's elk hunting."

"Well," Sam said, looking around. "I kind of like this area. It's a good example of the high plains. It's quiet."

"Windy," Nick added with a smile.

"Of course, you have to like grass and wheat," Sam added, ignoring the windy comment.

"Hot in the summer and cold in the winter," Nick said.

"It's sparsely populated."

"Hence the missile silos. You don't want to place the nation's strategic defenses in highly populated areas."

"Just what are your intentions regarding my daughter?" Sam said without warning, the words erupting from his mouth like bile from an unintended belch.

Nick seemed unaffected by the question. "You asked that once before. I assure you my intentions are honorable, sir."

"That's the same answer you gave me the first time I asked. And by the way, the 'sir' thing makes me feel as old as I sound."

"Yes, sir."

"It just seems to me that you two have been spending a lot of time together, and I suddenly realized that I know nothing about you or where this relationship is headed."

"Yes, sir. I understand. What would you like to know?"

Sam scratched the back of his head and looked down. "Well, it's not that easy, Nick. I don't have a list of prepared questions or a strategy to find out if you're worthy of my daughter's attentions. I think it's more a matter of getting to know you."

"Yes, sir."

"Are you aware of Sidney's condition?" Now he had done it. In an attempt to redirect the conversation from his poorly prepared assault to putting the young man on the defensive, he had opened up a can of worms.

"Condition, sir?"

"Never mind, Nick. Sorry I brought that up."

"You mean her hearing and vision problems?"

"It's a genetically transmissible condition known as Usher syndrome," Sam said, looking down.

"She mentioned it."

"Did she mention there was no cure and that it was progressive?"

"Yes, sir."

"And?" Sam paused. "I feel like I'm playing twenty questions with you, Nick. It's as if I'm having a conversation with Joe Friday."

"Joe Friday?"

"Never mind."

"Yes, sir."

"You're starting to piss me off, Nick."

"Yes, sir."

"Is your relationship with my daughter going somewhere?"

"Too early to tell, sir."

L2 yawned and looked up at Sam with an expression that said, "Shoot me."

Sam pulled out his pocket watch. "This has been most informative, Nick. It's been great talking with you. I need to get on down the road to Pine Bluffs before I lose my light."

"I'll let you go this time with just a warning," Nick said, attempting a smile.

"Excuse me?"

"This is private property, sir. You were trespassing."

CHAPTER 34
October 2012

What if? Those dreaded words often brought Sam to the brink of depression. Try as he might, he could not help asking himself what could have been if he had chosen the proverbial road less traveled in a life with Valentina Thompson. She had stood at that fork in the road, her huge dark eyes, alluring body, and inviting smile beckoning him to choose her, to rescue her from the mundane. He had taken the other road and too often stood looking back, wondering. Where would that road have taken him? The fields of ambrosia were mythical. He had made his choice and it angered him that, all these years later, he still on occasion asked himself, *What if? You only get one shot at life, yet so many ways to live it.* He supposed he could have made it work. He envisioned many scenarios, glimpses of a future without the necessity of a past. They could have been happy. More than likely, they could have been sad. What did it matter now? She was dead. Only the present was important.

"Earth to Dad. Hello," Sidney said from behind him.

Startled, Sam spun around from the kitchen window, where he had stood watching the heavy snow drift between the ponderosa pines, causing his coffee to slosh over the brim of his cup. "For Pete's sake, Sid, you ought not to sneak up on a guy like that."

"You ought not to ask the man I'm dating what his intentions are." She leaned slightly forward, hands on hips. "Stay the heck out of my personal life, Pop."

Sam studied his daughter. She had her mother's beauty, his temper, and her own combination of emotional traits that endeared her to him. He had chosen the correct path. It could have gone the other way. He was a lucky man and he knew it. "You're right, kiddo," he said, smiling tightly, nodding. "I'm sorry. It won't happen again."

Not prepared for his unconditional surrender, Sidney was speechless. Her eyes darted back and forth across his at the realization that he had taken the wind from her sails. The phone rang. "Get that and I'll start breakfast," she said. "I'm in the mood for French toast."

Without thinking, Sam walked over to the old-fashioned wall phone and lifted the receiver. "Hello," he said cheerfully.

At first there was no response. Then Hank Thompson cleared his throat and said faintly, "She sewed, you know," emptiness in his voice.

"Thompson?"

"She had a sewing room set up in the basement. After the diagnosis, she used it very little. The stairs were too much for her when she was taking the treatments. One night after dinner, she stood at the top the stairs looking down into the darkness and said she needed to get to work. She had nothing to wear to her funeral."

"Why are you doing this, Thompson?" Sam said softly.

"At dinner she would sit across from me without saying a word, staring down at the food that no longer had taste.

Toward the end, she had become an empty shell, skin pulled over bone. You wouldn't have recognized her, Sam." He cleared his throat again in an attempt to regain his composure. "In late spring she looked up at me and said she had nothing to show for her life. She stood up and made her way down into the cellar, where she worked sometimes day and night. She never talked about dying. She would send me off to the fabric store to buy material, thread, and needles. One night she pulled herself up the stairs and stood in the kitchen trying to catch her breath, three dresses over her arm. 'You choose,' she said to me. 'I won't care. I'll be dead. You must promise me to keep the casket closed, no viewing.'" Hank Thompson was silent.

Sam shifted his weight from one foot to the other. He too said nothing.

"After she died, I couldn't bring myself to go down there. It seemed like it rained every day for a month. One night I gathered my nerve and quietly descended the stairs. It was dank and musty smelling. I fully expected to see her usual mess of empty spools of thread, half-filled bobbins, jars of buttons, and fabric scraps all over the cabinet and floor. Instead, I found the room abandoned and cleaned, everything put away. Even the cord to the sewing machine had been unplugged and tightly wound up with a rubber band around it. Scraps of cloth had been neatly folded and stacked inside the cabinets. The clothes rack was empty, except for a single maroon-colored corduroy shirt. The 'cloth of kings,' Sam, it was soft and warm-looking with a button-down collar and flaps on the pockets, much too big for me. Imagine my surprise at the beautiful script in gold-colored thread above the left pocket, the one nearest your heart. 'STD' it read." He paused. "At first all I could think of was 'sexually transmitted disease,' having been around college students for so many years. When I discovered your middle name was Theodore, I realized she had made the shirt for you. Almost thirty-five years of marriage, Sam, and she never made me a single thing, not one thing." He exhaled heavily into the phone. "Enjoy the shirt, Samuel Theodore Dawson. Like the nighttime monsters from your childhood, it's hiding in your closet."

CHAPTER 35

October 2012

W as there anything missing?" Sheriff O'Malley avoided eye contact with Sam. Instead, he arranged the silverware on his napkin. The R&B Breakfast Club on east Lincolnway in Cheyenne was busy as usual. Privacy was not an option.

"I don't think so, at least nothing obvious. Look, Harrison, this lunatic was in my house and you're telling me there's nothing you can do?" Sam said as he leaned across the wood table covered with laminated photographs of Elvis Presley. Elvis memorabilia adorned every available surface of the restaurant.

"There's plenty I could do, if you could prove he actually invaded your home."

"The shirt—"

"Proves nothing, Sam. It's your word against his. There's no way a judge in Boulder County is going to issue a search warrant based on you finding a shirt in your closet. He's gonna say, 'Will the real lunatic please stand up?' If this guy is as slick as you say he is, they're not going to find anything linking him to the shirt anyway. Get real, my friend, there's true crime being committed every day in Boulder County, just as it is in Laramie County. And you want me to devote resources to chasing down the shirt monster?"

"Here you go," the waitress with an infectious smile said as she placed the huge breakfast burrito in front of the sheriff and the giant pancakes in front of Sam. "I'll warm that coffee up in just a minute. Anything else right now?"

"I think we're good," the sheriff said, smiling.

"So you're not going to do anything. Is that what you're saying?" Sam tried to sound incredulous, though he was distracted by the size of the burrito and the river of green chili sauce covering it.

"I didn't say that," the sheriff said with a wink at Sam, his mouth full of burrito. "I've reassigned Nick to your area. He'll be looking in on you and Sidney, mostly Sidney, until this guy stops pestering you or kills you, whichever comes first."

"Oh great, now you're playing matchmaker at my expense. Does this guy come with a food allowance? He eats like a hungry hippo."

"It's an investment. Love's in the air, Sam. Nick's a keeper, so don't screw it up."

"I think you're taking the 'serve and protect' motto a little too far."

"I've seen this guy on the range. He can shoot the pecker off a gnat at a hundred yards. Believe me, he's the one you want protecting Sidney."

"I'm thinking about getting a handgun," Sam threatened.

"Get a dog."

"I have a dog."

"I mean a real dog—no offense to L2. But you'll have to admit she lacks the intimidation factor."

"So do you. You're both old. I can't believe I voted for you," Sam said with a straight face.

"Does the shirt fit?"

"I don't know. I'm not touching it." Sam poured more syrup on his pancakes.

"You really should pull the stitches on that middle initial."

"Excuse me?"

"Having a monogram that reads STD is not exactly a chick magnet."

"Neither is green chili on your moustache," Sam shot back.

The waitress brought more coffee. "Can I get you anything else? Do either of you need a box?"

"Just the check, please," Sam said.

"Oh, that's been taken care of. A nice man came in and paid for your breakfast," she said with a smile.

Sam and the sheriff looked at her as if she had just announced they had won the lottery.

"He said to tell you that next time you should wear the shirt," she said to Sam.

Both men immediately turned toward the cash register by the crowded doorway, where patrons waited for tables, then locked eyes briefly.

"He also said to tell you that Sidney should have joined you."

The noisy restaurant suddenly became silent, everyone orienting toward the source of dishes clattering and silverware dropping to the floor as the two men struggled to their feet and raced toward the door.

CHAPTER 36
October 2012

Much later, it struck Sam just how incapable he was of putting into words the fear that seized him both mentally and physically. No parent should have to experience the uncertainty of potentially losing a child. He had been there before. Neither he nor Sidney had fully recovered from her abduction and attempted murder by a deranged killer four years earlier. Yet here he was again, careening toward the uncertainty of a parent's worst nightmare.

The thirty miles that separated Sidney from her father was a test for the Willys wagon. The sheriff's pickup, with its lights and siren clearing a path, faded away into the distance while the Willys shuddered along at almost half the speed, the front end vibrating wildly, L2 bouncing along in the passenger seat. Sam cussed the '53 as it crawled up the final escarpment west of Table Mountain. The cell phone, which he had promised Sidney he would carry, was still on the kitchen counter where he had left it. His teeth were clenched, his jaw set, and the tendons in his neck bulged as he jammed his foot to the floorboard. Fear and anger were the competing emotions that threatened to overwhelm him. This was the second time the coppery taste of fear had welled up from somewhere deep within him. The second time his daughter had been threatened by a madman. A sheriff's cruiser screamed by him, showering him with sand and gravel left over from the recent snow. Sam looked in the rearview mirror, expecting to see an ambulance following. Only a black ribbon of asphalt twisted between the snow-covered foothills of the Laramie range, the eight-thousand-foot escarpment that separated the eastern plains from the Laramie valley.

Three sheriff's vehicles were parked haphazardly between the house and barn when Sam slid around the last turn of the ponderosa-lined driveway. Laughter echoed from the mudroom that led to the kitchen. Sam burst through the door with L2 hurrying in after him. He glanced around the room. The scent of fresh-baked cinnamon rolls and coffee quickly arrested his alarm. He was speechless.

"Glad you could make it, Sam," the sheriff said, raising his coffee mug into the air. He held up Sam's cell phone in his other hand. "If you had taken your phone like you're supposed to, I could have called you. By the way, Deputy Rodriquez here"—he nodded across the table then continued—"said he clocked you going almost sixty-three miles per hour in a sixty-five zone." Everyone but Sam stifled a laugh. "The greenies will run over you if you drive that relic down to Colorado."

Sidney put down the coffeepot and rushed over to hug her father. "I'm fine, Pop. I was out feeding Daisy when the sheriff patched-through a call and I didn't hear the phone. Nick was the first to arrive, then the sheriff, then Ernesto." She pointed toward the second deputy. "I'm fine, really. Nothing out of the ordinary here."

Sam ran his fingers through his hair and tried to act normal without trembling. He looked at each of the deputies, their crisp uniforms adorned with law enforcement paraphernalia, before settling his gaze on the sheriff, whose oversized mustache made it difficult to read his face. The sheriff's pale blue eyes stared intently back at Sam and seemed to say, "Relax, Sam. I've got this under control." Sam swallowed hard, tucked his chin, raised his eyebrows, and flashed a menacing look at the sheriff. "You tried to stick me with the tip again at the restaurant."

CHAPTER 37
November 2012

October had typical fall-like weather right up through Halloween, Sidney's twenty-ninth birthday. November, however, was a different story. The winter winds started with a vengeance and promised not to let up until late May or early June. Sam cussed the wind during the day. At night he found its arrhythmic blowing soothing as he huddled within the confines of the home he had built, safe from the deadly cold chill they unleashed. He poked the coals in the fireplace and stacked more wood on the orange embers. The house was dark. There was something primordial about watching fire, hypnotized by the rising fingers of smoke then startled by the whoosh of combustion before the reassuring light and heat reflected from his face. In the end, the light and warmth brought reassurance and relief.

The mantle clock betrayed his comfort when it struck three. The house shivered, then seemed to hunker down in preparation for the next gusty assault. L2 padded over and sat by the fire next to Sam. Her light brown fur had lost its bronze sheen and her amber eyes had dulled. "Stink hound," he said softly, acknowledging her presence. She had just turned thirteen.

The kitchen phone sputtered, an incomplete ring followed by another that seemed cut short. Sam quickly answered, afraid that it would awaken Sidney. "What?" he said instead of his customary hello, agitation in his voice.

"I knew the holidays would be hard," Hank Thompson said.

"Do you know what time it is, Thompson?" Sam said, glancing at the clock again.

"She never really understood Thanksgiving. It seemed that every year I had to explain its origin and tradition to her. She was better at Christmas. At the time they left Germany, her family, who had been Evangelical, had settled along the Volga with the other Lutherans. The Catholics, Reformists, and Evangelicals never totally recovered from Stalin's purge of religion from the Soviet Union in the 1930s. They viewed religion skeptically. It was something that offered tradition, but it lacked the zealotry you see in this country. She would decorate the house, put up a tree in the living room, and buy gifts—never for me, however. Not once did she buy me a gift. Why do you suppose that is, Sam?"

"I don't know. Maybe it was because you're a mentally abusive jerk—always naughty, never nice. She despised you, Thompson. You expected her to buy a gift for someone she hated? She should have divorced your ass thirty-five years ago." Sam felt his pulse quicken.

"Why? So she could be with you?"

"No," Sam shot back. "So she could have found some happiness in her life. I've got to tell you, Hank, being married to you was probably pure hell for her. Can you imagine the hopelessness she felt, waking up every morning knowing she was wasting her life with a miserable bastard like you?"

"If this is your idea of a counteroffensive, Sam, it's not working. Don't try to make me out as the bad guy here. Let's not forget what you've done. And never assume that you understand the complexities of my relationship with my family. Don't you see, Sam, that's my goal, my sole purpose in life? I want you to understand. I want you to feel my loss, my betrayal. You have no idea what hopelessness feels like. Trust me, Sam, you are about to find out."

"Are you threatening me again?" Sam glanced at the kitchen clock. His heart pounded angrily in his ears.

"Not at all. I'm just prognosticating."

"See if you can predict this." Sam slammed the phone down. The wind pushed against the windows. It would never give up. Above the din he heard Daisy blow, followed by a protracted squeal.

Subdued, orange light reflected from the log walls and flickered around the room. Sam stared at the fireplace. It took a few moments for him to realize the illumination was too intense to be coming from the hearth. He stepped into the kitchen, hurried to the sink, and craned his neck to see out the window. The barn was on fire.

CHAPTER 38
November 2012

The Willys was conspicuous both visually and auditorily. He parked across the street a few doors down from Thompson's house. A light snow would indicate his path to intrusion. Sam had considered confronting him on campus, his office perhaps. There would be too many witnesses, too many distractions. He needed to focus. *An angry man without a plan is a dangerous thing,* he thought. Every conceivable scenario he had imagined on the drive down to Boulder had ended the same way—a series of smashing blows to Thompson's face. The consequences of such a physical altercation were hazy in Sam's mind. That was the problem with anger. It clouded his vision. He knew he should wait, allow the authorities to gather incriminating evidence, and proceed legally to ensure the accused's rights were not violated. That was much too civil for Sam. He needed to hurt the man, to inflict maximum pain and long-term suffering. He would beat him to a bloody pulp, then break both his arms. The mere thought of it all was satisfying. An elderly man opened the door of the house Sam was parked in front of, retrieved the mail from the box on the porch, and stared at the Willys. He continued to stare from behind the storm door glass before slowly closing the front door and disappearing. Five minutes later, the police arrived.

The drive back to Wyoming was depressing. He was unsure what to do next. There had been no "best laid plans of mice or men" to go awry. It was a thoughtless spur-of-the-moment act of vengeance. *Victimized and helpless!* His plan of taking the offensive was doomed for failure. He needed to concentrate on a defensive strategy, perhaps a security system with cameras and alarms. *What's with this guy?* Yes, he had shown up at her house, and drunkenness was no excuse. That was almost thirty years ago—and she was dead, for crying out loud. *What's with this guy?* Surely there was a statute of limitations on stupidity, one that included a special clause that considered how provocative she was, combined with his naïveté. *It takes two to tango.* Shouldn't her complicity offer him some leniency? He had been impulsive and irresponsible. She had been beautiful and seductive. What about redemption? Wasn't he eligible? Sam's jaw muscles were so tight, his ears ached. He had kept his secret. He had never told another living soul. Tortured by guilt, he was being held accountable.

The blackened remains of his barn jumped out at him as he made the final turn into the driveway. It could have been worse, much worse. Daisy could have been killed or injured. He was confident the horse would eventually enter the barn again without being led. The Laramie County Fire District #8 volunteers had arrived in record time with a pumper and manpower. Log buildings tend to burn more slowly than stick-built structures due to their lack of oxygen, so most of the barn had been saved. The bales of hay proved to be the most difficult to extinguish. The insurance adjustor came the next day and assured Sam he would be treated fairly. The fire chief was unsure of the cause. He suspected the wiring to the stock tank heater. Sam knew better.

Nick's cruiser was parked in front of the house. Sam was grateful for the added protection, even though Nick's presence was a little unnerving. After all, Sidney was his daughter. How was he supposed to feel? He found it increasingly difficult to talk to Nick. They had nothing in common, nothing except Sidney. He would try harder.

"Hi, Pop. Where have you been?" Sidney said cheerfully. She was making a plate of nachos in the kitchen.

"To hell and back," Sam said, eyeing Nick, who sat at the kitchen table with all his law enforcement junk hanging from his uniform.

"They wouldn't let you stay?"

"Closed on Mondays," Sam said without looking at her. Instead, he focused on the deputy. "Say, Nick, do you fish?"

"No, sir." He looked wide-eyed at Sam, surprised by the question.

"Hunt?"

"No, sir."

"Ski?"

"No, sir."

"Any hobbies?"

"No, sir."

"Nice talking with you, Nick." Sam turned and retreated to his study. "Now we're getting somewhere," he mumbled to himself.

CHAPTER 39
December 2012

Have you ever had a revelation, Sam?" Hank Thompson said as soon as Sam put the phone to his ear. Sam exhaled loudly through his nose as his head suddenly bowed forward, his chin nearly touching his chest. The coiled, cream-colored cord bounced against the kitchen wall.

Sam pinched the bridge of his nose and batted his eyes in an attempt to see through the cobwebs of sleep draped over his head. He tried to focus on the kitchen clock. It was too dark. He said nothing.

"I mean, a true disclosure that comes blazing out of the orderly cosmos straight at you, a fact that blindsides you with such force that you become paralyzed, unable to breathe, unable to deflect the next blow. The Earth tilts on its axis, the skies open up, and a bolt of lightning hits you so hard, your teeth shatter." Thompson paused, waiting for Sam to respond.

Sam rubbed the beard stubble on his chin and cheek. He remained silent.

"Of course, there is denial at first. Then comes some made-up story to help explain the inexplicable, a bunch of lies piled upon a lifetime of fiction. Maybe it's the time of year, Sam. The holidays are when families come together and grasp desperately for memories of their youth. They cling to the belief of their innocence, denying reality. All the while, they sing songs of joy and redemption in an attempt to escape the inevitable truth that man is unmerciful, that life is a constant struggle, that disappointment prevails. Do you understand what I'm saying, Sam?"

"I think so." Sam cleared his throat. He needed coffee. "You're basically saying whine, whine, whine, that you're a sad sack of shit and nothing's your fault." Now Sam waited for Hank's response.

"You know, you have a way with words, Sam," Thompson said politely. "I think you are missing the point, however. I was hoping you would acknowledge that nothing is as it seems, that life is a made-up story. Remembrances are not based on fact. We fictionalize them in order to disguise the truth. Everything is a lie. Sometimes it takes a death"—he paused then added—"or two, to make you realize how fragile your beliefs are."

Sam wished he had answered the cordless phone from his study. Then he could make coffee while listening to Thompson drone on.

"It was two years ago today when two men in uniform, both captains, showed up at our door. Val was horribly sick and home alone when they delivered the news of our son's death."

Sam straightened. Now he was attentive. His mind raced. Should he respond? Should he not respond? What should he say? "I-I'm sorry to hear that, Hank. I didn't know—"

"It was a roadside bomb, one of those improvised explosive devices that you read about. An incendiary device half a world away that kills and maims without prejudice. We hear about them on the news with such frequency that we've become immune, even impartial as to who's to blame. So many factions, so much hate that we barely give it a second thought as we bask in the luxury of our safe little homes. It's simply another statistic we don't understand."

Thompson was right and Sam knew it. He shuffled his feet and stared down at the floor. His silence was awkward. He wanted to hang up and make the coffee. The guy had lost his son and deserved sympathy, regardless of the fact that he was a whacked-out nutjob. "I'm sorry for your loss," Sam finally said.

"Which one?" Thompson shot back immediately. "My wife? My son? Or are you referring to my loss of time and place, my loss of faith, my loss of purpose, my loss of identity as a husband and father. Or maybe you're referring to my loss of compassion for those who have wronged me, for my total lack of well-being. That's what you should be sorry for, Sam. A man without fear is a very dangerous animal."

"Okay, here we go," Sam said, smiling as he lifted his head. "Here's the Thompson we all know and love. You're back to threatening me. You really had me going there for a moment, Hank. What's it going to be this time—plague, pestilence, fire and brimstone?" Sam nodded his head as he waited for Thompson's response. "Hank? Hello? You still there?" He waited. There was no reply. Thompson had hung up.

CHAPTER 40
January 2013

Greenhill Cemetery was an oasis on the western edge of the Laramie high plains. There was no hill. In the summer it was green with trees and shrubs that shot upward from the square of high mountain desert delineated by six feet of chain-link fence. In the winter, the evergreens appeared dark as they stood sentinel over rows of headstones. It had been one hundred and thirty years since the City of Laramie had attempted to consolidate a number of smaller cemeteries that lay in the path of development into a new location. During that time, the University of Wyoming campus had slowly surrounded Greenhill. The remains of approximately sixteen thousand people—and a few pets—were neatly arranged within the quiet sanctuary where old campus architecture met modern design. In the spring, flowering crabapple trees provided color, as did the sixty-two American flags that lined the circular drive. It was one of Sam's favorite Wyoming cemeteries. He eagerly took advantage of the sunny winter's day, with only a breeze, to start work on Albany County.

"To what do we owe this pleasure?" the old man asked as he shuffled up to Sam, who was placing his camera on a tripod. Sam's bulky, green parka and the evergreens provided the only color to the cold February morning.

"A grant from the Wyoming County Commissioners Association and State Parks and Cultural Resources," Sam said as he eyed the bent figure in front of him. "I'm doing a photographic catalog of the state's cemeteries."

"Why?"

Sam stopped what he was doing and studied the old man. He was underdressed in green janitorial clothes and an open Carhartt coat. He wore a snug ball cap atop a mop of white hair that billowed out from beneath it. He had on rubber irrigation boots with his pant legs tucked inside. He seemed permanently bent at the waist with a pronounced hump between his shoulder blades, and he needed a shave.

"To establish a historical record before they're lost. I believe that cemeteries remind us of who we were. They allow the future to see the past. By the way, I'm—"

"Sam Dawson," the old man cut him off. "I know who you are. I have your lost cemetery books. I heard you ran afoul of those idiots in Old Main last spring." He smiled from one side of his mouth as he winked up at Sam. He extended his gnarled hand. "I'm Lamar Preston. I'm the sexton here at Greenhill. I've been sexton since Moby Dick was a minnow."

Sam took his hand. "Pleased to meet you, Mr. Preston. I guess I should have checked in with you before setting up my stuff. It didn't cross my mind. There's not many of you guys left in the state."

"Oh, most cemeteries have a sexton. They're usually only part-time or unofficial lay people. The city has been waiting for me to keel over or retire so they can assign my duties to somebody in the parks department with no salary increase.

They'll be sorry when the university paves us over and builds a multistory building to house all their diversity administrators. I read the other day that the University of Michigan now employs ninety-three full-time diversity administrators. Penn State has sixty-six and Berkeley has a whopping one hundred seventy-five. I don't even know what LGBTQ stands for. I'm not sure I want to. Rest assured, as the university continues to grow, they'll want this land."

Sam frowned. "Surely, the city wouldn't let the university move the cemetery."

The old man chuckled. "The university is the dominant dog in this town. When it barks, the city wags its tail, rolls over, and wets itself. Besides, they've done it before. That's how Greenhill got its start. They disinterred the graves from several smaller cemeteries when the big dog lifted its leg and marked its territory. Those eleven graves you witched were just the tip of the iceberg."

"You think there's more?"

The old man scratched behind his ear and smiled. "There's a whole bunch more. It ain't just hearsay, Mr. Dawson. I've got all the records to prove it. One thing about us sextons, we're sticklers for keeping records. I have all the journals from my predecessors dating back to the 1860s. You know, Laramie was a pretty wild and woolly place back then. The railroad brought in everything from whores to grafters to rounders. Murder, mayhem, and disease made for a thriving burial business. The largest cemetery between Cheyenne and Salt Lake was right here in Albany County. It stretched from where 9th Street is now to 15th Street. Student Health, Merica Hall, Knight Hall,

Ross Hall all the way to Coe Library was once a cemetery. The city hired a flimflam man to move the bodies to Greenhill. The swindler kept his costs down by using children's coffins to rebury the remains. The city paid him so much a body. So the guy divided up every corpse two or three ways and tripled his income. He destroyed most of the markers, brought over a few wagonloads of boxed-up bones, and buried them in a common grave over there in potter's field." The old man flicked his thumb over his shoulder as he gestured to the north end of the cemetery. "Most of the graves were never moved. Every time a new residence hall was put up, they dug up a few more. I've been told that if you dig down to the footers of Merica Hall, you'll find some of the headstones cemented into the walls. That building gives me the willies."

Sam smiled and stroked his chin. "I wouldn't think a sexton would get the willies."

"Oh, don't get me started. I could tell you tales that would curl your hair. I knew this old girl who was the librarian, actually more of an archivist, for the extension service. Her desk was in the back of a basement room in Merica Hall where they kept all their publications. It was dark and creepy in the daytime. At night, it was downright terrifying. She was on a first-name basis with some of the things that go bump in the night. This woman was a straight shooter, as normal as apple pie." He scratched the back of his head. "She claimed to see things down there that would put lumps in your gravy."

Sam studied the old man, then smiled broadly. "I've heard some of the stories. They're just stories. I don't believe in that sort of thing. I've spent a lot of time in cemeteries and can honestly say I've never experienced anything out of the ordinary."

"It depends on your definition of ordinary. Everybody's different. I've been around a long time and I'm here to tell you that some people can see things that others can't. In my case, I hear things that other people don't. I have significant hearing loss in both ears and most of the time can't hear it thunder. Without my hearing aids you might as well be talking to a fence post. When conditions are right, though, I can hear the dead talking to each other."

Sam raised his eyebrows and attempted a smile. "Well—"

"Oh, I know what you're thinking. Crazy old coot spends too much time in a boneyard. Maybe you're right. I can't explain it. I'm just telling you what I know." The old man stared at Sam, his eyes cloudy and glassy. "The only two women I ever loved are buried thirty feet apart over there in Row K," he said, pointing with his chin. "They never knew each other in life. The one was a childhood sweetheart who stuck with me all through school and the war. When I came home from Europe we were going to be married. She died of pneumonia in the winter of '46. My wife of fifty-one years is just down from her. It wasn't planned. It just happened that way. Anyway, long story short, you should hear the two of them. When it's windy, especially on a cold winter's night, you can hear them plain as day arguing and sniping at each other. 'Catty' is the best way to describe it. Most of it you can't make out. But if you listen, it's easy to get the drift. They've been at it since 1998. You'd think they'd be over it by now, maybe get along. It's kind of like an endless loop of recorded squabble. I'm thinking about being cremated and selling my plot next to my wife to my girlfriend."

Sam could not help smiling and nodding his head in agreement. The old boy had a sense of humor. "We should all be so lucky, Mr. Preston, to have people we loved care for us after they're gone. I always believed the purpose of cemeteries was for the living. You've added a whole new dimension to that concept." Sam gave his chin a pinch. "I'll have to think about that one."

"Keep your ear to the ground, Mr. Dawson." The old man smiled and winked at Sam then abruptly turned and shuffled off toward the cemetery office.

The mood was gone. Sam took a few shots that anybody could have taken. His creativity was obscured by the confused, unintelligible dialogue of the four women he had loved—Val, Tommie, Marcie, and Annie. Their voices clamored for recognition, rising and falling with the Wyoming wind that had suddenly arrived. In his mind, Sam remembered each voice distinctly. The words meant nothing. He wondered what kind of auditory hell he would endure if he could hear the dead. The stark certainty and finality of his own death gave him pause. Centuries of lying cold next to someone yakity-yakking day and night sent a shiver down his spine. He would tell Sidney to spread his ashes in his secret, quiet glade with a tiny stream surrounded by aspen groves, in the national forest near his home. He would swear his daughter to secrecy for fear that Marcie—and her mother—would someday join him there. That thought alone was enough for him to pack up his equipment and call it a day. Lamar Preston's women had unsettled him.

CHAPTER 41
February 2013

I was too young to have a girlfriend," Sam said as if admitting an embarrassing flaw in his character.

"How old were you?" Sheriff O'Malley asked. "You gonna eat those fries?"

"I was sixteen, immature for my age, both physically and mentally." Sam pushed his plate across the table. His half-eaten burger and mound of French fries had lost their appeal. "Girls scared the crap out of me. Most of the other guys had girlfriends or were dating. It sort of went hand in hand with getting a driver's license and your first car. You know," Sam said with a shrug.

The sheriff nodded his acknowledgment as he scraped Sam's fries onto his plate.

"She could never be my girlfriend. She was a woman and I was just a kid. Hell, she had a kid of her own. Even if she hadn't been married, she was too old for me. We were just friends. She flirted with me constantly, and it made me nervous."

"How old was she?"

"She was twenty-one when we met. She might as well have been a hundred and one. I was just a kid."

"You keep saying that." The sheriff smiled. He held up the empty ketchup bottle for the waitress to see.

"I guess you could say she taught me how to kiss. Before that, I'd kissed a girl once, a dry peck on the mouth, sort of like kissing your sister. This woman, however, had it down. She knew how to do it, open mouth, tongue, the whole bit."

The sheriff raised his eyebrows and sat up straight. "You have the right to remain silent."

"Did I mention she looked like a Playboy model?"

"Anything you say can and will be used against you in a court of law."

"She was on me like a chicken on a June bug. I didn't stand a chance. She scared me half to death. She was the forbidden fruit that just hung there all ripe and red, tempting me to take a bite. I ran the other way. When I was in high school, I found a girl more my age, a sweet little thing just as dumb as me."

"There were two of you?" the sheriff said with a surprised look on his face.

Sam ignored him. "Everything was fine for the next three or four years. Then I got all boozed-up one night when I was in college and went by her place. By then I was old enough to know better. The beer and the hormones conspired to make me attempt to take a bite of that forbidden fruit."

"You have the right to an attorney—"

"I was pretty wasted and don't remember much of what happened. She cried as usual. It was sort of her thing. I think she was really unhappy in her marriage. Anyway, she stalked me for a time after that. I was married by then to a woman I met in college. I almost got an ulcer worrying about my wife finding out."

"If you can't afford to hire a lawyer, one will be appointed to represent you before any questioning, if you wish," the sheriff said, leaning back in his chair.

"I'd taken a vow to love, honor, obey, and all that other stuff. I had cheated on my wife—even though she wasn't my wife at the time and I didn't know she was pregnant."

"Ignorance is no excuse for the law."

"Did I mention how beautiful this woman was? She was really smart too. She had a wonderful sense of humor and, worst of all, she was in love with me. I think I must have been in love with her too. I thought about her every day for years."

"You can decide at any time to exercise these rights and not answer any questions or make any statements."

"I couldn't get the notion out of my head. … What if I had taken the other path? Would we have been happy? Could we have made it work? I think I loved her. I think I've always loved her. She was another man's wife."

"Say three Hail Marys and two Our Fathers." His hand raised in front of him, the sheriff traced the sign of the cross.

Sam stared with an incredulous look at the sheriff. "You think this is funny?"

"Look, Sam, I've heard this same story a thousand different ways from Sunday. It's the old eternal triangle excuse. I usually hear it right after some guy has beaten the living crap out of his wife, or some woman shot her husband a few times. If you're seeking absolution, talk to a priest. If you're looking for civil damages, call an attorney. If you're trying to prove to me that there is motive and opportunity for the jealous husband to whup up on you, say no more. It's a repetitive theme. Like

I've told you before, this isn't going to jump to the top of my investigations list. I've got a backlog of cases that keeps me up at night. This guy's veiled threats don't justify me reprioritizing any of my detectives' workloads."

"So what I hear you saying is that, until he hurts or kills me, you're not going to get involved."

"Yeah, pretty much. But don't overlook the fact that I have assigned a deputy to the far western edge of the county, where there is a total population of two, in order to keep an eye on you guys. I think the taxpayers would have my hide if they found out."

"I could hire a private security firm for less than what it's costing me in food for that deputy," Sam complained.

"I can reassign him," the sheriff offered.

"I'd love to take you up on that. He and Sidney have a thing going. I don't know what she sees in the guy. He has the personality of a road-killed toad. Plus, I don't see a future in their relationship. I've tried to ask him if he understands the nature of her condition and all I get are two-word answers… 'Yes, sir…No, sir.'"

"Maybe that's his way of saying, 'Mind your own business.' You want my advice?"

"No."

"Leave it alone. I guarantee you'll regret any involvement. These things have a way of working themselves out. Sid's a big girl, Sam. Besides being cuter than a speckled pup, she's really smart, unlike her father. Trust her." The sheriff smoothed the bottom of his mustache and softly repeated, "Trust her."

Sam stared at the sheriff for several seconds before responding. "Harrison, you should start writing an advice column for the newspaper. You could call it 'Dear Sheriff Dimwit.' People could write in and tell you their forlorn dilemmas: 'Dear Sheriff, a deranged psychopath calls me day and night threatening my life, and my exceptionally bright daughter has fallen head over heels for Joe Friday, her bodyguard.' And you could write back and tell them, 'Don't worry, be happy.' Is this what they teach you in sheriff's school?"

"Of course not. What they teach you is never to pick up the check when eating with a stupid person." Sheriff O'Malley winked at Sam, smiled, and pushed the slip of paper toward him before standing and walking away. "Oh, by the way, happy birthday, Sam," the sheriff called over his shoulder.

Sam pursed his lips and shook his head slowly. *Fifty-years-old and I'm still picking up the check.* "You'd think I'd learn," he muttered to himself.

CHAPTER 42
March 2013

Sam sat in his study brooding over what to photograph next. Albany County had fewer cemeteries than most other counties in Wyoming. Still, Sam wished he had established some criteria for his photographic catalog. Like the lone grave in Laramie County, it seemed a bit of a stretch to include two unmarked graves above the Laramie River near the mountain community of Jelm. Earlier in his career he had liked finding obscure cemeteries and graves off the beaten paths of Wyoming and other states. Back then, he had no thought of publishing them all between two covers. Rock River and Tie Siding cemeteries were easy finds compared to Mountain Home and the ghost town of Old Sherman. The northern half of the county was devoid of human settlement, except for the ranches, most of which had changed hands many times over the years.

Sam had already finished photographing the Marlow Cemetery, a tiny family plot near Wilcox on private land. He pulled the photos from his file. Little Alice Marlow's hand-lettered marker had faded a bit since he photographed her grave more than a decade earlier. The six-year-old had been sent to the barn to fetch her father for supper October 30, 1932, during a whiteout blizzard. They found her the next day a mile and a half away, curled up in a badger hole. She had frozen to death. Wyoming could be cruel that way. He was reminded of Hattie Ferguson, the first white child born in Laramie County. Her parents put the dead child in a box and placed her on the sod roof of their cabin until spring, when they could dig a proper grave. On a calm day, the remains of the family cabin can still be seen at the bottom of Granite Reservoir, large flowerpots at each end of the porch. The state was filled with such stories. Sam wished he had time to collect them and present them in a photographic tribute to their memories. It occurred to him that he could speed his project along if he used some of his earlier work on Wyoming's lost or forgotten cemeteries. After all, he had more than a thousand images of them cataloged and filed in his study. It would save both time and travel expenses. He smiled at the possibilities.

"Pop," Sidney said a little too loudly, poking her head in the doorway.

Startled, Sam spun around, somewhat annoyed. "Jeez O'Pete, you'd think my hair was on fire," he said, reciting a common exclamation favored by his late girlfriend, Annie.

Sidney smiled. "Nick has the day off. He'll be here in a few minutes. We're going to Laramie for lunch. Do you need anything from town?"

"Let's see…I could use an apology from the provost, a severance check from that little weasel—the president, and if you go by True Value or Ace Hardware, pick up a couple pounds of roofing nails. If we get a sunny day or two between spring snowstorms, I need to get Daisy's loafing shed shingled."

"Anything else?"

"No. Have fun, sweetie."

"There's leftover meatloaf in the refrigerator for lunch. I'm thawing a casserole for dinner. I have my phone. Call me if you think of anything else, okay?"

Sam heard Nick's pickup arrive, the door slam behind Sidney, and the noise of the truck's engine gently fade away. The phone rang.

"What'd you forget?" he said, picking up the receiver. Sidney had a habit of calling him shortly after she left to remind him of some minor detail she had failed to share with him.

"Did you know Saint Paul said all of us who were baptized into Christ Jesus were baptized into His death?"

Sam closed his eyes in a tight wince and dropped his chin to his chest. "What do you want, Thompson? I'm busy."

"Paul believed that we were buried with Him through baptism into death in order that, just as Christ was raised from the dead through the glory of the Father, we too may live a new life. If we have been united with Him in His death, we will certainly also be united with Him in His resurrection."

"That makes absolutely no sense, Hank. Speaking of a new life, though, you need to get one. If you don't stop bothering me, I'll see what I can do about uniting you with *Him*," Sam said, placing emphasis on the word Him.

"I have no fear, Sam. The Lord said He is the resurrection and life and he who believes in Him will live, even though he dies, and whoever lives and believes in Him will never die."

"Does this mean I have to put up with you forever?"

"Since you are an obvious nonbeliever, Sam, your days are numbered. You will not depart in peace. You have not seen or sought His salvation. He will not bless you and keep you.

His face will not shine upon you and be gracious unto you. The Lord will not lift up His countenance upon you and give you peace."

"Holy crap, Hank, I'm in a heap of trouble. Tell me, you sanctimonious, pious bastard, what should I do?"

"I should think it obvious. I shouldn't have to tell you to accept Jesus Christ, our Savior, into your heart. I shouldn't have to tell you to atone for your sins, to make reparations."

"Is that what this is all about, Hank? You want reparations? What will it take to make amends?"

"I've told you, Sam. Your reconciliation, just like that of God and humankind, can only be accomplished through suffering and death. He gave his only Son, our Lord, in order that your sins be forgiven. Our children, Sam—my son and your daughter, were not born children of God. They were born from the will of the flesh. To become the children of God they must accept His glory, His truth, and His grace. They must suffer and die as atonement for our sins, Sam, yours and mine. My reparation is complete. I have the tricornered flag to prove it. Your sacrifice awaits life everlasting."

The lines on Sam's forehead suddenly furrowed deeply. "What are you saying, Thompson?"

"An eye for an eye, Sam. It's Old Testament and is the only way. Can't you see the punishment matches the crime? If there is harm, you shall pay life for life, an eye for an eye. If you injure your neighbor, you shall be injured in the same manner. What could be simpler, more just than that, Sam? Two birds with one stone. You pay your debt to God, receive atonement for your sins, and I get justice for your crime against me."

"Are you threatening my daughter, you sick son of a—"
The line went dead. At the same time, he heard the approach of a vehicle in the driveway, followed by a knock on the door. He quickly hung up the phone, rushed to the door, and opened it.

"Hello, sir," Nick greeted. "Is Sidney ready to go?"

CHAPTER 43
March 2013

"Typically, we don't get too involved until someone has been missing for about three days," Sheriff O'Malley said, staring at the floor and twisting the end of his mustache. "I know there's some history here."

The veins in Sam's forehead stood out blue and his jaw tightened. "For Christ's sake, Harrison, we're burning daylight here. Call the FBI, put out an Amber Alert. Do something. Don't just stand there staring at my floor."

"The feds won't get involved unless they think she's been taken across the state line. The state takes jurisdiction. An Amber Alert is a child abduction alert system."

"She's my child," Sam said with an icy stare.

"She's over eighteen, Sam."

"This can't be happening again." Sam shook his head. His mind raced. His ears rang. The room seemed to recede, except for the empty chair where Sidney always sat. He saw only her face and heard only her voice. But she was not there. The frightening images from four years earlier flowed through his brain in vivid detail. There was no sound. Annie, his soul mate, lay in a pool of blood. Facedown in dirt and straw on the barn floor, Sidney was not breathing. Sirens whined in the distance.

"Sam. Sam," Sheriff O'Malley repeated. "Stay with me here, Sam. I need details. Did you see the vehicle? What time was it?

Where were you standing when you heard the vehicle drive up?
Who are her friends? What's her mother's name and where does
she live? Do you have her phone number? Did Sidney take her
cell phone with her?"

"I told you over and over for months this guy was a threat,
and you wouldn't do anything. Now he's got my daughter and
you're playing twenty questions with me?" Sam shot O'Malley
a look that said, "I told you so." He had long thought the sheriff
adhered to the adage, "Don't just do something, stand there."

"Tell me again what Thompson said. Did he threaten
Sidney outright?"

"Yes, for the umpteenth time. He was all religious again.
He said I had to atone for my sins, that reparations had to
be made, and that God wanted me to suffer. He babbled on
about giving his son as God had, and now it was my turn—the
old eye-for-an-eye crap. My sins were against Thompson, and I
needed to suffer the loss of my daughter as reparation. It was a
direct threat, Harrison. Quit screwing around with procedure
and get down to Boulder and find my daughter, because I'm
about on my way."

"Sam—" the sheriff started.

Nick rushed into the room and whispered something in
the sheriff's ear. Sam could not make out what was said. The
sheriff raised his eyebrows and started twirling his mustache.
"See if they can confirm the call," he said softly. "Get me
times." The sheriff looked at Sam. "Boulder police said the
young couple who live at the address you gave us—601 Spruce
Street—bought the house nearly eight years ago from a bank
in Boulder, which had foreclosed on the property the previous

year. Human Resources at the University of Colorado said they have no record of a Henry or Hank Thompson on their faculty."

Sam looked at him in disbelief. "What the hell are you talking about?"

"Sheriff," an overweight deputy called from the door to the kitchen. "We've got a hit from her cell phone. She's close."

Nick downloaded the GPS coordinates and took off down the driveway on foot.

Sam and the sheriff scrambled from the house in their shirtsleeves, oblivious to the cold. Nick ran past his pickup, toward the curve, and out of sight. Sam's heart was in his throat when he rounded the bend and saw Nick bent over in the snow-filled borrow pit, hands on his knees as if he were about to throw up, staring at something below the embankment. The sheriff grabbed Sam's shoulder from behind. The fat deputy wheezed in the distance. "Hold up, Sam. This is a crime scene," the sheriff gasped.

For once, Sam did not argue. His legs felt rubbery, his stomach hollow. He did not want to see.

CHAPTER 44
March 2013

In the stillness of the long sleepless night, he stared at the neatly made bed where she had slept. The bedspread, embroidered with forest green trees, brown moose, and a sky blue lake, was smoothed, as she had left it, with frivolous pillows arranged against the headboard. He saw her there as she had been, asleep and innocent. He saw the faces of his dead parents, older sister, and Annie, his love. He heard their voices, the unintelligible chatter of everyday things, out of context, unhurried, and unimportant. He inhaled the smell of bacon frying and fresh coffee bubbling in the percolator of his mother's kitchen decades ago. Every time he looked to the future, all he could see was the past. The middle of his life had long passed and he had nothing left, nothing to show for his wasted existence. He was lost. He had fallen into his life with no chance of righting himself. He had thought it was merely a stumble. Now he realized the seriousness of his miscalculation. He had caused injury and pain. Sam inhaled deeply and held it for a moment before releasing it slowly. He knew now how thin the line was between life and death, so much wasted on either side. When she was little, he had lulled his daughter to sleep with promises that all would be well in the morning, that when she awoke he would be there, her safety ensured. He had lied. He had failed. His life was more than half gone, and he had nothing.

His greatest accomplishment was missing—only missing, he reminded himself. Yet his grief was so intense that he wanted to collapse in a corner and let the spasms overtake him.

Her cell phone had been tossed out the window. It landed in the borrow pit where Nick found it. The sheriff had bagged it and tagged it and rushed it off to the crime lab to see if they could retrieve any fingerprints, and incoming and outgoing calls.

L2 padded into the room, her toenails clicking on the pine floor, head hung low, ears almost dragging. She had searched every room of the house. Finally, she curled up on the rug next to Sidney's bed and placed her head between her paws. She showed no guilt, no regrets, only what humans would label as sadness. Something was missing. Sam wondered if she knew what was missing or was simply responding to his own depression. Dogs and their thought processes were a mystery to him. Sidney would have told him that sadness is a human emotion and cannot be assigned to an animal. He was unconvinced. The phone rang.

"Harrison," Sam said excitedly. "Have you found her?"

"Every time I look to the future, I see the past," Thompson said. "I see photographs of my son framed ornately on shelves and walls. Photos of all the good times we had together, reminders of things that no one else understands."

"Thompson, if you harm a hair on her head, I'll—"

"I wish you could have heard him laugh. It made everything that was bad go away. I still hear him. Sometimes in a crowd filled with all the indistinct babble that humans elicit, I hear him laugh with pure joy and it makes me smile."

"Listen to me, Thompson—"

"When I'm gone there will be no one left to hear him. All the things that were meaningful to him, trivial fragments that represented things important to him and no one else, will be tossed out and pressed into the ground at a landfill. All thrown away by someone who doesn't care, someone who needs to make room for their own past."

"What do you want, Thompson? Money? A pound of flesh? What?"

"I want you to understand, Sam, to feel the magnitude of loss. To see the past each time you look down thinking it's the future, and all you see is her face. To see the places you used to go with her when she was alive and still see her there in your mind's eye. To feel the hollowness of something you loved that is no longer here."

"Is my daughter all right? Let me speak to her. Put her on the phone."

"I know he's gone. He disappeared down the road all living creatures take. Don't you see that I'm the only one who can keep him from insignificance?"

"Thompson, listen to me," Sam said sternly. "I don't give a damn about whatever you're trying to tell me, you sick bastard. I want my daughter back."

"And I want my son back."

Before he could let himself be drawn in again by Thompson's continual philosophical babble, Sam checked himself. He'd had enough. His patience was gone. "It's all about you, Thompson, as usual. I don't give a rat's ass about you and your totally screwed-up life. I'm willing to bet you got what you deserved.

Let me be very clear. If you harm my daughter, I'll hunt you down and kill you very slowly."

"I'm counting on it, Sam." The line went dead.

"All right, people, what have you got?" the FBI agent called out.

Sam glanced at the kitchen clock. It was almost six. The sun would be up soon. Strangers scurried in and out of Sam's study.

"Real time, people. Let's go," the FBI agent in charge yelled.

The guy with the headset, who hovered over the sophisticated electronic equipment on Sam's desk, shook his head. "There aren't enough base stations in this state to pinpoint anything smaller than New Jersey."

"Don't give me excuses, Larry. Give me a location," the agent shot back.

"We got two tower dumps so far. There were some intermittent pings. The perp was definitely using android. Our stingrays in Cheyenne and Laramie indicate few calls at the target time. Hold on, Sprint just downloaded." Larry pushed an index finger against his headset, then looked up at the agent in charge. "Scrambled! Our boy has some high-dollar technical gear. Sprint shows simultaneous call locations in Montana, Ohio, Tennessee, and New Mexico. What the hell? Over."

"Jesus H. Christ," the agent said, scratching the back of his head. "We've got us a sleeper here."

Sam could wait no longer. "Where is he?"

"We have no idea," the agent said, turning to face Sam. "This guy is using some very sophisticated equipment that sends out dummy signals that scramble any triangulation attempt by the phone company."

"What's a sleeper?"

"It's a ghost story, Mr. Dawson, and I'm not at liberty to tell it. Let's just say that it's above my pay grade."

"I don't understand. What are you saying?" Sam cocked his head as if trying to hear.

"I'm saying that, to my knowledge, damn few agencies have the technology to do that. The Chinese, maybe. They'll steal the pennies off their dead mother's eyes. The Russians, most certainly. And then there's us. The Bureau doesn't have it, but the Agency does."

"The Agency?"

"The Central Intelligence Agency, the ones with all the money, in Langley."

Sam frowned. "Langley, Virginia? Why would they be involved in this?"

"Exactly! The CIA doesn't get involved in domestic law enforcement issues. Pack it up, boys," he yelled over his shoulder. "We're out of here."

"That's it?" Sam's eyes narrowed.

The agent scratched the back of his head again. "Look, Mr. Dawson, I'm afraid we'll have to await further instructions. Most likely, we're about to be hit by a shitstorm of bureaucratic, interagency 'Who's on First' crap, whereby each agency tries to piss a little higher on the tree than the other one. Until I hear from my supervisor, who's undoubtedly being awakened as we speak, you'll have to rely on local law enforcement. I'm sorry; you're now dealing with the eight-hundred-pound gorilla that just walked through the door."

"What about my daughter?" Sam pleaded.

The man stared at him for a long moment. "We're here at the request of the locals. I'll do everything I can to honor that request. At this point I need to know who we're dealing with. Try to be patient, Mr. Dawson. I'll be in touch."

"When?" Sam demanded. "Everybody tells me they'll be in touch and that's the last I hear from them. When will you be in touch?"

The agent looked intently at Sam. "Oh, I imagine it will be very soon, Mr. Dawson."

CHAPTER 45
March 2013

I'm not who you think I am, Thompson. Whoever or whatever you think I am, I'm not. I'm telling you up front, fair warning, to be clear, I'm not what you supposed," Sam said aloud as he slid the last 30-30 round into the magazine of the old Winchester Model 94. It was the only gun he owned. He had thought briefly about the need for a personal defense weapon. He reasoned he was not on the defense. Rather, he was on the offense. His dad's old deer rifle had served him well over the years. Standing in his living room, he brought the gun to his shoulder, pointed it at the window set in the mudroom door, and looked through the buckhorn sight over the octagonal barrel. He watched a black Suburban pull into the driveway.

"Sam Dawson?" the older of two men called out as they approached Sam, who had gone out to intercept them. Sam did not respond. Instead, he inspected them cautiously. Dark suits, clean cut, Colorado tags on the Chevy. They had government written all over them.

⊷⟐⊶

"His name is Yevgeni Viktorovich and he was an agent of both the CIA and KGB, now the FSB, the Federal Security Service of the Russian Federation, since the Soviet Union is no more." The older man, who had not identified himself, got right to the point as Sam poured them cups of coffee.

"Are we talking about the same guy here?" Sam said with a troubled look on his face.

"Your Hank Thompson was born just outside Stalingrad in 1950," the agent said, his steely gray eyes not leaving Sam's. "He was a prodigy of sorts, has an IQ that's off the charts, speaks several languages fluently. He can cause a polygraph to spontaneously combust. Recruited by the KGB in 1972, he came into this country via Canada in '74, assumed the identity of a dead child in North Dakota, falsified degrees from Michigan and Pennsylvania, and conned his way into a faculty position at the University of Colorado a year later. His primary focus was our missile defense systems. As I'm sure you are aware, F. E. Warren Air Force Base, just down the road near Cheyenne, is one of three strategic missile bases in the U.S. To the south of Boulder is NORAD in Colorado Springs, charged with aerospace warning and defense."

"Wait, wait, wait," Sam interrupted, shaking his head. "Are you telling me Hank Thompson was a Russian spy?"

"That's exactly what we're telling you, Mr. Dawson. Actually, we use the term Soviet rather than Russian, and it's a little more complex than—"

"The sheriff said CU has no record of him on their faculty."

"We've scrubbed all references to Thompson—"

"His wife was a friend of mine," Sam almost shouted. "Did she know?"

"Of course," he said, dismissing Sam's question as naïve. "Her name was Ludmila Nikolaeva. They met at the KGB's Red Banner Institute outside of Moscow. They trained together."

"I don't understand," Sam said, still holding the coffeepot in his hand. "She was a spy too?"

"She was recruited out of East Germany when she was fifteen. Her father was a Russian border guard on the wall, her mother a German waitress. Her specialty was recruiting spies from high-ranking academics for the FSB. We refer to her as a 'swallow.'"

Sam shook his head. "I don't understand. What's a swallow?"

"It's the name we give to a female seductress within the category of espionage known as 'sexpionage.' She was trained at the KGB's State School 4 in Kazan, Tatarstan, southeast of Moscow. She was known only by the number 384. Viktorovich was her handler, her pimp, if you will. He would introduce her to high-ranking university administrators. She would lure them to the swallow's nest at their home in Boulder and he would film them from an adjoining room. It was a classic honey trap used to blackmail them into revealing classified information concerning defense projects under research at the university."

"She was a hostess at the Left Hand Lodge and Restaurant," Sam blurted.

"The Department of Defense funds research and development at University Affiliated Research Centers all over the country. The University of Colorado Applied Physics Laboratory is one of three major DOD-funded centers in Boulder. It was a gold mine for espionage."

"What's any of this got to do with me or my daughter?" Sam said loudly, his body tense as a coiled spring.

"Put down the coffeepot, Mr. Dawson, and sit down," the agent said forcefully. "As I said a moment ago, this situation is complex."

Sam reluctantly complied. The other agent stood rigidly at the end of the kitchen counter and stared a burning hole through him. Sam felt lightheaded. His stomach seemed to turn over at the realization that his secret from thirty years ago had never been a secret and the woman he had fantasized as his lover was someone else entirely. His mind raced. He was just a kid. What could a Russian spy possibly have wanted from him?

"Human emotions are unpredictable," the steely-eyed agent said without a hint of compassion for Sam's bewilderment. "We count on that in our business when it comes to counterintelligence. Viktorovich fell in love with his partner, an emotion apparently not shared by Nikolaeva even though she bore him a child. Unknown to him, we had funded his research on the Volga Deutsch dialect as part of a counterintelligence effort to possibly recruit him as a double agent. He was ripe. He wanted to set up house in Boulder and live the American dream, raise a family, become Joe Average for real rather than as a cover. We worked him for a couple of years, feeding him outdated and unclassified intelligence, before offering him a choice of life in a federal correctional institution that included accidental death by hanging, or life as Ozzie and Harriet in suburbia. He chose the latter." He paused and sipped his coffee like a debutante, pinkie finger raised. "He proved to be quite valuable to us. I needn't go into detail," he said with a flinty grin. "She on the other hand was a hard case. Viktorovich was her handler and her only link to the KGB. He cut her off completely, stopped the honey trap operations. He convinced her that she had been reassigned as his cover for a long-term operation that involved disrupting plutonium pit production at Rocky Flats. All the while he was feeding us names and locations of Soviet operatives in this country."

Sam was well aware of the controversy surrounding the Rocky Flats plant east of Boulder. Woody's and Chip's fathers worked at the plant that made components for the nuclear bombs that were assembled at Pantex near Amarillo.

"As it turned out"—the agent cleared his throat as if offering an embarrassing truth—"she was working as a mole for the KGB, who suspected Viktorovich was a double. The Left Hand Lodge, by the way, was where most of the organizers and peace activists of the Rocky Flats protests stayed. We long suspected Nikolaeva's role was more than that of an informant. The seventeen thousand people that joined hands around the plant in October of 1983, we believe, were coordinated at the Lodge with her help."

Sam suddenly felt even more agitated. He needed time to process all of this. "Again, what does any of this have to do with my daughter? Hank Thompson is crazy as a loon. He's taken her, and you're talking about ancient history. You obviously know his whereabouts. Quit with the spy versus spy crap and tell me where he is."

"First, Viktorovich is not crazy, perhaps a bit eccentric. I assure you; he's very calculating in his approach to everything. Second, you don't know if he has taken your daughter. You assume he has. Third, you need to understand who you are dealing with. He's a master of disguise and can hide in plain sight. He'll have you believe one thing while he's doing something totally opposite." He paused, then added, "This little history lesson was summoned when the FBI attempted to locate Viktorovich."

"Are you protecting this guy?" Sam did not avert his menacing stare. He looked as if he might pounce on the agent. "No more bullshit. Where is he?"

"We don't know." The agent was matter-of-fact, unapologetic. He simply answered the question.

Sam tipped his head and scrunched his eyebrows. His look was one of incredulousness. "A double agent and you don't know?"

"Have you ever wondered what becomes of old operatives, Mr. Dawson? Foreign or domestic?" he added as an afterthought. "Do you think they go on Social Security, cash in their 401(k) plans, move to Scottsdale or Orlando, spend time at the lake with their grandkids teaching them how to fish and reminiscing about the good old days? Most retire after twenty years and receive a full government pension, then go to work as contractors or consultants for either government or the private sector. Not so for a double. They generally don't achieve rank or title from either side. In the end, they have to choose one and hope to hell the other doesn't kill them. Cross and double-cross are the rules of the game. Negotiation is the monetary system. Nobody trusts anybody. These people don't get to retire. They become a footnote in some case officer's report to their chief of station. They're the fake line in the budget, the program that Congress doesn't get to see. Viktorovich chose to stay here and negotiated with the Agency for something akin to witness protection. We were in the process of dismantling Hank Thompson's fictional character when things started going south. His behavior became somewhat erratic after his son was killed in Afghanistan. When Nikolaeva died, he seemed to go off the deep end. A month ago he vanished. All attempts to contact him have failed. We now consider him an enemy of the state."

"Wait, wait," Sam said, straightening in his chair. "You're telling me you've lost this nutjob, the guy who has been calling and threatening me for a year and a half, the guy who kidnapped my daughter, the guy you've been protecting for years using my taxpayer dollars? An enemy of the state? What the hell does that mean?"

"We suspect Viktorovich took out his own insurance policy by gathering highly classified information about our operations in central Europe and, specifically, Russia. National security is at risk here, Mr. Dawson. We can't afford to have a rogue double. He's left the reservation and there are no second chances in this business."

Sam shook his head slowly. There were way too many loose ends. He suspected there was much more to this story than they were willing to share with him—or they were lying outright. His questions could wait. He just wanted Sidney returned unharmed. "Am I hearing you right? Are you telling me that my daughter's life is secondary to your primary mission of national security?"

"I'm telling you that we will bring the full weight of the United States government to bear on finding Viktorovich," the agent said without emotion. "And your daughter," he added as an afterthought, his flinty eyes offering no apology.

"And I'm telling you"—Sam said with all the determination of a threatened father—"if you want him alive, you better hope to find him first."

CHAPTER 46
March 2013

Sam remembered thinking "ontogeny recapitulates phylogeny" when he first saw the ultrasound image of what would become his daughter. Marcie's obstetrician was on the cutting edge of sonography as applied to obstetrics. Sam's freshman biology professor had called recapitulation theory biological mythology. However, the slides he showed of embryonic development and their similarity to evolutionary relatives told a different story. Sam and Marcie had gazed openmouthed at the screen as the black-and-white image of the big-headed, big-eyed tadpole suddenly appeared in the jumbled nursery of the womb. She resembled a seahorse. How was he to know this comma-shaped nymph—this tiny grammatical mark indicating a division, a pause in the sequential elements of everything he believed important—would punctuate his life? Looking back, he realized that she had been the teacher who taught him to let go. From that first ride on her bicycle—him jogging alongside out of breath, her finally straightening out and pulling away, shouting with delight, hair flying, growing smaller in the distance—to her graduation ceremonies, robed in black in a sea of black, setting sail for an independent life. She kept saying goodbye. He never took it seriously. She was gone now. He tried to remember if he had recently told her he loved her. Surely, he had.

⋅►═◑═◄⋅

The government spooks had left him with nothing. Not even hope. They operated in the shadows and delighted in secrecy. Sam suspected they knew much more about Thompson's whereabouts than they let on. They gave Sam the impression they were more interested in watching Thompson than bringing him back under their control. Sidney was a fly in the ointment and definitely secondary to their mission, whatever that was. Nobody was in charge and Sam felt helpless. The sheriff had been pushed aside by the FBI, who in turn had been trumped by the CIA, who had not even left him with contact information. Sam had failed to get the agents' names. He was on his own. He stared out over the valley below his deck. A rare winter fog had settled in over the trees and rocks, a smoky whiteness that made everything fuzzy. Over and over in his mind he debated whether to call Marcie. He rehearsed his lines, adding and subtracting pertinent information in an attempt to soften the blow. His conclusion was always the same. The last thing he needed was Marcie's drama. What he did need was a plan. "I guess it's up to us, ole girl," he said, looking down at L2 sitting next to him on the deck, the sadness in her eyes contagious.

⋅►═◑═◄⋅

The gloves were off. No more Mr. Nice Guy. Sam shook his head at the realization that he had spent his entire life trying to be good, at how much time had been wasted being mannered and proper. He was done being polite.

During his stint as press secretary to the governor, Sam had learned that—after disasters—the media loved most to expose government incompetence and conflict, and in so doing point a finger of blame at an elected official. In turn, politicians covered their butts by invariably overreacting with an over-blown preemptive strike. Nobody wanted to be left holding the bag. Politicians were scared to death of the media. Their entire careers—past, present, and future, were at stake. The media knew it and could be quite creative in how they assigned blame or assassinated a person's character. In essence, they were the unelected kingpin who governed by innuendo and outright intimidation. He smiled at the recollection of a paper he had written for a senior journalism class on Oswald Spengler's *The Decline of the West*, in which Spengler compared the press to an army, and readers to soldiers. Soldiers were taught to obey blindly. Likewise, the reader neither knew, nor was allowed to know, the purpose they were being used for. Freedom of thought was totally sacrificed while civilization and culture decayed. Sam had been a part of it. He knew how it worked and was good at manipulating the press to ensure the desired outcome. Sewage ran downhill. He would start at the top.

The press was a tight-knit, competitive group that, at the end of the day, enjoyed each other's company regardless of political affiliation. They were loyal to their profession and each other. Sam knew how to work with them. He picked up the phone, called in some markers, asked for a few favors, then prepared the copy. Give them the angle, do their fact-checking for them, and above all don't make them rewrite the release. The easier for them, the better—and the more likely it would run. Wyoming was a piece of cake compared to Colorado. He started with the congressional delegation, then implicated the governor before accusing the county commissioners. It was poetry in motion as heartstrings were tugged, injustices exposed, and government ineptness indicted. Wyoming's senior senator was on the Judiciary committee, the governor's director of the Division of Criminal Investigation was a holdover from the previous administration, and the chairman of the Laramie County commissioners was running for mayor of Cheyenne on a platform of law and order and government accountability. It was a perfect storm. The media was the judge, jury, and executioner.

"Jesus, Sam, do you have any idea what you've unleashed?" Sheriff O'Malley whimpered into the phone less than twenty-four hours after Sam's campaign began.

"The feds are protecting this guy. I want my daughter back. It's as simple as that." Sam was tired and in no mood to defend his actions.

"You know my term is up next year and that I'm running again?" Sam did not respond. He knew.

"My phone hasn't stopped ringing since the paper hit the stands this morning. Channel 5 is setting up in the parking lot right now. I'm on your side, Sam. I think the world of Sidney. Why—"

"I've not mentioned the sheriff's office."

"I'm the chief law enforcement official for this county. The buck stops here. What were you thinking?"

"I'll tell you what I'm thinking, Harrison. I'm thinking about my daughter who has been kidnapped, and everybody is standing around with their fingers in their butts saying, 'Not my job.' The feds aren't going to intimidate me. I'll hold them down on their backs and pluck off their legs one at a time until I get Sidney back."

"So I'm just collateral damage in this whole shitaree of yours?"

"I want the high muckety-mucks to put the squeeze on the feds until they give up Thompson. The media is going to demand answers. They're going to name names and assign blame. You know the drill, Harrison. You've been in this game for a long time. You can't be their friend; you can't be their enemy. Don't give 'em excuses, especially the old standby of not having enough resources. They'll tear you a new one. Don't worry about jurisdiction—you're their highest elected law enforcement official. Get out of the county and demand answers from those blue-blazered, penny-loafered twenty-two-year-olds that run our congressional offices. If you bow your neck and dig in your heels, the press will have you for lunch. They're on the hunt and they smell blood. My advice to you, Sheriff, is to get on board this train. It's about to leave the station."

"What? I'm sorry, I wasn't paying attention. I tuned you out when you started telling me how to do my job."

"Whoops, there's the other line. Gotta go, my friend."

"You only have one line, Sam."

"Help me find Sidney, Harrison."

"You know I will, Sam."

CHAPTER 47
April 2013

Sam's media blitz was complete. It was April Fools' Day, and Sidney had been gone for five days. He waited. The politicians had been quick to launch investigations and demand answers. Bucks were being passed furiously. The finger-pointing was directed toward political rivals, then subordinates. The local media, used to covering pothole repairs and high school sports, were quickly consumed by the larger, more powerful regional press. The syndicated media picked up the story and ran with it, a trail of yellow journalism in their wake. Sam had unplugged the phone. They would soon discover where he lived and swarm into the forest, each with an exclusive angle. He had to hurry.

The feds already knew where he lived. He counted on it. The black Suburban arrived with a spray of gravel as Sam finished packing the Willys. The gods were smiling upon him, he reckoned, when the same two CIA agents bolted authoritatively from the vehicle. "Good morning," Sam called cheerfully. "I was hoping it would be you."

"Dawson, do you have any idea who you're dealing with?" the older agent said sternly as they approached.

"I think so," Sam said. "You're the same assholes that were here earlier." He smiled as he smoothly pulled the old Winchester from the back of the Willys station wagon. The crescent-shaped steel butt plate caught the younger agent squarely in the face with a fleshy thud. In the same fluid movement, he chambered a round and pointed the muzzle directly at the chest of the older agent as the younger man crumpled to the ground. "If you so much as blink, I'll blow your spine all over the driveway."

"You've just unleashed a shitstorm, Dawson, the likes of which you can't imagine," the older agent snarled.

"No more Mr. Nice Guy," Sam growled. "I want my daughter back. We can end this right now. All you have to do is tell me where Thompson is."

"With all the attention you've rained down on the Agency, do you really think you can get away with this?"

"The hard way or the easy way," Sam stated matter-of-factly. "What's it going to be?"

"What? You're going to shoot me?"

"Heavens no," Sam said with a surprised look on his face. "I'm going to torture you."

⊷⊶⊷⊶⊷

"Do you know why Holden Caulfield in Salinger's *The Catcher in the Rye* gave up on his dream of escaping to a cabin in the woods, Agent…?" Sam asked as they ducked through the narrow passageway into the abandoned bunker that was now surrounded by national forest. Thrown off balance with his hands bound behind his back, the agent stumbled in. "In all the excitement, I forgot to ask your name."

"Up yours," the red-faced agent said defiantly.

"Yes, you're exactly right. It was the obscene graffiti that seemed to pop up everywhere. The carousel in Central Park, his sister's school, the Metropolitan Museum of Art—it was ubiquitous. He couldn't escape it. No matter where you go, you'll always find an 'up yours' scrawled on the wall. Even here in the middle of nowhere," he said with a quick nod toward the fortification, the 30-30 aimed straight at the agent. The walls were covered with lewd proclamations. "Before this was part of the national forest, it was Fort D. A. Russell, which, as you know, is now F. E. Warren Air Force Base. They used it as a bombing and artillery range during World War II. Can you imagine that? They blew up some of the most spectacular scenery in the world, all in the name of national defense." Sam paused, hoping the agent would see the parallel between sacrificing the environment and his daughter in the name of national defense. "I think this was an observational bunker rather than a gun placement. If you look out that little window you can see where the artillery range was." Sam had discovered the well-concealed bunker years earlier when searching for a lost post–Civil War cemetery at the former fort. The graffiti, smell of urine, and empty beer cans were attestive to others' finding it as well. Sam shook his head. "You know what's wrong with the public lands, Agent in Charge? The public!" he stated with authority, not waiting for a response. "You wouldn't believe how much damage they do with their soil-eroding four-by-fours, ATVs, and dirt bikes. When they're done destroying a wet meadow or a flower-covered hillside, they throw out a case of empties and their Big Mac wrappers."

"Look, Dawson, do you really think I'd tell you where Viktorovich is, even if I knew? Can you loosen the ropes? My hands are swelling from the altitude."

"A little swelling is the least of your worries, Agent in Charge. When I get done with you, there won't be anything left to swell. Now sit down."

"You'll spend the rest of your life in a federal prison. Turn me loose and I'll do what I can to get you a reduced sentence."

Sam pushed him to his knees roughly then forced him face-down into the litter that covered the floor. He quickly bound the agent's ankles together and tied a short rope between his wrists and his ankles. "Hogtied," he proclaimed cheerfully. Sam pulled the agent back up onto his knees so he could watch as Sam emptied the contents of his daypack onto a folded towel he had placed on the floor. Slowly and neatly he arranged the assortment of knives, scissors, pruning shears, pliers, fishhooks, and a large Band-Aid. He studied them quietly. "Now…I think pulling off fingernails or nipping off fingers is overrated. Same goes for waterboarding, even if I had water. What I think would be most effective is for you to see, with minimal pain, what is happening to you. Don't you agree?"

"Don't be stupid, Dawson. Quit while you're ahead. Plead temporary insanity. I'll back you up."

Sam opened the agent's white shirt violently, buttons popping and flying. "Last chance, Agent in Charge. Where's my daughter?"

"I don't know. I'll help you find her. I'll bring all the resources the Agency has to offer to find her."

"If you didn't know where Viktorovich was, you would have brought those resources to bear already. You're lying." Sam pulled on a pair of surgical gloves that he used for spraying pesticides to control the bark beetles.

"Don't do this, Dawson. Think what you're doing to you and your daughter's future. There's no going back."

Sam took the scissors and cut the man's tee shirt from the bottom all the way to the neck. He examined the agent's pale and flabby abdomen. "I should think right here is a good spot," he said, tracing a line with his finger on the man's skin. "Did you ever see the movie, *Braveheart,* starring Mel Gibson as Wallace fighting for Scottish independence? At the end they torture Wallace in order get him to plead for mercy. They open him up and pull out his intestines for the amusement of the cheering crowd. They disembowel him while he is still conscious," Sam added for emphasis. "I have to tell you, it'll make you squirm." He looked at the agent in charge pensively. "That's nothin'. I've got my own twist that'll make you think twice about protecting Viktorovich." Sam reached into the backpack and retrieved a small cloth bag with the opening tied shut. Cautiously he groped the bag as if trying to discern its contents, grasped something through the cloth, then slowly opened it. Carefully, he transferred his grip from one hand to the other, from outside the bag to the inside. Sam pulled out the small, agitated snake. "Found this little fella crawling across the road near Cheyenne. His name is Bill. He only has one button, young of the year. The venom, however, is more toxic than in older rattlesnakes." He held up the ten-inch-long squirming viper for the agent to see. Pleased with himself, Sam smiled broadly. "I'm going to make a small incision through the abdominal wall, insert Bill, then plaster that big Band-Aid over the hole so he can't get out. Where's my daughter?"

"Sounds like a plan, Sam. How can I help?" Sheriff O'Malley said from the entrance to the bunker.

Startled, Sam spun around to face him. "Harrison, what are you doing here? How did you find me?"

"Your cell phone, you big dummy. I have to tell you, Sam, you'd make a horrible criminal. Now put your little buzz worm back in the bag," he said, nodding toward the rattler Sam was still holding.

"Thank God you're here, Sheriff. Arrest this lunatic and cut me loose," the agent in charge commanded.

"Shut your piehole or I'll leave your sorry ass for the bears and coyotes. They'll untie ya. Now, I don't know what kind of sick pervert you are. I'm pretty sure it falls under the general heading of sodomy—forcing my friend Sam here to tie you up and play with serpents while you watched and achieved gratification."

"I'm Agent—"

"I know who you are," the sheriff cut him off. "I've got your partner down at Cheyenne Regional getting his nose reset. You should have done your homework before coming into my county and attempting to intimidate one of my citizens. Mr. Dawson here"—he said, nodding toward Sam—"is on a first-name basis with the former governor of Colorado, who, as you should know, ran for the U.S. Senate some years back and is now Chairman of the Senate Select Committee on Intelligence. Your Agency's budget, submitted by the president, was held over this morning pending further review of something to do with your Witness Protection Program. If I were you, I'd be pretty damn careful how you treat my whistleblowing friend here." The sheriff pulled out a pocketknife, cut the rope that bound the agent's ankles to his wrists, and dragged the agent to his feet.

"I'll have your badge for this," the agent in charge threatened.

"Hold up, Sam. Bring little Bill over here. Boxers or briefs?" he asked the agent in charge.

"What?"

"You heard me, boxers or briefs? You keep mouthing off like you've got a pair. Wait till you see how big they are after Bill gets done with you. Those babies will swell up like a couple of drowned puppies. You'll feel like a bull elephant is standing on you nuts."

"What is wrong with you people?"

"Welcome to Wyoming," the sheriff said and smiled as he gingerly took Bill from Sam. He pulled the agent toward him by his waistband and dropped Bill inside his underwear. "Sic balls, Bill," he said loudly, his grin stretching from ear to ear.

"You crazy bastard," the agent screamed as he started hopping up and down, his ankles still tied together.

"Let's give these two some privacy, Sam," the sheriff said, then ducked through the entryway onto the pine-covered hillside with Sam right behind him. A mountain breeze tousled the sheriff's moustache. He shook his head. "Where in the world did you find a hognose snake?"

"He was playing upside-down possum on the side of the road near Pine Bluffs. He's totally harmless."

"They look just like the real thing," the sheriff said. "They'll even shake their tail and mimic the sound of a rattler."

The screaming from inside the bunker suddenly stopped.

"I hope the old boy didn't have a heart attack. That could present a problem, Sam."

Both men rushed back into the bunker. The agent was lying on his side. Bill was splayed out, belly up, playing possum next to the man's feet. The sheriff quickly checked the agent's vitals. "I think he fainted." He looked up at Sam. "Did it ever occur to you that he really doesn't know where Thompson is?"

"I think they're trained to keep their mouths shut. He knows. If he doesn't, he's a poor excuse for a CIA agent."

The agent in charge moaned, blinked repeatedly, then opened his eyes fully. A look of terror swept across his face.

"Don't move," the sheriff said, unfolding his pocketknife again. "Bill gotcha in the gonads. I'm going to have to amputate. This might hurt. Sam, hold him down."

"Wait," Sam said. "Can't you call for a helicopter or something? If we got him to the hospital right away, they could give him antivenom and save both him and his manhood."

"Yeah, I could. I've gotta ask, what's in it for me?"

"Thompson," Sam said quickly. "If he tells us where Thompson is, you call in Flight For Life."

"I don't know. If he knew where Thompson was, he would've told us by now," the sheriff said, wiping the blade of his knife on his pants.

"I'll tell you," the agent said with a resigned exhale. "Now get me to a hospital."

CHAPTER 48
April 2013

He's a chameleon," the agent in charge said in desperation as Sam steered him through the forest and back down the mountain to rejoin the sheriff, who had gone ahead. "His disguises are the best in the business and change from day to day, as does his location," he said, panting as if he were in pain.

"Where is he?" Sam demanded. "Or you can walk to the hospital."

"We got a trace the last time you talked to him, Dawson."

"Wait, you tapped my phone?" Sam complained.

The agent ignored him. "He called from Laramie."

"He's in Laramie?" Sam said, wincing. "Why on earth would he come to Laramie?"

"He needs money and a place to hide. We think he's blackmailing the president of the university."

"What could he possibly have on that little twerp?" Sam almost laughed.

"Long before UW hired him as president, he was a midlevel administrator at CU in Boulder. He first came to our attention when he applied for a security clearance with NREL in Golden."

Sam was familiar with the sprawling complex near Golden, Colorado. "The little guy was involved with the National Renewable Energy Lab?" Sam scratched behind his ear.

"Specifically, the biohydrogen program in the bioenergetics section. He needed high-level clearance since his job was to coordinate the involvement of several other institutional collaborators. These included Lawrence Berkeley and Sandia National Laboratories. Viktorovich extorted top secret intel from him after luring him into his honey trap."

"Stop…You're telling me that Val had sex with that little dictatorial Ross Perot look-alike? The same weasel that fired me?"

"Apparently Viktorovich has the videotapes to prove it. Look, Dawson, I'm not feeling so good right now. You need to get me medical attention immediately or you'll get nothing more from me."

"That's why the sheriff went ahead. He's lining it up. Where in Laramie is Thompson?"

"He knew we would be tapping your phone. He knew when to hang up. We couldn't pinpoint his location other than it was from somewhere north of the fraternities and south of the Physical Plant on the east campus of the university. He was on a mobile. I don't feel well. I think my blood pressure is dropping like I might pass out."

Lost in thought, Sam did not hear him.

They emerged from the forest at the base of the mountain, the sun still high while angling to the west. Sheriff O'Malley was leaning against his pickup, peeling back the cellophane on a Slim Jim. "Get what you needed, Sam?"

"He's on campus in Laramie. I've got a hunch. Can you drop Agent What's-His-Face back at his vehicle?"

"Wait a second," the agent in charge protested. "I gave you everything I have on Viktorovich. You promised to get me medical assistance."

"No need for that," the sheriff said with a smile. "I'll give you a little Bag Balm for those rope burns and you'll be good to go."

Red-faced, the agent in charge looked as if he were about to explode. "I've been bitten by a venomous snake, I—"

"Who—Bill?" The sheriff took off his Stetson and wiped his forehead with his sleeve. "He's as harmless as they come. Looks like a rattler, acts like a rattler, but he's no rattler. When things get tense, old Bill rolls over on his back, sticks out his tongue, and plays dead. Maybe that's what you should have done, Agent in Charge. I'm sure your boss will be pleased with how easily you gave up sensitive information."

Decomposed granite popped and crunched from under the tires of Sam's Willys as it careened down the two-track toward the main Forest Service road.

"Woe be to the man who harms Sidney," the sheriff said pensively as he gazed after the disappearing vehicle.

CHAPTER 49
April 2013

Sidney had turned twenty-nine in October. She didn't need Sam's help negotiating life's obstacles. She would have left years ago had it not been for her affliction. He was both fortunate and cursed. Surely he had told her recently that he loved her. How long had it been since he put his arms around her and showed her true affection? Sidney had floated through his life—a wisp of late afternoon rain on a summer's day. Her scent lingered like the earthy musk of new life. He remembered how vulnerable she seemed as an infant, her swaddled body nestled against his chest, her head tucked under his chin. He would hold her until both she and his arms went to sleep. When she was older, she would wrap her arms around his neck, her skinny legs dangling as he trudged up the stairs to tuck her in, the day's light fading through her curtains. The line between adolescence and adulthood became gray and smudged from the stress of indecision, whether to remain a child or become a grownup. Neither of them knew how to act. Divorce had been a cold knife that sliced through his heart. It was Sidney who had stopped the bleeding. He had been useless. Had he told her he loved her? Surely he did, after the last time she was abducted five years ago. It's not always easy for a father to say the words. None of this was easy. He would do better when he got her back. It would be a new beginning.

Sam did not remember the drive to Laramie as the Willys slid to a halt outside the small brick building at Greenhill Cemetery. The temperature gauge indicated he had pushed the station wagon hard. The building's lights were off and the door was locked. He stepped around the corner and peeked through the window, cupping his hands around his face. Dusty boxes piled haphazardly on top of each other filled the small room. He pulled out his pocket watch. It was a quarter to five, normal business hours. At the maintenance shed he found a lanky young man with a long blonde ponytail working on a John Deere Gator. "Hello," Sam called out so as not to startle him as he bent over the engine compartment. It did not work. The guy convulsed upward, hitting his head on the cab roof.

"Can I help you?" he said with a flinchy grin, obviously embarrassed by his reaction.

"I'm looking for Lamar Preston?" Sam was proud of himself for remembering the name.

"Who?"

"Lamar Preston," Sam repeated. "The cemetery sexton."

The young man twisted his head like a robin listening for a worm, then shook it from side to side as he wiped his hands on a shop rag. "Sorry, nobody by that name here. We don't have a sexton. The cemetery is run by the city's parks department."

"Old guy, white hair, kind of hunchbacked," Sam offered.

Again, the guy shook his head, his blonde ponytail swinging from side to side. "Nope! There's nobody here by that description."

"I met him here last January."

He offered his sideways grin again. "I've been here for six years. Nobody like that works here."

Sam pinched his chin and shook his head slowly. "He told me where his wife was buried. He knew the history of the cemetery."

"Sorry," the young man apologized. "I can give you the contact information of the parks manager or the cemetery crew leader."

Sam's eyes narrowed and he froze, as though trying to understand someone speaking with their mouth full. The weight of realization settled across his shoulders and slid down his spine. His hunch had played out.

"They're over on Boulder Drive," the young man offered, seeing Sam's confusion.

"How do you heat this place?" Sam said quickly.

"What do you mean? In the winter?"

Sam glanced around the shop. He saw the ceiling-mounted gas heater up in the corner. "Not in here, the old building over there," he said, indicating the locked administrative building next door.

Ponytail looked at Sam for a long moment. "I'm not sure I—"

"In the winter, what's your source of heat?" Sam demanded.

"Um…"

"Is there a furnace of some sort?"

"Not really." Ponytail scratched behind his ear. "There's some kind of heat exchanger thing in there. The city cut a deal with the university a long time ago to provide steam heat from the physical plant next door." He pointed toward the coal-fired complex on the north side of the cemetery.

"So," Sam said a little too loudly, "Greenhill is connected to campus by a steam tunnel?"

"Yeah, I guess so."

Sam had heard various renditions of the popular urban legend that the campus was underlain by a series of inter-connected steam tunnels. Everything from hauntings, giant rodents, presidential escape routes, to corridors for wintertime access to classrooms, had been floated with each generation of students. Supposedly student use had been suspended after a brutal sexual assault had occurred somewhere in the labyrinth. He had been told that construction of the tunnels had begun in the late 1890s and that mules had been used to ferry out the diggings. Sam had to admit he had given little thought to the mountains of coal piled up outside the steam plant north of the cemetery, or the almost total lack of overhead electrical lines on the sprawling campus. The sort of plumbing required to centrally heat an entire university with steam heat fired by coal would need maintenance and access to the miles of pipes beneath the campus.

"Do you know where there's a tunnel entrance?" Sam asked excitedly, his patience worn thin as he studied the young man.

"Maybe," Ponytail said, weighing the question as if world peace hung in the balance. "The campus cops arrested some frat rats a couple years back. Seems they were trying to find their way to one of the sorority houses using the tunnels. They got turned around and surfaced across the street at Wyoming Hall. Some ROTC guys nabbed 'em. I was working late and saw the whole thing. Cops everywhere! I heard they got expelled. Anyway, the next day the Physical Plant crew came by here checking on things and I saw them go underground behind the admin building right over there." He pointed with a greasy finger. "There's a manhole cover on a cement pad back there. It has a big padlock on it. I thought it was for the sewer."

"Show me," Sam ordered. "Do you have a bolt cutter?"

"Uh-huh."

"Bring it. I'll get a flashlight," he said, turning and running toward the Willys. "Bring a crowbar too," he called over his shoulder.

⋆⋙⋘⋆

Cutting the lock off was easy. Sliding the manhole cover to one side required more effort. Ponytail refused to help, citing job loss as his concern. The smell of dank earth rose up from the blackness below. A steel ladder descended through the cobwebs into the dark unknown. "When I get down there, hand me my rifle," Sam said, nodding toward the old 30-30 he had brought from the Jeep. "Can you do me a huge favor?"

"I dunno, maybe," Ponytail said, rubbing the back of his neck and refusing eye contact.

"Forget you ever saw me. Can you do that for me?"

"I guess," the young man said with a crooked smile.

"Thanks. Hand me that rifle," he said, his hand reaching out from the cylinder of darkness.

"Watch out for giant rodents," Ponytail called down after Sam had disappeared.

The flashlight beam was pitiful against the total absence of light extending in two directions from the faded light at the base of the ladder. This was obviously an older section of tunnel, with walls constructed of stone blocks. However, the floor was cement and appeared to be newer. Asbestos-covered pipes and a mixture of galvanized and plastic conduit covered both walls. A simple light switch with a luminous toggle was fastened to the wall at the base of the ladder. Sam flipped the toggle up. Overhead lights came on in both directions, and Sam's heart and respiratory rate slowed noticeably. He assumed the tunnel to the left led under the street to the main campus. With one last look upward toward the manhole, Sam turned and hurried down the claustrophobic shaft that extended into the subterranean maze beneath the university.

Distances were difficult to determine. The air became more stale the farther he went. Numerous dark intersections would suddenly appear as black holes with a label painted on the wall displaying a combination of letters and numbers that meant nothing to Sam. The overhead lights ended at an intersection with a newer and wider section of tunnel. He turned left again. The light from his flashlight was a sickly yellow and offered no defense against overhead valves and dripping water. He had no idea where he was. Sam encountered another ladder and with it a light switch that illuminated a hub of intersections similar to a roundabout. The maze of pipes and electrical conduit was baffling. A poster-sized placard on the wall showed a schematic of the university similar to the one in the school phone directory. A circled red X marked his location, and heavy dark lines—each with a letter and number, showed the tunnel's destination. He was near the east end of Prexy's Pasture under the middle of campus, close to Half Acre Gymnasium and the Student Union.

Sam traced his finger over the map, repeating the letters and numbers and occasionally looking up to the corresponding signs at tunnel entrances. The older stone-lined tunnels headed west toward Old Main and Arts and Sciences, and south toward Ross, Knight, and Merica halls. Lamar Preston had mentioned Merica Hall and the spooky happenings there. "C-3" Sam whispered as he again turned left. The overhead lights faded behind him. He expected the flashlight to suddenly quit, just like in the movies. He would then bang it against his hand a few times and the light would come back on temporarily. That was not the case. Instead, the beam became less and less intense as the batteries drained their last bit of energy to the bulb's filament. Darkness overwhelmed him and brought him to a dead stop. His ears rang from the silence. Only his own breathing was audible—and that of someone or something else standing next to him.

CHAPTER 50
April 2013

M r. Dawson?" the familiar voice said calmly as the explosion of light from a flashlight assaulted Sam's eyes.

Instinctively, Sam shielded his eyes with his right forearm. "Nick? What are you doing here?"

"Looking for you, sir," Nick said as he shifted his night vision goggles to the top of his head. "Me, the campus cops, police and sheriff's office, everybody except the National Guard. They're all up there, armed and dangerous and quite prepared to shoot you. They take a man with a gun very seriously. I picked up the call as soon as I came off the pass. They were about to send in tear gas and play Whac-A-Mole when you popped up."

"How'd you find me down here?"

"Oh, they knew exactly where you were. They have motion sensors down here. Otherwise, the students would be playing leapfrog with one another in these tunnels."

"They sent you in to get me?" Sam winced. "Do they know who I am?"

"Yes, sir. You left your Jeep in the cemetery. If you don't mind me saying, you're a horrible criminal."

"So I've been told."

"I talked them into letting me come down and bring you out peacefully," Nick said.

"I'm in big trouble, huh?"

"Yes, sir, criminal trespass, property destruction, carrying a firearm on campus. You'll do hard time in the state pen for this," Nick said, smiling. "Then of course, there's the assault on a federal officer, kidnapping and torture of a CIA agent.... You're in a whole heap of trouble."

"What about Sidney? Thompson has her down here somewhere. I'm sure of it."

"Sidney is fine. She's topside waiting for you. She said you're going to need a good lawyer."

"She's all right?"

"Yes, sir. No worse for the wear."

"You're sure? He didn't hurt her?"

"No, sir, a little shaken up, maybe. She won't let them take her to the hospital for an exam until she sees you."

"What about her Pantoprazole? Without it she could have a seizure."

"Not to worry, sir. I brought it from your place and gave it to her already."

"Thank God," Sam gushed. "You're a lifesaver, Nick. What about Thompson?"

"Got him. He's in custody. Now let's get out of here."

"I'm with you, Nick. Lead the way. It's a little claustrophobic down here."

"Copy that, sir. There should be an exit with a light switch a little farther ahead, according to the map I saw. We're looking for tunnel entrance B-2."

They hustled along in silence for several minutes. The light from Nick's flashlight bounced erratically from floor to ceiling, making Sam a bit nauseous.

"Here we go," Nick said. "This should be it." His light illuminated the small placard next to an equally ancient stone-lined tunnel. A ladder shot upward. He reached behind it and flipped a switch. Lights exploded down the tunnel before them.

A lever-action rifle has an unmistakable sound when a round is brought from the magazine into the action and chambered, the bolt secured. No one spoke for what seemed an eternity.

"Don't turn around, Nick," Sam ordered. "If you so much as flinch, I'll send a hundred and seventy grains of Winchester Silver Tip into your back. The exit hole in your midsection will be the size of your fist."

"Mr. Dawson—"

"Shut up, Nick, and listen very carefully to me. Slowly place your flashlight on the floor and nudge it behind you.... Now with your left hand, I want you to remove your service pistol and place it on the floor, then gently kick it aside."

"Sir, you—"

"I'll not tell you again, Nick. Put the gun on the floor. Now!" Sam yelled.

Nick obeyed.

"Take off your shoes and socks," Sam ordered.

"Sir?" Nick hesitated.

"You heard me. Get 'em off now."

Nick knelt down, unlaced his military-style boots, and pulled them off, then his socks.

"Now, take out your handcuffs....First cuff your left hand....Reach up through the highest rung of the ladder you can touch by standing on the bottom rung, and handcuff your right hand on the backside of the ladder....No sudden moves now. The trigger pull on this thing is super light."

Stretched out on the steel ladder, Nick tried to position his feet to lessen the pain of the ladder rung against his tender soles.

"Does that hurt?" Sam asked.

"Yes, sir."

"Good. Pantoprazole, Nick, is a proton pump inhibitor taken for acid reflux. Sidney doesn't have gastroesophageal reflux disease, commonly referred to as GERD. Now, I'm going to ask you once—and only once, where Thompson and my daughter are, and if you don't tell me, then I'm going to take the butt of this gun and smash your feet before leaving you here to either hang by your wrists or stand on that ladder rung with broken feet. Your choice."

"B-2," Nick said, pointing with his chin to the left. "Then B-1 to the very end. You'll find a door and a set of stairs that will take you up to a room below Merica Hall."

"Does anyone know we're down here?"

"No."

"No cops?"

"No."

"If I find her and she's okay, I'll send someone for you. If I don't find her or she's not okay, you could be here for a very long, long time."

Sam gathered up the pistol and flashlight and started off down the tunnel marked B-2 before he stopped and turned back toward Nick. "One more thing, Nikolai—your mother may have been some kind of whore, but she deserved better than you."

CHAPTER 51
April 2013

The silence was deafening. Cold, dank air cut at Sam's lungs as he hustled through the underground maze. He dodged and ducked the overhead pipes and jutting electrical boxes that seemed to leap out at him at every turn. The beam of light from Nick's flashlight was wide and bright. He had not found a light switch since leaving Nick. According to the last directional placard, he should be getting close to Merica Hall. He rounded a sharp corner and was suddenly struck in his midsection, just below his ribs, by something fast and heavy. The blow to his diaphragm forced the air from his lungs and he fell to his knees, his mouth wide open as he sucked for air. The next blow caught him squarely across his back. Sam crumbled to the floor, the flashlight rolling ahead of him.

"I'll crush your head like a grape if you try to get up!" Her voice was frantic, yet unmistakable.

"Sid, it's me," Sam managed to expel, in spite of his deflated lungs.

"Dad?" she shouted. "Oh my God! Dad!" She dropped the long-handled shovel and rushed to her father.

They cried. Neither of them spoke. Stinging eyes, runny noses, and heaving chests captured the reunion. Words would come later. She was alive. That was all that mattered. Thompson was gone. There was no one to kill. Sam's rage turned to sorrowful and somewhat painful relief. He had so many questions, but the answers could wait. They drove home in silence. Halfway up the mountain, Sam reached over and gently squeezed her hand. "I love you, Sid," he said, his voice cracking.

"I know," she responded softly without looking at him. Outside it was snowing.

⟡══◉══⟡

While Sidney showered, Sam called the sheriff and told him where he could find his deputy. He asked for time, not for himself, rather for her. The sheriff agreed.

Sam watched his daughter sleep, her wet hair wrapped in a towel, her legs tucked up like a child's. With cracked ribs and a sore back, he dozed off in the easy chair across the room. The rifle leaned against the wall next to him. The phone rang. He answered it in the kitchen.

"Thank you for not killing him," Thompson said without emotion. He paused as if waiting for Sam to return the expression of gratitude.

Sam only listened.

"When Nikolai was a boy—maybe eight or nine, we sent him off to a camp in Estes Park, just outside of Rocky Mountain National Park, north of Boulder. It was a heart-wrenching experience for all of us. He had a backpack in which he had stuffed all the things he believed he needed to survive a week in the wild—Fruit Roll-Ups, a compass, a whistle, a couple of Tarzan books, underwear, and socks. All the necessities. I can still see that school bus growing smaller and smaller in the distance as I wondered if I had prepared him adequately for the world. Tragedy can occur in the blink of an eye. All I could think about was everything that could go wrong—the canoe flipping over, the wrong trail taken, the bear encountered. As a parent, I kept asking myself if I had equipped him for all of life's disasters. I remember how relieved I was when he returned home safely and told us with his nonstop chatter of all the things that were irrelevant. When do you stop? When do you let go and hope they swim rather than sink? Do you know what I'm saying, Sam?"

"Let's leave our children out of this, Thompson. This is between you and me."

"Agreed," Thompson shot back. "I can't help wondering, Sam, if you would have shown me the same mercy had you found me yesterday?"

"No. You signed your death warrant when you took my daughter."

"And now, with the children off the table, what will you do?"

"Gut you like a fish," Sam said. "There'll be no mercy. I'll not spend the rest of my life looking over my shoulder."

"That's the spirit, Sam. You've got your head in the game now."

"This isn't a game, Thompson."

"Oh, you're wrong. It is a game. Life's a game. To most, death is a consequence of losing—you lose, you die. To some, you included, death is viewed as a consequence of winning—you win, I die. Before this game ends, you'll hope and pray for death. It most certainly is a game. And I believe it's my move. *Dasvidaniya,* Sam."

When Sidney finally emerged from her room near noon the next day, Sam thought she looked older—not in a bad way, rather in a seasoned way. She was a person not to be trifled with.

"Pop, do you realize this is the second time I've been kidnapped and betrayed by someone I cared about, someone you went out of your way to offend? This is the second time I've been taken hostage by someone with a grudge against you. The second time my life has been endangered by a madman. You don't have to be a genius to figure out what the common denominator is."

Sam stared at her blankly.

"It's you!" she said, lowering her coffee mug and glaring at him. "Living with you is like being on death row with no appeals left."

"You're going to blame me for all of this? Don't you think that's being a little unfair?"

"Hold on, don't get all defensive. Here me out." She tried to smile but it came out crooked. "You're a magnet that attracts sick, warped people like bees to honey." She shook her head. "I gotta tell ya, I'm more than a little tired of being used as bait, of being the fall guy in your series of misadventures."

"I can't believe you're blaming me," Sam said, shaking his head.

"All I'm saying is why can't you leave me out of whatever vendetta is coming your way next time around? Maybe you could call up Rent-a-Daughter and they could send out a replacement for me. Someone, who doesn't mind being locked in an underground dungeon for a week."

"I can't believe you're blaming me," he repeated, still shaking his head. "If you hadn't escaped, I would have found you. And I wouldn't have bruises all over my body. I was almost there. You don't think you're being a little ungrateful?"

"I don't mean to be. I'm thankful, of course. Excuse me for being tired of having my life threatened, my relationships destroyed, my world turned upside down. I guess what I'm saying is I'm tired of being the patsy for everybody who has a grudge against you. I want a normal life. Did you ever consider that I'm tired of being abnormal? That I'm tired of being deaf and blind, without a future? That I'm tired of being used by people in order to get to you?" She put her coffee mug down and looked up at Sam, her eyes glassy with tears. "What's wrong with me, Pop? Why does this keep happening to me?" The tears finally came.

Sam looked down and shook his head slowly. He went to her, took her in his arms, and nestled her head against his chest. "There's nothing wrong with you, Sid, nothing that a father transplant couldn't cure. I can't begin to tell you how sorry I am. You deserve better. You've always deserved better when it comes to my parenting. There's no excuse for my screwups. I've done some pretty stupid things in my life, but I never meant for you to be hurt by my mistakes." Tears welled up in his eyes. "I love you, kiddo. You're the reason I exist." He looked away and hastily wiped at his cheek. "All I have to offer other than my sincerest apology is my pledge to do better if you'll give me another chance."

Sidney put her arms around her father and buried her head more deeply in his heaving chest. She loved her dad. She was skeptical.

CHAPTER 52
April 2013

Servicing the Willys was one of those mindless exercises that diverted Sam's attention from the frustration of indecision. A string of profane threats accompanied by a thrown wrench somehow helped put things in the right perspective. He was wiping the grease from his cold hands and inspecting the torn flap of skin on the middle knuckle of his right hand when the sheriff pulled into the slushy driveway.

"Sam," the sheriff greeted with a half smile.

"Come to arrest me, Harrison?"

"Should I?"

"Probably. Three squares a day and no vehicle maintenance sounds pretty good right now."

"How's Sidney?" the sheriff asked as he tipped his Stetson back on his head.

"Mad at the world, especially me."

The sheriff twisted the end of his mustache and nodded. "Can't say that I blame her." He paused and wrinkled his forehead. "Having a numbskull for a father can be downright irritating."

Sam nodded his acceptance of the criticism. "Well, let's have it."

"Have what?"

"The good news, the bad news, the other shoe that drops."

"What do you want first?" the sheriff said, looking down at the ground.

"Let's start with the feds."

"Haven't heard a word. The fact that you're still here tells me they're probably not going to pursue charges. The agent in charge had most of the wind taken out of his sails when he realized he'd been duped by a simple-minded photographer. The guy was obviously pretty embarrassed. The county sheriff being complicit added insult to injury. I'd say you're damn lucky they didn't nail you with assault on a federal officer, kidnapping, and a whole host of other related crimes. You should put out one of your phony press releases to let people know that Sidney was found unharmed. You could slobber a little over the CIA, maybe call off the dogs in D.C."

"The university?" Sam said as if reciting from a checklist.

"Not a peep. They had no idea that you or anybody else was in those tunnels. I guess I could have called in forensics on that room below Merica Hall. You know as well as I do, they wouldn't have found diddly. From the moment she stepped out the door here"—he said, gesturing toward the house—"and was stunned, Sidney never saw Thompson. Aside from sensory deprivation, she was pretty well cared for. The food, water, toilet, bedding had been long in the planning. He had help."

"Nick?"

"I've got nothing to hold him on. It's your word against his. He said he was trying to help you when you turned on him."

Sam's body tightened and he turned sharply toward the sheriff.

The sheriff threw up his hand to halt what he knew was coming. "I fired him yesterday. He'd lied on his application. We haven't quite figured out how he got through our background check. Most everything was true except his name. Sometime before he came to us, he had simply dropped his last name, Thompson, and used his middle name, Alexander. He said he was trying to get anonymity from his parents after he found out who they really were. It seems he had a little help from the feds."

"So now I've got two of them to look out for, father and son?"

"I don't know. I couldn't get a good read on how close he and his old man are."

"You don't think for a minute that this whole thing wasn't a setup, Nick and my daughter? They've been dating for over a year, for Christ's sake."

The sheriff looked down and curled the end of his moustache. "It sure looks that way, Sam. I feel for Sidney. She's been through this once before."

"There's nothing you can do?" Sam looked directly into the sheriff's eyes.

"There's plenty I could do in terms of protecting you and Sidney, if I had the money and manpower. As far as pursuing a kidnapper, with the feds protecting him I don't have a chance."

"He called the other night," Sam said, squeezing his chin. "He agreed that we should leave our children out of this."

"You don't trust him, do you?"

"Of course not. It's pretty clear he's going to keep coming at me. So far it's been his little cat-and-mouse game. He's just playing with me. At some point, when he's tortured me enough, he's going to make his move. I don't think he wants to kill me. He could have done it a dozen times already. He wants me to suffer. He wants me to endure emotional pain for a long time, and there's only one way to do that."

The sheriff stared at Sam for a long moment before speaking. "You want me to put her in protective custody?"

Sam worried the stubble on his chin. "I've thought about that. I'm afraid it would push her over the edge. Right now she's pretty fragile." He looked at Sheriff O'Malley. "Something's been bothering me. Thompson lied to me about his son being killed by a roadside bomb—in Afghanistan, according to the agent in charge. They both lied. Obviously Nick is alive. Why the lie? Thompson led me to believe that I had to make reparations, pay my debt. He said our children must suffer and die as atonement for our sins. God had given His son, Thompson had given his son, and now it was my turn." Sam pursed his lips and slowly shook his head. "He's not done, Harrison. He's coming back at me." He bowed his head, his chin almost touching his chest, his eyes closed. Suddenly Sam's head bolted upright and he stared into the sheriff's eyes. "Damn it, Harrison, don't you see it? The yarn about his son dying in Afghanistan was a metaphor for his wife's death. Valentina Thompson was the reparation he had paid, not his son. Oh my God—"

"Dad!" Sidney screamed as she stumbled from the door. Tears streamed down her contorted face. "Dad!" she screamed again. She shook her head and closed her eyes, stopped, and bent over, placing her hands on her knees.

Both Sam and Sheriff O'Malley rushed to intercept her. "What is it?" Sam demanded as he took his daughter by the arm.

"It's Mom…it's Mom," she sobbed. Her chest heaved as she looked up at Sam, her face contorted. "She's dead. Mom's dead. Someone killed her."

CHAPTER 53
April 2013

In Denver, Pat Bateson—Marcie's husband and Sam's ex-publisher, greeted Sam warmly. When he hugged Sidney, emotion overcame him once again. His dark kippah slid precariously to one side before he righted it on the back of his head. Sidney wiped the tears from her cheeks. She was a mourner, Sam was not. Divorce—or perhaps Marcie's mother, had taken that right from him. He would join the general congregation in Temple Emanuel, the synagogue where the family worshiped.

It had been a hectic twenty-four hours since Marcie's death. Sidney had gently made her case to allow for an autopsy. She had been overruled by her grandmother, who stubbornly declared it a desecration of the body. To Sam it was open and shut. Her throat had been slit. Even though Marcie's mother knew nothing about Hank Thompson, she somehow knew Sam was to blame. The look she gave him said it all. It was the same look she had always given him. The assignation of guilt was her specialty.

The simple pine coffin without metal embellishment appeared small, dwarfed by the enormity of the room. For once, Sam was glad Marcie was Jewish. He could not have endured an open casket and the ritual of viewing. Sidney was ushered off to a separate room with the other mourners. Sam was given a kippah and shown a seat midway back in the chapel. After the attendees were seated, the mourners entered solemnly in single file and were directed toward the front, each with a black ribbon attached to their clothes, symbolizing a torn garment. First there was the opening prayer—something from Psalms, then the brief eulogy, more for the comfort of mourners than an essence of the life of the deceased, Sam thought. It was painfully short. This was followed by the chanting of the final prayer with the congregation standing, and finally, the recession of the mourners and removal of the casket. Sam felt stunned by the efficiency and brevity of the service. It allowed no time to grieve.

At the cemetery, the procession of attendees gathered at the wet grave and silently waited for the pallbearers to bring the casket. A cold breeze helped preserve the snow in the shaded areas and sent a shiver down his back. Another series of short prayers was delivered. The mourners recited, in unison, a prayer that extolled the virtues of God. The casket was lowered, and everyone lined up to symbolically place earth on top of it with an upside-down shovel. Then it was off to Pat's house for the traditional shiva, a reception of sorts where the attendees formed two lines and the mourners passed between them as comforting Hebrew words were recited.

Sam had no time to think of Marcie and the years they had spent together. Maybe that was the purpose of the highly ritu-alized ceremony. Pat's house was foreign to him. No pictures were framed on the walls to remind Sam of his life with Marcie, nothing that told of her past or her daughter's. Instead, modern art—bright and confusing, with straight lines and sharp angles, competed with the soft, curved lines of traditional furniture.

Sam's pictorials were conspicuously absent from the wall of books in the den. Gone were the personal souvenirs that told the story of a beautiful young woman who had a life before Pat, before Sam, the inspiring detritus that declared her an individual with dreams of the future. Where were the black and whites of dead pets, dead relatives, and trips to the lake? Where was Sidney, her hair in braids, poking an insect with a stick as late afternoon shadows gave way to a soft light that accentuated her cheeks? They had been happy. They had been hopeful. Someday the remnants of her existence would be sent to a dump or scattered across a table at a garage sale. How could she have known?

Sam scanned the faces in the crowd, a moving collage of somber heads straight out of a Hitchcock movie. Tears were dabbed, muted expressions of sympathy were offered, and all the while morsels of food were stuffed between their moving lips. He felt dizzy. He wanted to scream, "She's dead!" Of course, they all knew that.

"You okay, Pop?" Sidney said as she came up alongside him.

"No," he whispered. "I need to leave."

She looked into his eyes and could see he was serious. She nodded almost imperceptibly. "I'll get my things."

⊷═◉═⊷

They drove home in silence, remembering.

CHAPTER 54
May 2013

Sidney's cold indifference was palpable in the days that followed. She, too, was a victim of Thompson's assault. Kidnapped, betrayed, and half-orphaned, she had seemingly lost hope. Once again she blamed her father. Sam's grief, on the other hand, had turned to anger. Denver police had labeled him a person of interest in their investigation of Marcie's murder. A Denver Police Department detective, accompanied by Sheriff O'Malley, had driven up to Wyoming to interview Sam. Both Sidney and the sheriff argued that Sam should retain counsel. Sam politely asked Sidney to sit in on the interrogation. She reluctantly agreed and, in addition to serving as his legal advisor, provided collaboration for his alibi. They had been home together when Marcie was murdered.

In the days that followed, it was more than anger that dominated his feelings. It was hate. He could not remember feeling so strongly about anything in his life. He hated what Thompson had done to his family, his life, his world. He hated Thompson and secretly vowed vengeance. He determined that none of this would go away until he found Thompson and killed him. Who could blame him? Maybe that was what Thompson wanted. The final nail in Sam's coffin would be his prosecution and conviction for murder. The fact that Sam believed it might be worth it troubled him. He had to be smart. His plan had to be faultless. He could not believe he was having such thoughts. *Surely, I cannot be capable of such savagery.*

"If you want something for supper, you better take it out of the freezer this morning," Sidney said in a monotone as she shuffled through the kitchen. "I don't care for anything."

Sam glanced at the kitchen clock. It was after ten and she was still in her pajamas and robe.

"How 'bout I fly you to New York for a pizza at Lombardi's?" Sam said cheerfully.

"You don't have enough money to fly the forty-six miles from Cheyenne to Laramie," Sidney said dryly.

"You could loan it to me, moneybags. We could eat pizza until we were sick. Then we could grab a cab and go over to Katz's Delicatessen on the Lower East Side and have a pastrami sandwich to hold down the pizza."

"You don't have enough money for cab fare."

"Speaking of Katz's Deli," Sam said, "that reminds me… you got a call from a Denver attorney, a Mr. Katzenstein, this morning while you were still in bed." He knew who Katzenstein was. He had been Marcie's attorney and, before that, her family's attorney.

"What'd he want?"

"He didn't say. I told him you'd return the call sometime when you weren't wallowing in self-pity and misplaced anger. His number is on the table."

Sidney glared at him. Her eyes narrowed and she shook her head slowly. She was about to speak, to tell him he was an insensitive jerk and that she would move out as soon as she found a place to live. She thought better of it, shuffled back to her room, and closed the door.

Sam believed his future murder conviction was sealed with a court-appointed public defender. His daughter would not represent him.

⊷══◉══⊷

On the way to Laramie, Sam envisioned several scenarios of how to confront the university president, who was protected by at least six layers of staff in increasing order of importance, all trained to filter out nonessential callers and visitors and keep him on schedule. Old Main, the oldest building on campus, still possessed the Victorian charm of its original design inside and out. The president's office on the second floor was the largest in the building, with the exception of the conference room where the trustees and deans' council met. The first layer smiled pleasantly up at Sam when he approached. "Hi, I'm Drake Sebastian with the *Casper Star-Tribune* here for my two o'clock interview with the president." Mentioning the state's most widely read newspaper would demand their attention. The receptionist looked confused. She called the second layer, the president's staff assistant, who in turn called the third layer, the executive administrative assistant. The three of them conferred briefly before calling the fourth layer, the special assistant to the president, who seemed skeptical, although professional.

"I'm sorry, Mr. Sebastian, there seems to be a scheduling error. The president is unavailable. Are you sure you weren't scheduled to meet with our vice president for Institutional Communications?"

Sam pulled out his pocket watch and looked at it. "I'm on deadline for the morning edition. My office called and arranged for me to get a statement from the president regarding the governor's recommendation of a twenty percent budget cut to the university for the next biennium. All I need is a response. Otherwise, I'll have to report 'no comment,' which runs the risk of angering both the trustees and the governor." Sam raised his eyebrows and stared at the special assistant without smiling.

"The president is not here," she said, returning his stare. "Let me see if our Communications director is available."

"I'm out of time. I've got to call this into my editor now. The headline editor is holding up the entire front-page copy for this story. I'll just go with 'no comment.' Thank you for your time." He turned and started for the door.

"The president is meeting with the faculty senate in the west ballroom of the Wyoming Union," she said. The irritation in her voice was obvious. "You may be able to catch him as he leaves. He has a two-thirty here."

Sam rushed from the office and the building. He knew she would call the president. Like all politicos, he hated to be surprised.

The little Ross Perot look-alike seemed confused when he stepped out of the faculty senate meeting with staff layers five and six trailing hurriedly behind. "Dawson, what the hell—"

"Dismiss your staff and walk with me now," Sam demanded.

"Why should—"

"Valentina Thompson," Sam said, stepping closer and looking down on the president.

He turned and said something to his entourage. They walked slowly back toward the ballroom while repeatedly glancing over their shoulders at Sam.

"I've got a copy of the videotape," Sam whispered as he maintained eye contact with the president. "You screw with me, and I'll drop copies in the mail to the trustees, your wife, and your children. Do you understand me?"

"That was a long time ago," he whined through short vocal cords.

"Time isn't relevant when it comes to perversion and betraying your country. Let's see, how old were your children when you were giving up state secrets and humping a Russian spy? I'm sure with a little digging I can come up with more recent indiscretions. A leopard doesn't change his spots. You're as phony as a rubber dick."

"What do you want, Dawson? Money? You're just a petty extortionist, no different than Thompson."

"I want Thompson. I know he's in the area and he needs money. Has he contacted you yet?"

"What's in this for me?"

"You're in no position to bargain, you little shit. You tell me where Thompson is and I won't splash your naked ass on billboards all across the state," Sam said, leaning in closer for emphasis.

"How do I know you have the tape? Thompson said he had the only copy."

Sam smiled. "Have it your way." He turned and started to walk away.

"Dawson," the president barked like a terrier. "Wait, I'm sure we can work out a deal."

Sam turned toward him. "Here's the deal. I want Thompson. When I get him, I'll give you the tape and whatever amount of money he's extorted from you. It's a win-win for you. You go back to being the dictatorial little prick that you are. You can brush off your curriculum vitae and start shopping around for a university that someone has actually heard of. And you'll never hear from me again. Now what's it going to be?"

The little man's big ears glowed red. "He called me three days ago. He wants half a million dollars in cash by Saturday."

"When and where?"

"I don't know. He said he would call with instructions."

"Write this down," Sam said. He recited his cell phone number slowly. "Call me." He hurried toward the stairs, paused, and called over his shoulder. "Don't forget, you have a two-thirty in your office."

Halfway to his Willys in the metered lot outside the library, Sam's hands began to shake.

CHAPTER 55
May 2013

Sam had not taken time to mourn. He sat with a cardboard box between his ankles, fumbling with a bruised photograph of Marcie taken the year they were married. She was standing ankle-deep in Boulder Creek, her shoes dangling from her right hand, looking down at something in the water. Her long, dark hair flowed over her exposed shoulders in the flowery sundress she wore. Sam wondered if she knew then how beautiful she was—"flawless" came to mind. She was probably four months pregnant that late spring day and not yet showing. They had been married for only a few weeks, and Marcie was worried how to tell her parents about the baby. Sam had been working two part-time minimum-wage jobs while carrying a full load of classes. Marcie's parents were wealthy. Determined to make it on his own, he steadfastly refused their offers of help. Sam and Marcie fought about the new things that would suddenly appear in the tiny one-bedroom apartment—a bassinet, an expensive crib, clothes, toys. Her trust fund was equivalent to the GNP of a small country. In her parents' eyes he was an underachieving gentile, a commoner unworthy of the princess he had married. He found it amazing the marriage had lasted six years.

Sam's flip phone vibrated in his pocket. The prefix indicated the call was from the university, the call he had been waiting for. Sam answered with a simple "Yes."

The president's falsetto voice was unmistakable. "Tonight, eight o'clock at the Maverick Bar on North Second. You know where it is?"

Sam knew where it was. Everyone in Laramie knew where it was, especially the police. "Seedy" was too polite a description for the bar popular with blue-collar barflies and local toughs looking for trouble. The place took on the mystique of an urban legend a few years earlier, when it was rumored that one of the university's football coaches had sex with a barmaid on the pool table during happy hour. It was the last place a university president would want to be seen. "Uh-huh," Sam said, his mind racing as to why Thompson would choose such a public place. "You'll be recognized," he added.

"There's no chance of that," the president said, cackling like a bantam rooster. "He wants you to deliver the money."

Stunned, Sam did not respond for several seconds. "You implicated me?"

"No. Of course not. Apparently, he knew somehow. You know what I think? I think the two of you are in league together. You're playing the 'good cop, bad cop' routine with me. The problem is, I can't tell which one is the good cop."

Look who's calling the kettle black, Sam thought. "I told you you'll get the tapes and your money back. All I want is Thompson."

"If you cross me, Dawson—"

"Do you have the money?"

"Meet me in Laramie behind the band shell in Washington Park at seven-thirty."

⊷══◉◉══⊷

Sam was nervous. He checked his watch again, then glanced at the briefcase on the passenger seat of the Willys. His rage had been replaced by fear. The whole thing was ill-conceived. He did not even know what Thompson looked like. He assumed Thompson would recognize him. Sam slid the briefcase under the backseat and covered the area with a serape. At precisely eight he locked the Willys and walked into the Maverick Bar. It smelled of stale beer, urine, and cigarettes. Smoke drifted across the room in a haze. Obviously, they had not received the no-smoking order from the city. "Smoky the Bar," a polka-like country tune, emanated from the gaudy Wurlitzer at the end of a makeshift dance floor and seemed appropriate. Men sat on stools, hunched over the bar, nursing longneck bottles of Coors and Budweiser. A few couples sat in dark booths along the far wall. Sam approached the bar.

"Hi, Professor Dawson," the blonde barmaid said cheerfully.

Stunned, Sam stared at her. His eyes narrowed. "Brittany?" He almost said "Juicy," since that was printed across the rear end of the sweatpants she wore to his first Introduction to Photography class.

"You remembered," she said, smiling broadly.

"How could I forget?" He remembered that she never took notes, did not have a clue about the basics of photography, and turned in a final photographic essay that featured her nude body with several erotic tattoos. All were done using the concepts of light, contrast, depth of field, focal length, and composition that he had been lecturing about all semester. "What's it been…four years?"

"Five…I'll graduate in a couple of weeks."

"Then what?"

"Don't know yet. I'm taking my time, keeping my options open. What can I get you?"

"How about a Pepsi, no ice?" He watched after her as she walked to the fountain drinks station. She wore a short denim skirt with cowboy boots and a sleeveless blouse tied in a knot above her waist, baring her midriff. Officially spring, early May nights were cold for exposed skin in Laramie.

"Here you go," she said, placing the drink on the bar in front of him.

Sam reached for his wallet.

"It's on the house." She smiled again. He could tell she wanted to say something else. Instead, she turned and attended to other customers along the bar.

Sam studied the patrons. *Motley*, he thought to himself. Plus, the mood was depressing in spite of the bouncy, honky-tonk music coming from the jukebox. In most places, "Cab Driver" followed by "A Six Pack to Go" would be toe-tappers. This crowd seemed unaffected. A bony old man with a gray ponytail sat closest to Sam. His T-shirt proclaimed "Sturgis" and featured two dogs copulating next to a motorcycle. His upper arm showed the faded remnants of a snarling red-eyed bulldog wearing a drill sergeant hat, a fat stogie clenched in its teeth. "USMC" in blue-green block letters was arced across the bottom. It was meant to be a message to all that he was not to be trifled with. That message had been lost over the last forty years, his vanity sagging amid the wrinkles of time. A silver chain hung in a loop from his belt to his wallet. What was left of this month's Social Security check was tucked beneath the coaster under his beer bottle.

"She's somethin', ain't she?" the old man said as he exhaled a plume of smoke from between white-whiskered lips and nodded toward Brittany.

Sam did not respond.

"Reminds me of a sweet little thing I knew in Da Nang."

Sam looked at his watch. It was quarter past eight.

"She could suck the chrome off the bumper of a '58 Buick."

Another song started on the jukebox, a lively melody with a repetitive chorus that an elderly couple could not resist. They were surprisingly spry although a little stiff in the joints as they two-stepped beneath their matching Stetsons.

"How about a dance, Sam?" a woman's voice asked from behind him.

Sam turned around to face a weather-beaten old woman who was missing several teeth. He looked at her skeptically.

"It's 'Squaws Along the Yukon,' one of my favorites," she said, extending a hand as if she were a socialite at a debutante ball.

"Do I know you?" Sam said.

"It's Wyoming. Everybody knows everybody. Come on, let's give it a twirl."

"I'll dance with ya, sweetheart," the old man next to Sam said.

"I weren't askin' you, Lefty. I was askin' Sam here," she said, smiling demurely.

"How do you know my name?"

"Better dance with her, Sam," the old man said. "She won't take no for 'Go to hell.'"

Sam glanced at Brittany, who nodded approvingly as she polished a shot glass.

"C'mon, young fella, I'm startin' to dry up here. This is my favorite Hank Thompson song," the old woman shouted above the music.

Sam stood up sharply. He looked quickly around the room through the smoky haze at each patron. "Did you say, 'Hank Thompson'?" Sam asked, his voice faltering.

"It's Hank Thompson night," she said, as if everyone should know the country music legend. "All the songs are Hank Thompson's hits. It's the best of Hank Thompson," she said, smiling through a toothless grin. "Don't you just love that smooth baritone of his?"

Sam suddenly felt dizzy. He ran from the Maverick and burst into the parking lot like a drowning man breaking the surface. The Willys was still locked. He fumbled with the key, then threw the door open. The serape was folded neatly on the backseat. The briefcase was gone.

CHAPTER 56
May 2013

Both the sheriff and Sidney sat silently at the kitchen table; seemingly stunned by the story Sam had just finished telling them. The sheriff twisted the end of his moustache then shook his head. "This just keeps getting better all the time." He took a long, deep breath and released it slowly. "Did it ever occur to you that law enforcement agencies have training and established protocols for dealing with this sort of thing? What were you going to do if you actually caught him? Did you think about the consequences?"

Sidney looked like she had swallowed a bone. "I just lost my mother to this maniac. What were you thinking? If you're going to make me an orphan, the least you could do is get your affairs in order. Oh, wait! It was one of your affairs that got you into this mess." She pointed an index finger at her father.

The sheriff interrupted. "Did you get the videotape?"

Sam shook his head.

"Have you told the president?"

Sam nodded. "He thinks Thompson and I are in this together. He wants the half million back or he's going to the authorities."

"That's what should have been done in the first place," the sheriff said sternly.

"Don't give me that crap, Harrison. You're complicit in all this."

"I gotta tell you, Sam, I'm damn sorry I ever let it get out of hand. I think it's time we bring the FBI back into this. We've got kidnapping, murder, extortion—"

"The FBI rolled over and wet all over their selves when they found out the CIA and national security were involved," Sam complained.

"I'm here to tell ya the Bureau gets madder than a wet hen when they find the CIA messin' with domestic issues. Those two agencies have a long history of turf wars," the sheriff said.

A knock on the door startled all three of them. Sam opened it cautiously with the sheriff backing him up. It was FedEx with an overnight delivery, a package the size of a shoebox, addressed to Sam. The return address was from a Theodore Kaczynski, ADX Florence, Florence, Colorado.

"Christ in a nighty," the sheriff whined.

"What?" Sam asked, shaking the box.

"Kaczynski is the Unabomber," Sidney warned as she backed away. "He's doing life at the federal maximum-security prison in Florence, Colorado."

"Put it down outside, Sam," the sheriff ordered. "I'll call the bomb squad."

Sam placed the package in the middle of the parking lot between the house and barn. "Hold up, Harrison. I've got a better idea." He grabbed the old Winchester 94 from behind the door, chambered a round, and took aim at the package.

"Sam, I wouldn't do that if I were—"

The blast from the rifle cut the sheriff off. Bits of paper floated to the ground around the box. There was no explosion. Sam nudged the box with the toe of his boot, then swept it up and took it into the house.

"The bomb squad would have handled that a little differently," the sheriff said.

Sam carefully opened the package and lifted the lid from the Nike shoebox inside. It was filled with money, crisp hundred-dollar bills, many of which had chunks torn away by the hundred-and-seventy grains of bullet that had ripped through the box. Sam read aloud the note he found on top of the mutilated money: "Sam, here is your half. Good work."

The three of them stood speechless, looking at the box full of money. Finally, Sam said, "Sid, we're rich."

Sidney rolled her eyes, threw up her arms, and turned away.

The sheriff gave Sam a gentle shove, taking the note from his hand and placing it back in the box. "Don't contaminate the evidence, Sam. Forensics will want to examine this." He nudged his Stetson back on his head. "This guy delights in playing games. He figures I will arrest you on suspicion. If I didn't know you, I would. He's put me in a tough spot too."

Turning back around, Sidney said, "Let's not forget he's a cold-blooded killer. This isn't a game."

The sheriff pulled a handkerchief from his rear pocket and carefully lifted the stacks of bills. Underneath was an intact videotape. "Do you have a VCR?"

⋆⟹⟸⋆

Sam had argued that the video might affect a woman's delicate sensibilities. The truth was he could not bring himself to watch a pornographic movie with his daughter. Fortunately, Sidney was of like mind. Violence, language, adult situations, and drug use were tolerable. When it came to viewing sex and nudity in each other's presence, both of them were uncomfortable. Sidney retreated to her room.

It was a grainy black and white with no audio, as if taken with a cheap security camera. The Ross Perot look-alike was much younger then, but unmistakable. Except for an occasional click of the tongue and loud exhalation from Sam and the sheriff, the room remained silent throughout the short video. When it was over, Sam grabbed his chin between his thumb and forefinger and the sheriff twisted the end of his moustache. Finally, the sheriff spoke, first clearing his throat. "I take it that wasn't Valentina Thompson?"

Sam shook his head slowly. "Is there a statute of limitations on something like this?"

"I don't know about Colorado. Here it's generally four years. In this case—involving a minor, it would be eight years. I think I remember Colorado extending it to twenty years for sexual assault on a child. In any case, those timelines have all passed. I'd have to consult with the AG. Do you have any idea who the girl is?"

"No, she couldn't have been older than fifteen or sixteen. What would be the statute of limitations if I were to rearrange his face with my fists?"

"Don't even go there, Sam. It'll all catch up with him someday. What goes around comes around." The sheriff paused then looked at Sam intently. "It's stuff like this, Sam, that makes me hate my job. It's bad enough dealing with the dregs of society. It's when the pillars of the community are scummy you start to lose faith in humanity."

Sheriff O'Malley's words seemed distant, echoing with a hollow resonance from somewhere beyond Sam's comprehension. He could not sustain a complete thought. Jagged images, seemingly unrelated, flashed in his mind. The common denominator was Thompson, an evildoer of epic proportions.

"Sam," the sheriff said sharply. "Are you listening to me?"

"No. Should I?"

"Only if you want to catch Thompson."

CHAPTER 57

May 2013

The plan was simple enough. The difficulty was sticking to it. If Thompson had a weakness, it was his intense hatred of Sam. He wanted Sam to suffer. They all agreed they would stop responding to Thompson's plan. They would refuse to be treated like pawns in his perverse game of chess. Sam was skeptical, Sidney reluctant, and the sheriff over his head.

"All right, people, listen up," the sheriff said to the gathering of uniformed and plainclothes officers assembled in the sheriff's conference room. "This isn't rocket science. We know who the perp is. His name is Yevgeni Viktorovich, better known as Hank Thompson. We're pretty sure he's holed up somewhere in this two-county area. Even though we've potentially got kidnapping, murder, and extortion, the Bureau is hesitant to get involved. They believe the folks in Langley are protecting, perhaps abetting Thompson. We don't know to what extent. They say he's a rogue double agent who has highly classified information that threatens national security. He was or still is in some sort of protection program. He's a master of disguise and often hides in plain sight. He's highly trained and extremely dangerous. Our job, people, is not to find him. Rather it is to allow him to find us. Specifically, he wants Sam or his daughter, Sidney, or both. They're the bait and we're the trap. It's as simple as that.

"The devil is, of course, in the details," Sheriff O'Malley continued. "The Dawsons' remote location is problematic, as is the absence of people in the surrounding area. We can't easily blend in by assuming roles of the general public. So we're moving them into town. They will be the victims of a tragic auto accident. Sidney's in ICU and Sam will be clinging to life in the burn unit at Cheyenne Regional Medical Center. We've located a Willys wagon in a salvage yard in Greeley. We'll burn it and place it in our impound lot. Again, details, people. If you think of something we've missed, speak up. There will be no obvious police protection, the key word being 'obvious.' Lives are at stake here. If you let your guard down, this guy will take advantage and someone will die. We're talking Academy Award performances by each of you. You'll live, eat, and sleep at the hospital, assuming your specific roles twenty-four seven. Undercover is an understatement, folks. Officially, you're attending a training program at the academy in Douglas. Don't jeopardize your family by telling them anything different. Undersheriff Piccard will brief you on your assignment and pair you with hospital staff for a little OJT. Don't ask me about overtime. It won't happen. After your briefings, go home and pack a bag and report back here. You'll be smuggled into the hospital via emergency services. Good luck."

⋯⊷∈⊷⋯

"This is your idea of a safe house?" Sam said, taking in the stark surroundings of the historic home located in the heart of the Avenues area of old Cheyenne. The few furnishings were covered with plastic drop cloths. The walls, some of which were lath and plaster, were scraped clean. Baseboards and ceiling molding were masked off. It was a work in progress.

"This is Laramie County, Sam," Sheriff O'Malley said, readjusting his Stetson. "We don't have money for a safe house. My wife and I bought this a couple of years back. We work on it when we have the time. When I get voted out or retire, whichever comes first, we plan to move in."

"It's lovely, Harrison." Sidney elbowed her father. "The homes in this area have so much historic charm. I love the carriage house in the back and those giant cottonwoods out front. I'll bet they're beautiful when fully leaved."

"Brenda, my wife, stocked the refrigerator and pantry for you. Let me know if you need anything."

"I need my life back," Sam whined. "Where's my dog?"

"I've got L2 at my house. She's fine. You'll have round-the-clock protection. During the day, the drywallers, plumbers, electricians, and painters will be our people. There will be someone in the carriage house at night. And Sam, if I hear you complain one more time, I'll take Sidney home with me and leave you here by your miserable self. I'm out of people and out of money. The commissioners will have my hide when they find out about all this."

"We appreciate everything you've done for us, Harrison. We really do," Sidney offered. "Please give our thanks to your wife too. I'd love to meet her sometime. Hopefully, everything will be over soon and we'll look back on this as an effort well spent."

54848484848484848484848484848484848 STEVEN W. HORN

The sheriff put his arm around Sidney and gave her a hug. "Are you sure you're related to him?" he said, motioning toward Sam.

"I'm pretty sure there was a mistake in the maternity ward. My real father was a gentleman."

⊶⊷⊷

The Wyoming wind hummed, whistled, and played an odd basso cantante as if from a bassoon nestled somewhere in the cottonwoods. Their branches scraped against the upstairs windowpanes, adding to the confusion.

Sidney lay awake, the covers pulled up to her chin. It was more than the strange noises and unfamiliar surroundings that kept her from sleeping. She felt sorry for herself. She had no one to explain her misfortune or confide her tangled thoughts to—thoughts that repeatedly returned to the cemetery after her mother's funeral. Like a yo-yo tossed out into a fog, they came slapping back with the sound of dirt hitting the casket lid. Most of her mother's family were buried there, one after the other, in two or three rows. None of them had ventured far from home. She saw her mother's relatives with stone markers in the perfect symmetry and ear-ringing silence of a well-designed cemetery. They kept their secrets with the same stoic silence they exhibited at a holiday meal. Their tight lips and knowing eyes held back the things a young girl wanted to hear. Her mother was with them now and the secrets were shared. Sidney was curious. Not that curious. She could wait.

Sidney heard the floorboards creak outside the door to her room. She looked at the red numerals of the clock radio on the nightstand. It was 2:06 a.m. The weather service had warned of a spring snowstorm. Rain or sleet pattered lightly on the roof.

"You asleep?" she heard her father say.

"Yes."

"Me too. You hungry?"

"No."

"Me neither. You want to see what's in the fridge?"

"Okay."

The stairs creaked horribly as they both made their way down to the kitchen. Sam found a box of frozen waffles in the freezer, a bottle of maple syrup in the pantry, and a toaster oven on the kitchen counter. A Mr. Coffee coffeemaker and a bag of Starbucks Colombia completed the provisions. "Life is good," he proclaimed.

They ate quietly in the subdued illumination of a nightlight. At 5:20 a.m., lightning flashed above the Avenues for a flickering second, long enough for them to see the snow-covered man staring at them through the kitchen window.

CHAPTER 58
May 2013

A brief news story buried on page four of the *Wyoming Tribune Eagle* reported the fictitious rollover accident. It gave no names of the injured but mentioned the Willys wagon. At the hospital, none of the police detail wanted to lie motionless for hours on end waiting to be murdered by Hank Thompson, so resuscitation dummies were bandaged and placed beneath sheets. The green and blue of the pastel walls was broken by moving splashes of colorful hospital scrubs darting back and forth. Voices were muted. Everyone scrambled around with efficiency. Rank was not apparent—no bars, oak leaves, eagles, or stars, no chevrons on their sleeves to discriminate between rank and file. Some wore lab coats, many had stethoscopes slung around their necks. Like ants tending their queen's eggs, everyone had a specific role in what appeared to be an avant-garde theatrical production. Resuscitation Annie, the CPR doll, was attended to with earnest competence. Few realized it was snowing outside. The bomb threat was received at precisely 6:00 a.m.

⋯⊨◌⊨⋯

Sidney provided the deputy with a towel to blot up the melting snow, while Sam popped two more waffles in the toaster oven and poured him a cup of coffee. The pistol beneath his jacket was clearly visible under his left arm as he dried his hair.

"Sorry," the deputy repeated. "I saw the light on and thought I better investigate."

"I saw you in the window and thought I better evacuate my colon," Sam said with mock seriousness.

"Not funny, Pop," Sidney said, pushing her plate away.

"Aren't you a little old to be a deputy sheriff?" Sam said a minute later as he delivered the waffles to the sodden deputy.

"Dad," Sidney scolded.

"That's all right." The deputy smiled. "It's my second career. I retired from the Air Force Security Forces at the base a few years ago. My wife and I liked Cheyenne and decided to settle here."

"Where did your wife graduate high school?"

Sidney scowled at her father.

"Minocqua, Wisconsin," he answered quickly and pushed back from the table.

"When?"

"Nineteen eighty-six. Look, Mr. Dawson, I can play this game all day. Why don't you call the sheriff's office and give them my badge number? They'll verify my identity."

"That won't be necessary," Sidney interrupted.

"He could have stolen his badge," Sam said from the corner of his mouth. "Are you forgetting Nick?"

"Enough, Pop."

The deputy's cell phone vibrated in his shirt pocket. He excused himself and stepped into the living room. Less than a minute later he returned. "There's been a bomb threat at the hospital. They're evacuating. My orders are to secure the premises and await further instructions. I'm going to check the perimeter. Please stay inside. Don't answer the phone or let anyone in. Lock the door after me, Sam." The deputy slipped quietly out the kitchen door into the backyard.

Sam snapped the dead bolt into the locked position. "I guess it could be unrelated. Or it could be a diversion," Sam said, squeezing his chin. In the distance he heard sirens rising and falling in the damp morning air.

Sidney shook her head. "Have you ever heard of a bomb threat in Cheyenne?"

"Nope."

"Me neither." Sidney pulled her hair back tightly and circled a rubber band around her ponytail. "I'm going upstairs to take a quick shower. I have a feeling we could be moving in the very near future."

"You go ahead. I'll clean up the kitchen and keep an eye out for Anthony Perkins."

"Who?"

"Norman Bates."

Sidney scrunched her eyebrows and made a face. "Who's Norman Bates?"

"Never mind." Sam smiled. "Take your shower."

Sam tidied up the kitchen. He wished he had not challenged the deputy. *The poor guy never got to eat his breakfast.* He heard the water pipes squeal and yelp upstairs. He rubbed his chin stubble and thought a bath and shave sounded good to him too.

"Knock, knock," a woman's voice called from the entryway as the front door creaked open. "Hello?"

Sam stepped into the front hallway to see the older woman coming through the door, keys in one hand, a bag of groceries in the other.

"You must be Mr. Dawson," she said, her voice a squeaky soprano. "I'm Brenda O'Malley. Harrison wanted me to bring by a few things and see if you needed anything."

Surprised, Sam was at a loss for words. She wore a gray, pleated skirt that hung well below her knees, stopping at the tops of her bulky, rubber rain boots. The yellow boots matched the hooded raincoat. Her thick glasses made her watery eyes look huge.

"I've got eggs, a pound of bacon, and some things for lunch too." She brushed by Sam and headed for the kitchen. He followed. "Harrison would have brought these things himself. He had some sort of emergency crop up this morning. He went flying out of the house as he yelled instructions to me. I hope you don't mind."

"No, of course not," Sam stammered. "We're thankful for your hospitality, Mrs. O'Malley. Did you happen to see the deputy outside?"

"Oh please, call me Brenda. Yes, the poor dear is covered with wet snow. You know, I've heard so much about you, I feel as if I know you." She started unpacking things from the grocery sack. "I brought something special just for you." She reached deep inside the bag. "Look, Sam," she said in a man's voice. "It's a TASER Pulse stun gun," he said as he turned and fired. The thin, flexible wires, attached to the two projectiles, struck Sam squarely in the chest.

Sam fell back against the refrigerator then slid to the floor. His body convulsed spasmodically. He was unsure if he had lost consciousness after the initial pain. He was unable to move or speak. His entire body tingled, especially his fingers and toes. His clenched jaw prevented him from crying out.

"That stupid bloodhound of yours was a dead giveaway," Thompson said as he rolled Sam to his stomach and used heavy zip ties to bind Sam's wrists, then ankles, behind his back. "The sheriff should have taken it to the pound instead of bringing it home with him." He grabbed a small sponge from the sink and stuffed it into Sam's mouth, pulled a roll of duct tape from the grocery sack, and taped over the sponge and Sam's gaping mouth. "I hope that's not too uncomfortable, Sam. I want you to save your suffering for later. I want you to feel what I felt. I want you to experience the helplessness of watching someone you love die." Thompson looked upward at the sound of the water pipes rattling shut. "She's such a pretty girl, Sam," he said, smiling with red-covered lips.

CHAPTER 59
May 2013

Sam could not inhale without his chest sputtering, less from the high-voltage assault in Cheyenne than from the emotion that threatened to overtake him. He stood outside the door to Sidney's bedroom at the log house, afraid to enter. L2 sat at his feet, repeatedly glancing upward with quick, bloodshot eyes as she attempted to understand his reluctance to step forward. The space behind Sam's eyes was filled with sorrow. He forcibly held back the flood of tears. His dry lips were speechless. Sidney was not there to hear him. His eyes searched the room filled with the things she loved, all silent and unmoving. Items representing how she used her life, important only to her, things that would someday be discarded by an auctioneer as rubbish. She was not there to explain. The pain behind his eyes grew. Thompson had said their children were off the table, then killed Marcie to prove it. But it had simply been a diversion. Thompson had lied to him. Killing Sidney had been his plan all along. Sam had suspected as much but had let his guard down nonetheless. He could not swallow his gullibility. How could he have allowed this to happen a second time? There was no excuse, no forgiveness. Still, how could a drunken mistake just out of adolescence haunt him this many years later, and cause so much pain to the innocent? He would repent if he knew how.

L2's toenails scraped across the floor as she awkwardly ran to the front door. Sam turned. She had heard something he had not. Opening the door, he came face to face with the agent in charge and his trusty sidekick, whose black eyes contrasted with the white tape holding his nose in place.

"If you so much as blink sideways at us, I'll put three slugs in you before you can reconsider," the agent in charge said.

"Fair enough," Sam said, stepping aside with an unspoken invitation.

Sam made a fresh pot of coffee.

"This is what happens when amateurs take over," the agent in charge said, his gaze locked on Sam.

"I just want my daughter back."

"Thompson is no ordinary psychopath. Killing means nothing to him. It's just a means to an end. It's all about the game and following his rules. He's a genius who delights in teasing and staying one step ahead. You can't match wits with this guy. He'll win every time."

"Why are you here?"

"You got your daughter back the first time and he changed the game. He killed your ex-wife. He knew you'd come for him. Did you really think you could catch him at that bar in Laramie? I'm sure he was delighted to detour your little hospital ruse in Cheyenne. You're lucky he didn't kill the lot of you."

"You're here to tell me how stupid I am?"

"Of course not, we're professionals. However, you're as dumb as a box of rocks."

Sam smiled. "Okay, now that we have that out of the way, why are you here?"

"Oh, you really are stupid," the agent in charge said with a grin. "We're not here. We've been reassigned. We'll be delving into the exciting world of industrial espionage by China. We leave for San Francisco tomorrow. A new team who can't find their ass with both hands will be arriving in Denver as soon as they're potty-trained. In the meantime, Mr. Dawson, you're on your own."

Sam stared at the agent in charge. Confusion wrinkled his forehead and he shook his head slightly. "And the reason you're here is?"

"God, you're stupid. Didn't I just tell you we're not here?" He nodded to his junior G-man partner, who resembled a raccoon.

The younger agent stood and left the house briskly. The agent in charge sipped his coffee. A few moments later the door opened and Nick walked into the kitchen, followed by the younger agent. Sam jumped up, propelling his chair backward. "Where's my daughter, you son of a bitch?"

"Go easy, Mr. Dawson," the agent in charge commanded. "He's here of his own free will—aaaand," he added, drawing out the word, "the avoidance of facing some minor charges of falsifying his employment records, specifically his federal firearms permit."

"That's bull and you know it," Sam said. "You've been protecting him all along."

"We want Thompson as bad as you do."

"No you don't," Sam said. "You couldn't possibly want him as much as I do."

The agent in charge did not respond immediately. "My interests are about national security. Yours have to do with flesh and blood. It gets pretty sticky when trying to compare the two. Believe me, my partner and I have seen firsthand how motivated you are. We both have children too." He paused. His lips tightened. "That's why we're giving you this little token of our appreciation for the dilemma you're in." The agent in charge stood up. "Listen to him, Mr. Dawson. He has some very interesting things to tell you. Good luck. If you are ever in San Francisco, stay the hell away from us." The two agents started for the door.

"Wait," Sam called out. "What am I supposed to do with him?"

"Not our problem," the agent in charge said. Then he smiled at Sam. "You really aren't very bright. We leveled the playing field for you and now you want us to give you the playbook too. We're finished here, Mr. Dawson." With that, the two men walked out, leaving Sam and Nick staring speechless at one another. L2 came padding up to Nick, leaned against his leg, and wagged her tail.

CHAPTER 60
May 2013

"He's not my father anymore," Nick said softly while looking down at the floor, as though admitting a truth that had been brewing a long time. "He's gone too far."

Sam could feel the rage building. "Gone too far?" he repeated in a mocking tone. "He killed an innocent woman—my ex-wife, the mother of my child, just to show me he could. Gone too far," he said again, this time with incredulity. "He took my daughter—again. The first time you helped him. You're probably helping him now."

"No, sir," Nick said, looking directly into Sam's eyes. "You don't understand. You'll never understand."

"You better make me understand, Nick, because your life depends on it. The only reason you're still standing and breathing is you have value as trade bait, nothing more." Sam's jaw was set, his fists clenched.

"I love Sidney," Nick gushed. "I don't know if you can comprehend that right now, given your state of mind."

"That's bullshit. How can you possibly say that after you tried to kill her?"

"That's not true. I was trying to save her after everything went south with my father."

"You betrayed her. You used her. You took advantage of her trust. And now, you worthless piece of crap, you have the audacity to stand there and tell me you love her? If you didn't have trade value, I'd dig a hole right now and put you in it."

"Hear me out, Mr. Dawson. That's all I'm asking," Nick said without averting his gaze.

Sam pondered his request for several seconds. "I'm listening, but if you so much as flinch, if you stutter, I'll take you out."

"Have you ever truly loved someone, Mr. Dawson? I mean in a grownup romantic way."

"Yes," Sam said, looking squarely at Nick. "Twice, and they were both killed by crazy bastards. So excuse me if I don't get all warm and fuzzy as we walk down memory lane together."

Nick pursed his lips and tucked his chin. He was obviously frustrated with Sam's inability to listen impartially. "Then you understand the conflicting emotions of love and hate."

"Don't tell me, punk, what I do and don't understand. You haven't a clue."

In an attempt to defuse Sam's anger, Nick asked, "Can we sit down?"

Sensing a long story, Sam wanted to sit in the overstuffed chairs of the open living room. Instead, he motioned toward the hard-backed kitchen chairs nearest them.

"This story has many chapters and goes back a few years. You need to hear all of it before you rush to judgment."

⊷══◉══⊷

Sam wanted to scream, "Stop!" He had lost interest and was out of patience. He wanted to toss civility out the window and ask Nick how his self-centered confessions aided in getting Sidney back. Sam glanced at the kitchen clock and held his tongue.

Much of Nick's narrative consisted of the usual family drama that shaped the storyteller's life and accounted for all the things that did not conform to what the narrator thought was normal or usual. The neglect, the unfairness of parent-child relationships, the mistakes of parenting that resulted in the shortcomings of adulthood, and, of course, the offspring's desperate attempts to win parental favor. It could have been anybody's story.

The next chapter depicted a man falling in love, finding that one person who gave meaning to his life. At the same time, it spoke of a father's betrayal and a son's realization that the man he had looked up to all his life was not only fallible, he was also deranged. The story was complex, and hard for Sam to listen to since it involved his daughter. Or, perhaps, it reminded him of his own tragic relationships. Equally troubling was how convincing Nick was. Sam believed him. Unlike Sam, Nick had found his path to redemption. His repentance had turned into penitence. His regret was now the basis for his self-imposed punishment. He would pay for his wrongdoing by betraying his father. He had gone over to the other side.

Sam shook his head. His patience was gone. "How does any of this help find my daughter?" The ringing of the phone only added to his frustration. He answered with a rude "What?"

"Sam," Sheriff O'Malley said excitedly. "We may have a break. The other morning when Sidney was abducted, a realtor for Century 21 was taking photos of the house next door for a listing. One of her shots has a black Plymouth Fury parked two doors down from us, no snow on it."

"Uh-huh," Sam heard himself reply as if he were awakening from a deep sleep.

"Chrysler hasn't made that car since the late seventies or early eighties. We ran the plates and discovered they were stolen. The car itself was reported stolen last week in Fort Collins, Colorado. Only a crazy man would steal an oversized muscle car and drive it around town like he owned it. We put out an APB on it and got a hit from the state patrol in Carbon County, west of Laramie. A trooper saw it near Arlington yesterday and an Albany County sheriff's deputy spotted it twenty-five miles west of Laramie near Centennial this morning. We're checking campgrounds and cabins along the Sand Lake Road between Highway 130 and I-80."

Sam stared at the floor. His mind raced. He saw much of his life flutter rapidly before him, like images from a picture book fanned by an imaginary thumb. He needed to concentrate. He needed to prioritize. Sidney was at the top of the list.

"Sam, are you there?" he suddenly heard the sheriff asking.

"I'm here," Sam said weakly. "What can I do to help?"

"Stay put and near the phone. I'll let you know if we find anything. And Sam…" He paused.

"Yes?"

"Don't do anything stupid," the sheriff cautioned.

Sam hung up the phone and looked intently at Nick. "Does Sand Lake, Deep Creek, Trail Creek, or Rock Creek mean anything to you?" Sam's passion for fly fishing had familiarized him with all the trout-bearing waters of that part of the Medicine Bow National Forest.

"Yes, sir," Nick answered quickly as he rose from his chair. "We camped in that area when I was a kid. There's an old logging camp—"

"Saddle up." Sam cut him off as he grabbed the Willys's keys from the hook near the back door and the Winchester from above the door frame. He suddenly turned and faced Nick. "You cross me and I'll kill you. Understood?"

Nick nodded his acceptance of the threat and the two men stared at each other.

L2 waited for a command. Sam patted his leg and the dog tottered out the door ahead of them.

CHAPTER 61
May 2013

It was obvious Nick had more chapters to read from his life's story. Sam did not prompt him. He wanted to shout, "Tell somebody who cares!" Sam tried to pull things from Nick's confession that might help negotiate Sidney's return. Too many questions remained unanswered. Thompson's behavior was erratic. He was an unpredictable psychopath, and he had Sidney. Sam needed to focus. Everything else could wait.

After the two men left the house, they did not speak in the hour and a half it took to reach the turnoff to Sand Lake in the Snowy Range of the Medicine Bow Mountains between Laramie and Saratoga. The Willys rattled and bounced along on the miles of washboard gravel that snaked through the Medicine Bow National Forest. Pockets of snow remained on the north slopes. The forest was a patchwork of uneven mature spruce and pine with interrupted clear-cuts of uniform replanted pine trees. In the rearview mirror, Sam could see the Snowy Range descending into Colorado, the peaks and valleys defined by shades of undulating darkness.

Sam had fished most of the streams in the region. He remembered taking Sidney camping on Deep Creek as it tumbled recklessly from Sand Lake to Rock Creek. It was during her undergraduate years at UW. She had protested the imposition on her overachieving class schedule, combined with her social agenda. He had thought they would catch only brook trout beneath the shaded banks and in the swirling eddies behind giant boulders. When she pulled out a seventeen-inch rainbow, her attitude suddenly changed. He would never forget the smile on her lips and the gleam in her eye as she held up the fish for his inspection, late summer wildflowers ablaze in the background.

"Here," Nick suddenly shouted as the Willys bottomed out on a valley floor and crossed over a large culvert that carried a mountain stream. "I'm pretty sure this is it. What creek is this?"

"Trail Creek," Sam answered. "The last valley was South Fork. Up ahead are the Middle Fork, then North Fork and Deep Creek."

"It's down that way," Nick said, pointing to the east. "Maybe a mile, then there's a bigger stream."

"That would be Rock Creek," Sam said. He pulled over and stopped the Willys.

"The logging camp is east of that. It's buried back in the timber on a plateau above the creek."

"You sure?"

"Pretty sure. It's been a long time. This looks familiar. I remember the ruins of a barn where they kept their draft horses, a springhouse over an ice-cold wellhead, even an old outhouse. There must have been half a dozen log buildings at one time. They were all in ruins, except one with a tin roof. It even had a small woodstove. We used pine boughs to sweep away the pack rat droppings—"

"This is the only road for miles," Sam said, interrupting Nick's walk down memory lane. "He had to hide the car somewhere close by. Keep an eye out." He let out the clutch and drove slowly to the north. Sam scanned both sides of the road, thick with mature lodgepole pine. He stopped and let L2 out. She urinated, her nose held high, testing the mountain air. A hundred yards down the road, she veered off into the timber and he lost sight of her. Sam brought the Willys to an abrupt stop, jumped from the Jeep with the Winchester, and scrambled into the forest. Less than thirty yards into the timber, he found the Plymouth covered with fresh-cut pine limbs, the hood still warm. L2 waved her tail.

Twenty minutes down the deadfall-littered trail, Sam and Nick struggled to keep up with a thirteen-year-old dog who suddenly acted young again. "Does any of this look familiar?" Sam asked.

Nick shook his head. "I don't know. It was a long time ago."

Sam remembered fishing the confluence where Trail Creek rushed from the narrow gorge into the broad, rocky meadow that surrounded Rock Creek. They would be exposed if they tried crossing the larger stream there. Through the trees, he could see they were approaching the valley. "We'll stay in the timber, skirt Rock Creek upstream, and look for a place to cross. And Nick, one false step and I'll blow a hole in you and leave you for the bears." It was too late. L2 had lowered her head and started to run. Short of putting her on a lead, which Sam had forgotten to bring, there was no controlling her. She loped into the open meadow, plunged into Rock Creek with the grace of a train wreck, crossed the stream, scrambled up the embankment, and disappeared into the forest. "We've got to move fast," Sam yelled above the roar of rushing water. "How far is it to the logging camp?"

"Not far, maybe a hundred yards," Nick called back.

The two men splashed across Rock Creek and scrambled up the steep embankment where L2 had disappeared. The forest was suddenly eerie. Sam noted the almost total lack of understory. The mature lodgepole pine had taken away the sun and created a dark and dank forest floor that was spongy with duff. The smell of decay filled his nostrils. The logging camp was as Nick had described, dilapidated and rotted. Roofs had fallen in, walls had collapsed, and trees had grown up from the ruins more than a lifetime ago. Stillness hung over the scene with a deathly quiet that caused the hairs on the back of Sam's neck to stand up. His thumb felt absently for the hammer on the Winchester.

Nick pointed to the one structure that was still standing, a windowless cabin not much bigger than a single-car garage. The remains of what appeared to be an outhouse stood twenty yards behind it. L2 waited quietly outside the door of the shack, waving her tail. She looked back over her shoulder at Sam then pawed at the door. Nick held up his fist, signaling Sam to stop. He tapped his ear and turned his head sideways toward the cabin. He listened, then shook his head.

Winded, Sam stood motionless. He was scared of what he might find. Ugly images flashed in his mind's eye.

Without warning, Nick kicked in the door with a thunderous crash and charged into the cabin right behind L2. Sam brought up the rear, his rifle held at port arms.

Sidney was huddled in a dark corner of the cabin. She was bound to the wall and gagged. Her eyes showed relief then concern. Thompson was not there. L2 nuzzled her, then turned her attention to investigating food wrappers and other trash strewn about the floor. Nick removed the gag as Sam cut the ropes. Sam grabbed her and pulled her to his chest, an embrace that told her everything he wanted to say but could not find words for. "I can't believe this has happened again, kiddo," he said.

"I gotta tell you, Pop, this is getting really old," she said sarcastically and much too loudly.

Sam fumbled in his shirt pocket and pulled out her hearing aids, which he had brought from home. From his other pocket he produced her eyeglasses.

"Are you okay? Did he hurt you?" Sam blurted, holding her by the shoulders at arm's length.

Sidney did not answer. Her attention was drawn to Nick, who stood somewhat sheepishly behind Sam.

"He led me here, Sid."

She gently pushed past Sam and stepped in front of Nick. Neither of them spoke. Nick continued to look down while Sidney inserted her hearing aids.

"He said he loves you. He's either a damn good liar with a loose screw or he means it. We can sort it out later."

Sidney glanced at her father then turned back to Nick. "Is that right?"

Nick nodded without looking at her directly.

Sidney's eyes narrowed and she shook her head slowly. "I'm not buying it," she said as she stepped closer and examined his face. "But I'll hear your arguments."

"That can wait. Where's Thompson?" Sam said hurriedly.

"He was just here," Sidney said. "He grabbed the toilet paper and headed out the door maybe five minutes ago."

"The outhouse," Sam almost yelled. He rushed toward the door.

"Wait." Nick stepped in front of Sam. "Let me talk to him."

Sam stared back at him with a puzzled look.

"He's my father," Nick said.

Sam's eyes darted back and forth across Nick's face. "I'll cover you. Go."

The two men exited the cabin and carefully eased around the back corner, where the logs overlapped each other. The board-and-batten outhouse stood rigid, door open, revealing its empty interior.

CHAPTER 62
June 2013

Sam's semiannual report to the County Commissioners Association and Wyoming State Parks and Cultural Resources was two weeks overdue. In disgust, he tossed the two-page account on his desk. It was the work of an eighth grader lying about having done his assignment. They were threatening to pull the plug on his project unless he showed significant progress, of which he had none.

Sidney had mastered the art of the cold shoulder. She was civil, while distant and apathetic. Sam knew she held him responsible for her mother's death. The sheriff held him responsible for Thompson's escape and would not take Sam's phone calls. Nick had hired out as a sales rep with a private security company in Fort Collins and was attempting to sell his wares in Cheyenne. Sam believed most of Nick's sales pitches were actually to Sidney, based on the number of phone calls he made to her. She remained aloof, even guarded. She was unconvinced, and that was fine with Sam.

"Pop"—Sidney said as she stepped into Sam's study—"I haven't been out of this house in over two weeks. Nick's coming up this weekend and wants to take me to dinner and a movie in Cheyenne. I told him no, but unless you take me to town for dinner and a movie, I might accept his offer."

"Not a chance, sweetie. When Nick's crazy father is dead or behind bars, I might let you out of my sight. Until then it's house arrest."

Sidney crunched her eyebrows together. "You can't do that. I'm twenty-nine years old. You don't make the rules anymore."

"I can and I do." Sam smiled. "How about I fix you a big plate of nachos and a DVD, one we've only seen a dozen times so far?"

Sidney huffed, spun around, and stomped out of his study. Sam called after her, "How about we hike into the headwaters of Horse Creek tomorrow and catch a mess of brookies?" He heard her door slam shut. "Or maybe not," he mumbled to himself. Absentmindedly, Sam picked up the phone halfway through the first ring.

"No one knows how a young man chooses the things that interest him," Thompson crooned. "I suspect it's no different than catching a common virus like the chicken pox. For me, it was Valentina's total indifference to my advances. For Nikolai, who knows? Perhaps it was your daughter's flawless skin and perfect body that inspired his betrayal."

"You killed my wife, you sick piece of shit." Sam was ready to explode.

"Ex-wife, Sam. You had discarded her decades ago. It was good seeing you at the funeral. You looked upset. I was right behind you in the fourth row. I wore my best funeral clothes. It was fun to be with old friends I have never met, to kiss their sad cheeks and offer my deepest sympathies. They were Jews, Sam. You would think they would have been used to tragedy."

"Stay away from my family, Thompson. If you—"

"Spare me the threats, Sam."

"No threats. I was going to tell you that only an impotent sissy with a penis the size of a peanut would attack women. If it's revenge you want, why not come after me?"

"In due time, Sam Dawson, in due time. I had thought I made it clear to you. First, you must suffer as I have suffered. I want you to have the time to reflect on what you have done, to see the consequences of your actions. I want you to intervene. I delight in seeing your futile attempts to stop the slaughter of the innocents, people that mean something to you. Death is too quick for you, Sam. Likewise, physical pain is too fleeting. It's the everlasting emotional suffering of knowing that you are responsible for the death of someone else that I'm after. Something you are forced to live with for the rest of your days, however few remain."

Sam's mind raced. He had acquaintances rather than friends. The people he cared most about were already dead, except for Sidney. "Stay away from us, Thompson. Two can play this game. I—" He stopped himself.

"Go on," Thompson coached.

"I…won't hesitate to put a bullet in Nick."

"That's the spirit, Sam. I was hoping you would say that. It would save me the trouble of having to deal with his betrayal. And as an added bonus, your daughter would hate you as my son does me. Checkmate, my friend."

Sam heard him chuckle. He seethed with anger as a result of having nothing to offer.

"It has been fun talking with you, Sam. I really must go. There is so much to do. Oh, I almost forgot. Do you remember

Thomasina Tucker? Of course you do. No one forgets their first true love." He chuckled again. "Now there's a blast from the past. Just when you thought I might have run out of moves."

Sam heard the distinctive click of Thompson hanging up the phone. He could not control the trembling in his hands.

CHAPTER 63

June 2013

"Cat Girl? How the hell should I know? Christ, Dawson, I haven't heard from you in years, and you call me up looking for a chick from high school?"

"Look, Woody, it's really important," Sam pleaded.

"Oh, why didn't you say so? Let me check my Rolodex. Nope, she's not in there. Wait, I was looking under her maiden name. Maybe she's under Weaver. Yeah, she was under Weaver all right. She got knocked up by that dirtbag."

"Do you know if she's still in Boulder?"

"Let's see, we graduated high school thirty-two years ago, she was a year behind us, so she wouldn't have come to any of our class reunions, and since you didn't come to any of them either, Chip and I thought maybe the two of you had reunited and were living somewhere in paradise. Hey, do you remember the words to our little ditty?"

Woody was on a roll and Sam could not stop him.

Woody began to sing. "Sammy had a girlfriend. Her name was Tommie Tucker. He took her in the backseat to see if he could—"

"Yeah, I remember," Sam said, cutting him off. "How could I forget?" Listening to Woody was like being in a time warp, Sam thought. He was still as sarcastic and repulsive as he was in high school. Sam was losing his patience. "Do you know where she is or not?"

"Not a clue," Woody shot back. "Have you checked the local animal shelter? Meow."

"Thanks for nothing, Woody."

"Anytime, Sam. It was great talking to you."

⊹═◉═⊹

"Easy as pie, Sam," Sheriff O'Malley said coyly as he leaned back in his squeaky chair and placed his hands behind his head, his fingers interlaced. "Like falling off a log," he added with a smile. "Do you care to share with me why you want her address and phone number?"

"I think she's Thompson's next target. He called this morning and threatened her."

"And she is...who?"

"She was my girlfriend thirty-two years ago."

Sheriff O'Malley raised his eyebrows and inhaled sharply.

"Quit with the third degree, Harrison. I know you're mad at me. We can work out our differences later. Right now I need to warn this woman that her life is in danger."

"Have you ever listened to hear the number of times you use the personal pronoun 'I' when speaking, Sam? I don't know why we have this web of law enforcement agencies throughout the country when all we really need is Sam Dawson, photographer of cemeteries."

"Look, we can work out—"

"Hi, Harrison," Sidney said cheerfully as she rushed into O'Malley's office, brushing past her father to give the sheriff a hug as he stood to greet her. "Come on, Pop, I'm starving. Can you join us for lunch?" she asked the sheriff.

"I'd love to. Does he have to come?" The sheriff flicked his thumb toward Sam.

"I'm afraid so. He hasn't let me out of his sight since the last kidnapping. He's like one of those ankle bracelets the court requires when sentencing someone to their home. The only reason we came to town today is because you won't take his phone calls. Give him what he wants, Harrison. Otherwise, he'll make your life miserable."

The sheriff pushed a button on his intercom. "Bridgett, please get me the contact information for one Thomasina Tucker, last known address: Boulder, Colorado. Call me when you find it."

The Plains Hotel in downtown Cheyenne was crowded with a mixture of tourists and local merchants eating in the subdued atmosphere of the historic landmark. Sidney had wolfed down her Cobb salad and was snatching fries from Sam's plate, where his bison burger sat untouched. The sheriff eyed her skeptically. He turned to Sam. "Don't you feed her at home?"

Sam had not said two words during lunch. The sheriff studied him and seemed about to offer a comment when his cell phone buzzed. He pulled a pen and a small pad of paper from his shirt pocket and began jotting something down. "Thanks, Bridgett." He folded the flip phone and put it in his pocket, then carefully wiped his moustache with his linen napkin. "You're in luck, Sam. She's just down the road in Berthoud between Longmont and Fort Collins. She goes by the name of

Weaver now." He slid the page torn from his notebook toward Sam. "There's her address and phone number."

Sam eagerly took the paper and stared at it as if it required deciphering. "Thanks, Harrison. One more big favor?" he asked. Sam looked at Sidney, who was cutting his burger in half. "Could you take her with you back to your office and lock her up until I get back?"

"Sam, Berthoud is in Larimer County. I know the sheriff well. Why don't you let me call him and have her put under surveillance until we find this guy?"

"I need to explain to her what's happening before cops start showing up on her doorstep." Sam slid from the booth. "Will you watch Sid for me, Harrison?"

"You know I will."

Sidney looked up at her father, her cheek ballooned out with burger. "Be careful, Pop."

"Trust no one except Harrison, kiddo," he said, looking directly into her eyes. "I'll be back by close of business. Berthoud is only an hour or so from here." Sam turned and walked briskly away.

"Can you believe that guy?" Sheriff O'Malley said, shaking his head. "He finally stuck me with the check."

CHAPTER 64
June 2013

The Willys rumbled slowly over the railroad tracks and down Mountain Avenue—the main drag of Berthoud, two blocks of unique stores and eateries. The town straddled the Weld and Larimer County lines. Sam remembered it as a small farming community that, with the help of water diverted from both the Big Thompson and Little Thompson creeks, grew everything from sugar beets and corn to wheat and cabbage. He recalled the stench of sheep grazing on cabbage residue in the fields east of town, the methane from the woolies' passing gas bringing tears to his eyes. Agriculture had since been overtaken by rural subdivisions with an insatiable thirst for the water that sustained family farms. The sugar factory in Longmont had been the first to close, then the meat processing plant, the vegetable stands, and the slow trickle-down of economic and cultural loss that supported an agrarian lifestyle. It was quickly supplanted by rooftops and paved-over parking lots of trendy communities, the inhabitants of which got in line every morning to slowly commute to jobs in Denver forty-five miles to the south. Berthoud had made the transition much better than most towns along the Front Range of Colorado. It retained the flavor of a slightly mid-West farm town with cottonwood-lined streets and Longs Peak as a backdrop.

Sinclair Lewis could easily have used it as the mythical Sauk Centre in his novel *Main Street*.

Sam read off the street numbers of businesses on Mountain Avenue. He began to worry the address the sheriff had given him was wrong. He expected it to be in a residential neighborhood. Instead, it was one of the more historic red brick buildings in the center of town, three stories with a facade. The store's name was arched gracefully across a large picture window: "Western Pleasure." A smaller subheading underneath read "Treasures from the Past." It was an antique store. He assumed there must be an apartment or two above and looked for a separate entrance.

Sam parked the Willys in front of the store but did not get out. Instead, he sat gripping the steering wheel, looking at the storefront. He remembered the pleasant innocence of his youth and his girlfriend, Tommie Tucker. He thought he might not be able to bear another disappointment, one more calamity, another stain on his memory of, perhaps, the best years of his life. He had been incredibly selfish and stupid when he walked away from her without an explanation. They were too young to harbor so much love. The world was waiting and he was too impatient, too inarticulate to offer clarification. He simply faded into the background. The blemish of a past love, along with all the other stains, was still there. More than thirty years of shame was bottled up inside of him. He was no more prepared now than he was then to stumble through the ignorance of human emotion, and the guilt he harbored for unilaterally deciding to end it for his benefit, not hers. Until the last few years, his life had been blessed. And what about hers? He had treated her badly. What could he possibly say to change that?

Bells tinkled softy from above the door when he entered. The fragrant aroma of scented candles and soaps wafted gently over him. Music played softly in the background. He tried to recall if they had a song way back then that defined them. Nothing came to mind. What he remembered was how compatible they were, how each liked what the other liked. They chided but never argued. Sam knew, at the time, how perfect their union was. He also knew that someday they would discover their differences and grow apart. He would come to resent his lost opportunities. Only now was he beginning to realize that love can offset the uncertainty of dreams deferred.

The floor creaked from the direction of the counter, and movement caught Sam's eye. "There is hot water and a nice selection of teas at the back of the store," a woman called out.

Sam recognized her voice instantly. She stepped from behind the counter. Elegant as a model, she had retained her athletic figure and well-proportioned stature. He was suddenly reminded of the fact that she had been the only cheerleader who could do the splits perfectly, her long legs splayed in opposite directions, a smile on her face. She wore a dark red shirtdress, a cameo pinned to the lapel. Her hair was shorter and darker with silvery streaks that belied her flawless complexion. She looked like she had just stepped off the cover of a fashion magazine catering to middle-aged women.

"Is there anything I can help you—" She stopped and her eyes slowly grew larger. "Sam?"

"Tommie," he said, smiling slightly and looking directly into her eyes. It was not a greeting of surprise. Rather, his inflection connoted an attainment of purpose.

Both stood silently, awkwardly staring at each other. She was the first to speak. "What...?" She cocked her head slightly. "How...?"

"You haven't changed a bit," Sam said, smiling. "You're still as beautiful as you were in high school."

"And you're still, how should I say..." She twisted her lips in a crooked smile. "Full of beans. How long has it been, Sam?"

"Thirty-two years or so, I think."

"Hmm," she said, lowering her chin. "I believe it's more like thirty years if you count the time you snubbed me in Walgreens."

"You saw me?"

Tommie smiled broadly. "What brings you here, Sam? I'm going to assume this isn't coincidental."

"No, it's not. That can wait. First things first. How are you?"

"I'm fine, thank you."

"Is this yours?" he said, taking in the space with a broad gesture.

"Yes," she answered quickly. Her gaze became more intense.

"How about your folks?"

"They're well. They moved to Scottsdale a couple of years ago."

"Paul?"

"He's selling used cars in Denver. He found it safer to sell them than steal them. We divorced between incarcerations over a quarter century ago. Next."

"Children?"

"My daughter is a physician's assistant at Sloan Kettering in New York. Look, Sam, we both have a million questions."

He could not stop staring at her. She was beautiful, and he suddenly felt intimidated by her intellect and good looks. He was remembering the passion-filled nights in the backseat of his Comet convertible parked amid the tombstones at Green Mountain Cemetery. He thought of the choices he had made in his life—some good, many bad, a winnowing process that kept him up at night. "It's your turn," he said.

She pointed toward a bookshelf behind him where his books were neatly displayed. "The backflap of the dust jacket tells me everything I need to know. Why are you here, Sam?"

"Is there someplace more private we can go?"

"No."

"I'll take you up on that tea, if you don't mind." His mind raced as to how to broach the topic of a psychopathic killer who was threatening her.

They sat at a small, antique ice-cream parlor set. Two uncomfortable wrought iron chairs were separated by a crooked table that tipped back and forth each time Sam rested his arm on it. A tag taped to the table had a price of $275 written on it. "How's business?" Sam asked out of the blue, knowing he was the only other person in the store.

"I've thought about this day many times," Tommie said as she slowly stirred her tea bag around the inside of her fine bone china cup. "What I would say to you, what questions I would ask. But it doesn't matter anymore. It was a long time ago, Sam. We were just kids." She squeezed her tea bag in her spoon by wrapping the string around it. "We didn't have a clue about the future. It took me a long while to get over the pain of rejection, of not knowing why. I was very depressed and then I was angry. My whole life had suddenly changed. I was pretty lost. Paul Weaver took advantage of that and I let him. I was helpless then. When my daughter was born, she became my sanctuary, my purpose to go on." She stopped and looked up at Sam. She smiled. "This isn't what I had rehearsed over and over in my mind, should the day come when you walked through that door." She shook her head slowly. "Did you know that I never finished high school? I was too embarrassed. I moved to Colorado Springs and lived with my grandparents for almost a year. I saw a therapist." She sipped her tea and kept her eyes turned downward, not at Sam. "Eventually, I got my GED and went to a community college off and on for a couple of years. My parents were saints. Long story short, after a series of dead-end jobs, I mortgaged my soul and bought this so I could be my own boss. End of story."

Sam studied her. Troubled, Sam said, "Tell me more about your daughter."

Finally, her eyes came up to meet his. "No," she said definitively and kept her stare. "What brings you here, Sam? Why now after all these years?"

It was Sam's turn to fix his eyes on the table. "All the way down here I tried to rehearse in my mind what I would say to you." He paused. "I kept getting distracted by old memories of the two of us." He paused again. "We had some good times, didn't we, Tommie?" He looked up at her and smiled.

She did not respond.

"I've often wondered if we were too young or if we were like most kids and just experimenting with biology. How much was real and how much was just hormones? I guess it didn't matter at the time. I think we both believed we were in love. I'm not sure we understood that concept. I'm not sure I understand it yet. We were young," he repeated. "The whole world was ours for the asking. Everything was new and exciting. There was so much to look forward to. I-I mean us." He paused. "I think we were headed for a pretty bleak future if we had taken on the responsibilities of adulthood and continued down the path we were on. I wish now I would have confided in you and that it had been a mutual decision to go out and discover the rest of the world." Sam paused again. This time he looked squarely at her. "I was scared, Tommie. Too scared to face you and tell you we were too young to make such a commitment."

"It took you thirty-two years to overcome your fear and tell me now? Frankly, Sam, I don't care anymore. I did at one time and, yes, I was hurt. I got over it and moved on with my life. It doesn't do any good to sit and wonder what your life would have been like had you made different choices. You play the cards you're dealt and you play to win."

"And did you? Did you win?" Sam asked.

"Is this why you're here?" she shot back. "You look me up after all this time in order to tell me you were scared and how has my life been? I'm not buying it." Her eyes narrowed. "There's something else, isn't there? What is it you are not telling me?"

⋯⇒◉⇐⋯

Sam felt foolish. As soon as he finished, he regretted it. He had presented the *Reader's Digest* version, leaving out names, dates, and places. "I know it sounds stupid. Believe me, this guy is relentless. He will stop at nothing to inflict emotional pain on me. If he thinks I care for you, and I do, he'll prey on that feeling. He killed my ex and kidnapped my daughter twice. He's an evildoer, the Devil incarnate, and he means business, Tommie. I think you are in danger."

"Wait a second," she said, her eyebrows furrowing. "You care for me? Not a word from you in over three decades and you suddenly show up on my doorstep and tell me you care for me?" She shook her head from side to side. "I gotta tell you, Sam, this just doesn't compute. I don't know what universe you live in. It's not this one. I won't let you come in here and drag me into your deranged fantasy world. Life is good for me right now. Like I said before, I've moved on. I have my own business and I've started dating someone. He's older and worldly. If I needed protection, and I don't, Hank would be there for me."

"Excuse me?" Sam blurted out aggressively. "Hank who?"

Tommie sat up straight. "Not that it's any of your business, his name is Hank Thompson."

CHAPTER 65
June 2013

Snapshot memories of hours spent with Tommie back in high school were projected in his mind's eye like old photographs pasted in an album. They were of good times, smiles that radiated promise. Their possibilities were endless. Sam thought it strange that neither of them could see the bad in the world hurtling straight toward them. Like most young people, they seemed to live for the moment. The past was irrelevant and the future unpredictable. They would have followed each other off a cliff in those days. Now Tommie viewed him as mentally deranged. At first he saw the confusion in her eyes, then skepticism, and lastly the sympathy of a stranger being approached by a raving maniac. She wanted rid of him.

Of course Sam had forgotten his cell phone and was forced to realize that pay phones had disappeared off the face of the planet. He found one outside the trucker's shower room at Johnson's Corner, a landmark truck stop in northern Colorado, and dialed Sheriff O'Malley. The sheriff would call his counterpart in Colorado and alert the Denver authorities that their prime suspect in Marcie's murder was about to strike again in Berthoud. Sam stood staring at the wall after he hung up the phone. The realization of his helplessness overpowered him.

The scent of fresh-baked cinnamon rolls, the restaurant's trademark, filled the truck stop. He bought three of them on the way out, a peace offering for the sheriff and Sidney. In the parking lot, a man with a turban and full beard stood admiring Sam's Willys. Sam had noticed a growing number of truckers wearing turbans—red, white, black fabric headdresses. Sam guessed they were Sikhs, though he knew little of their religious beliefs.

"She's a beauty," the man said with the upswept syllables typical of India. "What year?"

"Fifty-three," Sam responded proudly.

"My father's brother had one in Punjab when I was a boy."

Sam wondered why the man didn't use the word "uncle."

"It was the only one in the region. He used it to haul his goats to market."

Sam hesitated. He looked at the man skeptically. "I thought Punjabi Sikhs were vegetarians."

It was after midnight when Sheriff O'Malley arrived at Johnson's Corner. Flashing emergency lights surrounded the Willys, its doors still locked. A white paper sack with three cinnamon rolls inside lay on the pavement next to the passenger door. A row of semi-tractor-trailer rigs, their engines running noisily, sat impervious to the investigation. Cars chased their own headlight beams north and south on I-25. The sheriff rubbed the beard stubble on his chin, his eyes bleary with fatigue. He was scared.

CHAPTER 66
June 2013

It was more than dark. There was a total absence of light. Sam was confused, like waking from a disturbing dream. He tried to open his eyes. Something held them shut. His arms tingled as if asleep. At first, he could not tell if he was lying down or sitting. He listened. The only sound was the ringing in his ears. As the fog started to lift, he inhaled through his nose. Sam stretched his fingers. He could not move his hands. His wrists were bound tightly by something tough and thin. Likewise, his ankles were lashed together, preventing any movement. His feet felt as if they were cast in concrete. He could only wiggle his toes. He attempted to swallow the dry lump in his throat but was hampered by something made of cloth tied tightly between his upper and lower jaws. He couldn't bend, turn, or stand. Slowly he came to the realization that he was blindfolded, gagged, and bound to a chair. He could lift and turn his head.

"You should let go of the dead, Sam," Thompson said from somewhere behind him, his voice calm, almost melodious. "We needn't pester them with our thoughts of pity and remorse. They had a job to do and dying was part of it."

Sam made a sound like a man drowning, his tongue held down by the gag.

"We're the ones who need help in reconciling their deaths. Leave them out of it. They're dead."

Sam turned his head from side to side as he attempted to locate the source of Thompson's voice.

"My son was not the only one killed that day. There was little left of him and the others. They could have sent him home in a shoebox. There's no dignity in that. Can you imagine six uniformed pallbearers carrying a flag-draped shoebox from the back of a military transport?"

Sam attempted to move his legs. His feet were all pins and needles.

"It took several days before we were notified. They knew who had been killed but they wanted to get it right. You know, send the families the right remains."

The gag cut deeply into Sam's cheeks. It took great effort to swallow.

"They had to identify what was left by doing DNA analysis. Normally, they wouldn't have told us Jack Squat. There were extenuating circumstances, you see. I needn't bother you with the details, Sam. Let me just say that you have no concept of real grief. Pain that great is indescribable. You have to experience it to understand it." Thompson almost chuckled. "Really, you have no idea. Nothing was as it seemed. Everything was an illusion. I shouldn't have been surprised. My life had been an illusion, totally fabricated." He snorted. "Still is!"

Sam wanted to scream that Nick was his son and that he was alive and well in Fort Collins. *Why continue this charade?*

"When you're in my line of work, there's no place for proper grieving. The horror of not formalizing his death, of

not honoring his life was more than I could bear. There were no
burial clothes to pick out, no hymn to choose for a service that
would not be held, no obituary to write, no ground to purchase
for a place to memorialize him. My grief, as you might expect,
was explosive. How could this have occurred? My cooperation
with your government was provisional. Strings had been pulled
and arrangements made to ensure his safety. Policies were over-
ridden, orders handed down from above so that Nikolai could
watch over his little brother." Thompson's voice softened. "They
got separated when their unit was hurriedly dispatched to some
squalid village where suspected insurgents were hiding. Nikolai
was one hundred feet behind when the IED was detonated."

Sam stopped struggling. He inhaled deeply through his
nostrils and turned his head toward Thompson's voice.

"The boys were as different as night and day."

Sam could hear amusement slip into Thompson's words.

"Samuil was the favored son. In his mother's eyes, he could
do no wrong. Bright as a new penny, with a wit that could
cut you to the bone or win over those who dared to disagree.
Good-looking to a fault, if he wanted something, he got it. If
you stood in his way you would soon be made a fool. For him
there was no distinction between truth and a lie. He was a
fast-talker whose exaggerations were legend within our family.
He was in and out of juvenile hall, mostly for possession of
drugs, always with a smile. The more outlandish his behavior,
the more girls were attracted to him. He consumed them like
potato chips. I wouldn't be surprised if there were fatherless
children or aborted fetuses in his wake. He put ketchup on
everything, even soup. He could silence a room with flatulence

that shook the walls. There wasn't a game invented that he couldn't cheat at. He rarely slept more than a few hours, wore sandals in the winter. He never finished a can of beer, and never failed to tell us he loved us, always with a toothy grin and a gleam in his eye. Perpetually broke, he stole from both your wallet and your heart. He threw open his arms to life, gathered as much of it as he could, and laughed at the rest. It was a judge who saw through him and set his fate. One pool-hall fight too many had been the last straw. He was given a chance to channel his anger toward a legitimate foe by accepting military service over prison."

Sam waited. Thompson had paused. He heard the man's feet shuffle on the floor.

"Nikolai's job was to protect his brother. Did you know that Nikolai wanted to be a dentist? He had been accepted at Creighton when Samuil was given his choice. There was no convincing Nikolai of his job. He faithfully accepted it. It was what family did. They protected their own. I had what your government wanted and traded information to keep my boys together." He paused again. "A hundred feet was all that separated them. A hundred feet kept me from losing two sons that day. This is all ancient history, Sam. You needed this in order to understand my motivation. You see, I live by a simple code that dictates there is neither friend nor foe who I haven't repaid in full." He chuckled. "Imagine my surprise when I found out that my son had a half sister around the same age."

It took a moment for Thompson's last comment to register. Sam tipped his head sideways in puzzlement.

"Oh, the Army wouldn't have said a thing. It was a botched attempt by your CIA to extort more information from me that led to the discovery. The extensive testing performed on Sidney while unraveling her heritable disease established the baseline that popped up like a neon sign. She and Samuil shared twenty-five percent of their genotype, different mothers, same father."

Sam did not comprehend immediately what Thompson had said. The sound of his own coarse breathing resonating from his hollow chest took priority. A feeling of lightness flowed from the top of his head, spread across his shoulders, descended his spine, and radiated down each leg. He thought he might pass out. He could hear his heart thundering in his ears. Fear suddenly gripped him at the realization he had been drugged. He felt paralyzed.

"Try to imagine my anguish, Sam. My son, the boy I raised, the boy I loved, had just been killed. I then discover he was not really my son. He was sired by some man I never heard of, a photographer in Wyoming. On top of all this is the issue of infidelity by my wife, a woman dying of cancer. The news was all bad and it just kept coming. Are you imagining my agony, Sam?"

Sam was nauseous. He panicked at the possibility of vomiting with his mouth gagged so tightly. He would drown in his own puke. He inhaled deeply and tried to suppress the thought.

"I'm one of those people, Sam, who when angered gets relief—albeit temporary—from exacting payment out of those who have wronged me. To be fair, restitution should be equal.

Hence, my failed attempts to seek compensation by taking your beautiful daughter from you. Granted, a daughter, in my estimation, is not equal to a son. However, it was a start. Watching you lose someone you loved was the prologue to my epic tale. Slicing the throat of that Jew-bitch wife of yours was exciting, as will be putting the knife to Tommie Tucker. However, they are just hors d'oeuvres, rabbit trails in the narrative, if you will, to keep you off balance. Sidney will be the final chapter for your enjoyment. She will die as you watch. And you, Samuel Dawson, will be the epilogue, a satisfying conclusion that ties the follies of your worthless life together. Trust me, Sam, the crescendo leading to your demise will be worth staying awake for. A death so exciting you won't want to miss it."

CHAPTER 67
June 2013

Sam was unsure if he was awake and had been dreaming, or if he was asleep, dreaming he was awake. He felt numb. He and Sidney had picked out the clothes she wanted to be buried in. She held up the flowery sundress her mother was wearing standing ankle-deep in Boulder Creek when she was pregnant with her. He shook his head. Muted chatter from the next room distracted him. His sister smiled at him, then licked the frosting from the knife she had used to cut one of several cakes on the kitchen table. She wore her cheerleading outfit. Tommie, Valentina, Marcie, and Annie all suddenly stopped talking and turned toward Sam, each smiling pleasantly at him. Their faces showed no tears or grief, no scorn, no recriminations, no expressions of bad blood—just four women smiling.

"Dad," Sidney called from the adjoining room.

Sam looked suspiciously at the four women. He turned and walked into the living room. Sidney lay in her mother's stark coffin, her hands folded across her stomach, her pallid face drawn and masklike. Sam's mother stood next to the coffin. She held out a box of chocolate-covered cherries as though offering them to Sidney for her journey.

"How do I look?" Sidney said without opening her eyes.

"Fine," Sam assured her.

"Don't forget, when L2 dies, have her cremated and sprinkle half her ashes on my grave and the other half on his." Without looking she pointed a bony finger past Sam.

Thompson stood behind. Dressed in black with a clerical collar, he clutched a Bible to his chest. "Remember, we should let go of the dead, Sam," he said, his voice confident and reassuring.

"Then why don't you?" Sam mumbled into the gag. The ends of his fingers felt like they were about to explode from lack of circulation.

"What was that, Sam?" Thompson said.

"Let go of the dead," Sam answered unintelligibly, still groggy with sleep or drugs. He was unsure which.

"You're probably asking why I've gone to so much trouble. Why I feel the way I do. I've thought about that for some time. Why should Samuil's death haunt me more than that of a family pet? I wasn't related to him, after all, at least genetically. I raised him. I cared for him when he was young, watched over him when he was sick. I trained him to be the adult he became. But why should I bereave him more than a beagle who runs out into the street and gets hit by a truck? There was no biological linkage. He was just something I fed and watered and picked up after. When I found out he was your son, I felt cheated more than I felt loss. I had been betrayed. It's a common tale— an unfaithful wife, a bastard child, an unsuspecting spouse, a story as old as life itself. Like the cuckoo that rolls the eggs of its victims out of the nest, then replaces them with its own to be raised by the hapless stooge as if they were his own. It's biological fraud, Sam. The penalty must fit the crime, don't you think? You cheated me out of my rightful contribution to the future. It's only fair that I take yours. What a shame. She's such a beautiful girl, despite being genetically flawed. What were you thinking, marrying a Jew?"

The fog was dissolving. The pain in his hands was quickly becoming unbearable. Again, he tried to talk.

"Those are some nasty-looking fingers, Sam," Thompson said, tipping his head to one side. "Perhaps you would like me to loosen those ties a bit?"

Sam nodded, his nostrils flaring in pain. He could hear Thompson rustling behind him.

"Not a chance. You think I'm a fool?"

Sam felt the sharp prick of a needle in the side of his neck. He tried to pull away. Thompson yanked him back by his hair.

CHAPTER 68

June 2013

Harrison," Sidney said softly from the door to the sheriff's office. "Any word?"

He looked up from his desk and slowly shook his head. "Not yet, Sid. They're still interviewing potential witnesses and gathering evidence. These things take time." He noted her puffy, reddened eyes.

"It's been almost forty-eight hours."

"This isn't your standard kidnapping, Sid. I doubt we'll be contacted with a list of demands. All we can do is wait and let the professionals do their job. How are you holding up? You need anything?"

"I need to go home and get a few things."

"I promised him I would watch over you," the sheriff said, settling back in his squeaky chair and smoothing out his moustache. "I can't do that very well from an unsecured location. Plus, I don't have the manpower to spare in order to protect that godforsaken wilderness you call home. I've got DCI and CBI crawling down my back, wanting more than I can give them. The FBI thinks they're in charge and somehow believes I'm their lackey."

"All I'm asking is to make a quick trip home, feed the horse, take a shower, pack a bag, and get some of L2's dry meal and her dog bed. I promise I'll come right back."

L2 heard her name and raised her wrinkled head from the black sweatshirt rumpled on the floor behind the sheriff's desk.

"Maybe you could send Bridgett with me."

The sheriff raised his eyebrows and seemed to ponder the thought. Bridgett was clerical. She had trained at the academy at least two decades ago. She was never given a chance to work in enforcement. Built like an offensive lineman, with no neck and a face similar to Jack Dempsey's, she guarded the sheriff's office from all with no exceptions. Her protectiveness was legendary within the department. He smoothed his moustache again. "Bridgett," he barked into the intercom.

⊷═◉═⊶

Hot water sprayed over Sidney's head, ran off the end of her nose and chin, then circled the shower drain before descending into darkness. The warmth caressed her slender body and soothed her tired mind. Without her hearing aids and glasses her world was encapsulated within her mind. She neither heard nor saw him enter the bathroom.

CHAPTER 69

June 2013

Harrison O'Malley was the longest-serving sheriff in the history of Laramie County. He had never shot a person. In fact, he had never drawn his gun either offensively or defensively. He seldom wore his sidearm. It was too heavy and invariably elicited smart-alecky comments from his coworkers or other law enforcement officials. The weapon of choice by most in the business was a Glock 22 9 mm/.40 cal. with the firepower of fifteen rounds, or some variant of the Colt 1911 in .45 cal. The sheriff carried a Smith & Wesson Model 29 revolver in 44 Magnum with a six-and-a-half-inch barrel that fired a 275-grain hollow point. The foot-pounds of energy at fifty yards would be similar to being hit by a truck while standing on the freeway. Clint Eastwood's character, Dirty Harry, in the 1971 movie by the same name, proclaimed it to be "the most powerful handgun in the world," a quote that took on a life of its own among gun enthusiasts. That was all the endorsement a rookie sheriff's deputy needed. It was a real wrist-breaker and would render him deaf for at least an hour after firing it. He never practiced marksmanship at the range and never cleaned his weapon. There was no need. He jokingly told people he couldn't hit the broadside of a flock of outhouses with it. It was, however, a head-turner on the big man's hip and inspired cooperation.

As it happens, the sheriff's favorite weapon was not his gun, but his intuition. He never called it a "sixth sense." Instead, he referred to it as a feeling, usually a bad feeling. He could look into a suspect's eyes and tell if he was lying—not if he was telling the truth, only if he was lying. The back of his neck got stiff when things did not feel right. He would rub it, wincing with pain, and proclaim he didn't like the look of things, never quite able to put his finger on the exact cause. As soon as Bridgett and Sidney left in the cruiser, the sheriff's hand went to the back of his neck. The feeling continued as he turned off the highway onto the Forest Service road that led to Sam's property. The sheriff was wearing his revolver.

⋅→═◉═◄⋅

Three sheriff's cruisers were parked haphazardly in the driveway, lights flashing. Bridgett, unconscious, her head wrapped in bloody bandages, was wheeled into an ambulance while Sidney cried uncontrollably in the sheriff's arms. Nick lay dead in the driveway, three feet back from where the bullet had struck him in the chest. The sheriff's ears rang almost painfully.

CHAPTER 70

June 2013

Sam listened intently before lifting his head. Wind. It hummed intermittently through something outdoors—trees perhaps. No other sounds offered hints of his surroundings. He needed to urinate. He had no idea how long he had been asleep. The distention of his bladder told him it had been some time. His fingers and toes burned with numbness. There were no birds, no planes, no traffic sounds. Just wind. The air was dry. He was pretty sure he was not in a basement—the ground floor perhaps. The wind humming through the trees was above him. He raised his head slowly. His throat was painfully dry. He tried to swallow. It was like swallowing razor blades. A faint odor, almost imperceptible, lingered just beyond his ability to make a quick association—the Willys, a chainsaw, a lawnmower. It was gasoline. The smell had not been there before, but it was unmistakably there now.

"Are you thinking you'll get a second chance?" Thompson said from somewhere behind him. There was a slight echo as though they were in an empty room with nothing to absorb the sound of his voice. "Personally, I don't believe in them. To me, a second chance connotes failure. What we have are options with an array of choices, each with a list of pros and cons. There are no second chances, Sam. You have to make do with your first choice, draw upon your past experiences before you can make that choice. If you don't look behind you, you can't see what's in front of you. Unfortunately for you, my friend, the choices you made were the wrong ones. The consequences of those poor choices don't go away. They're always there, lingering in the murky past, waiting for just the right time to pop up and surprise you."

Sam attempted to tell him that he had to pee. It came out garbled and unintelligible.

"I'll bet you need to see a man about a dog," Thompson said merrily. "Bleed the old lizard, take a whiz. I'll bet your back teeth are starting to float and your eyes are turning yellow. Well forget it, Sam. What I have in store for you will cause you to piss your pants in one last moment of terror and relief. Before death comes for you, you'll watch your beautiful daughter burn alive before your very eyes. I'll tape your eyelids open so you won't miss a thing. You'll hear the sizzle and pop amid the screams of agony. You'll smell hair burning, fat boiling beneath skin that's searing, and finally the odor of meat cooking. When death walks through the door, you'll beg him to take you to that dark place, to hustle you through that quagmire of pain and redemption. Near the end, I hope you'll ask yourself if your life was worth it. You shouldn't have to wonder if your contributions were real and lasting or simply the brief flailing of the proverbial actor upon the stage. I hope you can be honest with yourself as you breathe in the cold, eternal darkness that awaits you. Please know that I will be smiling, knowing that payment has been made, the debt fulfilled."

Sam snorted his skeptical response through his nose and shook his head slowly.

"If you're hoping I want to hear what you have to say, forget that too. I couldn't care less."

Sam heard Thompson begin to pace impatiently, grinding his shoes against the floor at the end of each straight lap. Finally he stopped—silence, then the soft tapping of a cell phone being dialed.

"Who's this?" Thompson demanded.

Sam sat straight and still to listen.

"Who? Where's my son, O'Malley? Put my son on."

Sam oriented toward Thompson, who was silent. He heard the flip phone click shut.

"It seems that our plans have changed somewhat, Sam. Nick, who was to deliver your daughter, has been delayed. Not to worry, my friend. I'll deal with her later. Rest eternally assured that she will follow you into damnation."

Sam inhaled deeply and dropped his chin to his chest. Nick, that traitorous bastard, had fooled him again. He had lied with total conviction. His relationship with Sidney from the very beginning had been a ruse. He had played both of them. His job all along had been to deliver Sidney and him to Thompson, who needed both to carry out his twisted plan. Sidney was safe with the sheriff. For Harrison to have Nick's cell phone was reassuring.

Liquid splashing, first to his right, then his left, in front of him, and behind him caused Sam to orient spasmodically to the sound of gasoline being poured on the floor and walls around him. The smell was overpowering.

"Here we go, Sam," Thompson said reassuringly as he untied Sam's blindfold. "Remember, I said you wouldn't want to miss this. That's half the fun, watching you react to your death. Suffering can be quite exhilarating. Now, one of the problems with being burned alive is that the victim typically runs out of oxygen or scorches his lungs and suffocates before experiencing the total effect of toasting nicely. I want you to roast slowly, or as they say at the gym, 'feel the burn.' So here is the very mask firemen wear when going into a burning building, complete with your own oxygen supply." From behind, Thompson placed the mask over Sam's head and pulled the adjusting straps securely to his face. "There we go. Comfy? I'll be right over there." To his right, Sam could just glimpse Thompson's hand pointing toward a window across the barren room. "I'll videotape your performance to show Sidney before I do the same to her. Now, let's see, what did I do with those matches? Oh, here they are," Thompson said as he stepped from behind Sam to face him. He held a book of matches out for Sam to see.

Instead, Sam gazed directly at Thompson's face. It was the first time he had seen him as himself. His features were typically Slavic—a pointy chin, high cheekbones, narrow eyes, broad forehead, and pasty complexion. He looked Russian, older than he had envisioned, altogether ordinary—like someone who could easily get lost in a crowd or a disguise.

Thompson tore a single match from the book. "It says, 'Close cover before striking.' Safety first, Sam. We wouldn't want to start a fire." He laughed, then smiled broadly at Sam. "You know, God has a nasty temper when provoked. Any last—"

A muffled shot came from outside, through the window glass. It struck Thompson in the back of the head. Blood, brains, and bone fragments sprayed against the clear face shield of Sam's mask before Thompson crashed to the floor at Sam's feet with a deadweight thud. A crimson pool of blood spread slowly from around his head. Without further warning, Sam's bladder released. Embarrassment quickly overrode relief and he was able to stop the flow, but not before a dark, wet blotch appeared on the right leg of his khakis. A gurgling sound came from Thompson's body. A door behind him opened and someone entered the room.

"Saaam," she said with her short vowel. "Long time no see."

CHAPTER 71
June 2013

Through the tops of pine and aspen, the night was filled with stars, bright flashes of heaven, as the Land Rover sped along the mountain road. The Milky Way arced luminously across the sky. Sam had no idea where he was and did not care. At one point, he saw the lights of civilization far below them, clustered in the center, less dense toward the edges. Valentina Thompson drove without speaking. Faint traces of her perfume drifted across the center console and the decades that separated them. Sam studied her outline in the green glow of the instrument panel. She was fifty-five and as beautiful as he remembered.

"You smell like pee," she said, her eyes on the road.

Sam rolled down his window a couple of inches. The heavy, night air swirled around them, a cold embrace that caused the hair on his arms to stiffen and made him shiver. "Sorry," he offered apologetically. "You smell pretty good for a dead woman."

Val flashed a fleeting smile through dark red lips. "It was plan. I give state secrets, they give immunity and protection. They say I must die before I start over."

"Hank too?" he asked.

"Agreement was for separate plans. I want protection from crazy partner. Everything blows up when Samuil die. Mother

Russia want me dead. Crazy husband want me dead. CIA could not control him or protect me. It was—"

"Samuil was my son?" he said, looking directly at her.

"*Nyet,*" she said softly, still staring straight ahead. "I want to tell you he was yours. There was no good in it. For you or me," she added. "It was very hard time. I had Nikolai to think of too. That day I come to see you in capitol, I come to say you have son. I chicken out. You married...little girl...What good was there?"

"I don't understand. Why would you..."

"Because I want him to be yours, not crazy husband's who force himself on me. I want start over, do again. I make bad choices when young. I want normal life, *E'merikan* dream, jes?"

"Are you sure? Thompson seemed pretty convinced. The DNA identification—"

"No DNA test. All Hank lies." She paused. "I tell him Samuil is yours to make him go away. Plan not work. He try to kill me, then you. Big mess."

"But that night..."

"That night you come to house, you drunk. I give you more beer, you pass out. Spend night on bathroom floor then go home in morning. Nothing happen. You still virgin."

"We didn't..."

"*Nyet.*" She turned and gazed at him sternly. "History now. You forget. Nothing to gain. Samuil is dead. Crazy husband is dead. I still have Nikolai. Hank fill him with lies about me."

"Does Nick know you are alive?"

Valentina nodded her head and smiled. "He's a good boy. He will join me in exile one day."

"Exile?"

"I have no country. I betrayed my homeland. I have nothing left to give this country. My death was part of cover-up. Relocation was final stage."

"Where?"

"Why? You come visit me?"

Sam turned away to keep from showing his amusement. She was the same Val he had known long ago, always putting him on the spot. He could see her folding napkins at the Left Hand Restaurant, bent over the table across from him, her cleavage beckoning the awkward busboy. He was still frightened by her. More than that, he was angered by all the things in the past he could not control.

"What about the honey trap?" The question was his way of lashing out at her.

"Old history. Not me. I do set up and run camera. Use local whores. Not me. I am still virgin, no?" She smiled and shot him a quick look. "You think I'm whore?"

"Val, I don't know what to think. I need time to process all of this. Your husband or partner, whatever he was, put my daughter and me through living hell these past two years because of the lie you told him. He murdered my ex-wife, for Christ's sake. He kidnapped my daughter. Twice! Then he tried to kill me." He glanced at her to see if she would respond. She did not. "To find out the woman I grieved is still alive…"

"You grieved me, jes?"

"Of course I did. I thought about you often over the years. I may have even been in love with you at one time. You seduced me. At least I thought you did. That's not easy to forget."

"Love?" she said, turning toward him again.

"I was young, impressionable, and horribly conflicted. You have no idea of the guilt I suffered all those years and the fear I had of being exposed. And now I find out it was all a lie. What am I to think? Your lies have caused me and my family unspeakable pain. What am I supposed to do about all this?"

"You can start by not being victim. This not all about you. Samuil was my son and I loved him more than you will ever understand. Crazy husband love him too. You think you mad? Hank mad more than you. He tried to kill me with nerve agent. I spend three weeks in Houston hospital. I'm glad to kill him. I save your life, jes?"

Sam stared at her in the subdued light. "Yes. Thank you," he said weakly. The five years between them had completely evaporated. She had been a woman when he was a boy. He had been a man, however, when he thought he finally had succumbed to her wiles and his impetuous hormones. Now, three decades later, it boggled his mind what that lapse in judgment, even though nothing happened, had cost him and those he loved. He had read once that the American male doesn't mature until he has exhausted all other possibilities. Deep down, he knew right from wrong. The mistake could not be taken back. "Thanks for the shirt" sputtered from his lips, coming from nowhere.

"What shirt?" She looked at him quizzically.

"The one you sewed when you were supposedly dying of cancer."

"I don't sew, never."

"Hank or Nick put it in my closet. It's corduroy with my initials on it."

She seemed to ponder that for a few moments. "Don't wear. Cloth trapped vapors of military-grade nerve agent, give secondary contamination. No antidote. Much worse than sarin. Body heat activate it. Absorbed through skin. Ask me how I know. You call hazmat for disposal. Very bad."

"This whole thing has been very bad," Sam said softly. He leaned forward and looked upward through the top of the windshield. The constellations were all in place. He had lost all sense of time and had no idea where he was. Still in the northern hemisphere, he reasoned. "Where are we?"

"We come to Steamboat Springs soon. Can get room, clean you up. Jes?"

"No, Steamboat is only two and a half hours from my place. I need to get home. My daughter…I need to call my daughter. Do you have a phone? What time is it?"

"No phone." She pointed toward the green numerals in the center of the dash.

He stared at the clock. The time did not register with him. The digital clock read five thirty-six. "Is it morning or night?"

"Morning," she said, then looked at him skeptically. "Is new day, Saaam." She pointed to the jagged, thin pink line that had appeared on the eastern horizon.

Sam inhaled deeply. "Is new day," he whispered and closed his eyes. He erased the horrors of the day and the image of Thompson's gruesome death, supplanting it with the thought of his homecoming with Sidney. The dawn of a new day, like new days everywhere, offered hope, not to start over, rather to begin anew. He knew there was no turning back. The past with all its ugliness was history. The future was being born on the other side of darkness and Sam was eager to greet it. He was determined to make the most of his second chance. He slept.

CHAPTER 72
June 2013

Sam, deep in thought, had said little during the remainder of the trip. He offered directions for the fastest route to Laramie and his Pole Mountain home. Conflicted, he had barely thanked Valentina for saving his life. His indebtedness and emotional history were clouded by the horrific events and consequences of her lies. Marcie was dead. Both he and Sidney had been traumatized, scarred for life, because of her. Valentina offered no apologies and showed no remorse. Sam was at a loss for words. He hated her.

Emergency vehicles were scattered across Sam's driveway when he and Valentina arrived. Undersheriff Piccard intercepted them. Seeing the panic on Sam's face, he said, "Your daughter is fine, Dawson. She's in the house. Nick Alexander, on the other hand, is dead. The sheriff shot him. Who's this?" he said, looking across the front seat at Val. Sam bolted from the car, nearly knocking Piccard down. He ran across the parking area—dodging people in various uniforms, and into the house, yelling Sidney's name.

"Dad!" Sidney sobbed as she rushed into his arms. "Dad!" she repeated as if attempting to convince herself that he was really there or, perhaps, as an exclamation of grief for Nick's death.

"I'm here. I know," Sam said, covering both possibilities. Sidney continued to cry.

When Sam returned to the driveway, Val was gone. He doubted he would ever hear from her again. Piccard said she had cried at the news of Nikolai's death. He again asked who she was. Sam did not respond. She had been spared seeing the body of her dead son, since the coroner had completed his investigation and transported the corpse to the morgue. Time and cause of death had been quickly determined. The medical examiner would take a look, but there was no need to send Nick's remains to the pathologist for an autopsy. Piccard said Harrison O'Malley had placed himself on administrative leave pending a full investigation. Sam had asked where his Willys was. "Greeley. Sheriff's impound," Piccard said brusquely, then turned his back and walked away. The undersheriff had disliked Sam ever since Sam decked him the day Annie was murdered, and the feeling was mutual.

It was dinnertime when the last sheriff's department cruiser left Sam's driveway. All that remained was yellow crime scene tape that warned the reader not to cross, a chalk outline of Nick's body surrounding a rust-colored pool of dried blood, and several small, numbered plastic tents placed on the ground where critical evidence was found. Sam had showered and changed clothes. He stood in the entryway of the mudroom looking out at the remains of the investigation. His stomach growled. He had not eaten anything since he and Val had split a box of Little Debbie snack cakes when they stopped for gas in Walden, just south of the Wyoming border.

Pans rattled from the kitchen behind him. "Are you hungry?" Sidney said flatly as Sam approached her.

"I could eat," he said, stuffing his hands in the front pockets of his jeans.

"I didn't thaw anything, so it's catch-as-catch can," she said without looking at him. She opened a tube of biscuits and a can of Dinty Moore Beef Stew. Sam set the table and fed L2 and Daisy. He busied himself. He did not know where to begin. Should he even tell her of the horrific fate Thompson had in store for both of them, and why? *It was over now,* he thought. *Let it be.*

They ate without conversation. Neither wanted to share what had happened to them. It was too soon. The words would come later. So would the hurt, the recriminations, sorrow, and pledges of new beginnings.

While clearing the table, Sam glanced at his fishing vest hanging next to the door and his fly rod leaning in the corner of the room. "You think a little brook trout therapy might help us?"

"Couldn't hurt," Sidney said, with a forced smile.

CHAPTER 73

July 2013

Sam's phone calls to Tommie in Berthoud, went unanswered at first. Gradually she allowed him back into her life, though with reservations that seemed insurmountable. He had hurt her once before and she believed he would do it again. He knew it would take time and effort to regain her confidence. Neither of them had mentioned Hank Thompson. Sam never would.

Often at night, with the Wyoming wind buffeting the house, he lay awake wondering why he felt compelled to renew his relationship with her. Guilt could not be ruled out. If it was indebtedness, would there be a final payment? If so, what was it? Could it be that he still loved her after all these years? Or was he attempting to move on after Annie? What were his intentions? Questions and answers that swirled in his mind made no sense when dawn came just a few hours later. He concluded he still had feelings for her. He had caused her pain and knew her wounds would never heal completely. He would not forget Annie, nor did he want to.

Sidney had asked him if he thought he was suffering from post-traumatic stress or simply midlife crisis with early-onset male menopause. She suggested that, in either case, professional counseling might help. She believed part of the solution was for him to immerse himself in work for profit. Sam was reluctant to admit she could be right on all counts. He secretly thought about therapy. But first, he would give fly fishing a chance.

⋯≡◎⧲⋯

Sam's drive to Berthoud was pleasant. Tommie had invited him to dinner at Western Pleasure, her antique store. Tommie had laughed that the table settings would consist of all the antiques she couldn't sell. It would be an early-twentieth-century exercise in etiquette.

The sign said closed. The door was unlocked. The bells overhead tinkled invitingly when he entered, the obligatory bottle of wine in his left hand. The smell of fresh-baked bread was almost overpowering.

"Just in time, Sam," Tommie said cheerfully from the back of the store, where she was arranging a table that Emily Post would have been proud of. "How was your drive down?"

"Good until Fort Collins, then traffic was somewhat heavy." Sam presented her with the wine, the bottle wrapped crudely with a piece of paper and a rubber band. He awkwardly attempted what he thought of as a polite hello hug.

Tommie looked at him strangely. "Relax, Sam. It's just dinner. What's this?" she asked, removing the rubber band and unfurling the paper with a child's drawing of a bus on one side and a penciled note on the other. She stared at the drawing for a long moment. "Yellow Blue Bus? I'm not sure I understand."

"It's what I had for wrapping paper," he lied. "Someday I'll explain."

He looked at the table in an effort to change the subject. It was perfectly set with fine china, about which he knew nothing.

He touched the edge of a plate hand-painted with a delicate floral pattern.

"Dresden," she said, smiling.

Sam scanned the table. He recognized a soup tureen, a gravy boat, bread plates, crystal stemware, and ornate flatware all beneath a giant chandelier. Troubled, he searched the table again, counting silently—three place settings. He looked at Tommie.

"My daughter that I told you about," she said lightly. "She's visiting from New York. She'll be joining us for dinner. I hope you don't mind."

"Mom"—a voice came from the back of the store—"I think the potatoes are done."

"Honey, come out here. I want you to meet someone," Tommie called over her shoulder.

Sam heard the rustling of dinnerware in the kitchen, then a woman appeared, pulling off an apron. She was neatly dressed, slender, in her early thirties. Her shoulder-length light brown hair was pulled loosely into a ponytail. She smiled broadly and approached Sam confidently. She had piercing blue eyes set in a familiar face. She looked like her mother.

Tommie turned to him with an intense look and a nervous smile. "Sam, this is my daughter, Samantha."

EPILOGUE
September 2013

In the movies, circling buzzards signal death below. Sometimes, Sam believed, the birds just liked to fly. From the deck, Sam and Sidney watched them go around and around above the valley below the house. Their muffled wings—spread over the thermals and updrafts from the uneven earth below, allowed them to spiral on the edge of those unseen currents in defiance of gravity. Their giant black bodies were held upward by the force of air rushing over their perfectly tilted wings, providing lift and reducing drag. Surrounded by blue sky, no frenzy of beating wings was needed to prevent a downward tumble to the unyielding earth, just a seemingly motionless balancing act of mass versus the laws of physics. Circles in the sky.

"It's a certain kind of poetry in motion," Sam said without looking at his daughter. Steam rose from the mug of coffee held between his hands.

Sidney pushed a wisp of hair away from her eyes as she turned toward him. "You mean, what goes around comes around?"

Sam managed a quiet smile. Time and togetherness—father and daughter—would heal their wounds. Each understood that forgiveness had to be earned. Sam loved his daughter. He was committed to regaining her trust and proving his self-worth. The new leaf he had to turn over was heavy. They would both bear scars, scars worn like badges of honor, proving their resilience and love for each other. Whether they faded over time would depend on the depth of their wounds.

"Like so many things in life"—Sidney said, looking up at the buzzards—"they have a kind of beauty from a distance. Up close, however, there's a sobering repulsion. Not even the Wyoming wind can cleanse them of their ugliness."

Sam sipped his coffee and stared into the distance of the mountain morning. That same Wyoming wind mesmerized him with the silvery flutter of aspen leaves in the valley below. He was unsure if the analogy she was implying referred to him or Nick. He had chosen not to tell his daughter about Nick's brother, Samuil. Sidney seemed indifferent to the fact that the alleged affair with Val never occurred. She knew the intent was there. If, however, she was referring to Nick, it was a mystery to Sam how the dead could be forgiven. Perhaps she had loved him. Sam was puzzled as to how she could love someone who obviously did not love her back. But like the rest of his family, Nick was a convincing liar. Resolving her feelings for him was one more thing that would take time.

Neither did he tell her about his near fainting spell when Tommie introduced her daughter, Samantha. He was still unsure if Tommie had named her after her grandmother as she claimed. What he was sure of, however, was that he and Tommie had never consummated their union. Sam could read in Tommie's eyes that she thought he had overreacted at meeting Samantha. She might have accepted his stuttering and momentary disorientation if she had known what he had been through with Hank Thompson.

Sam held Valentina responsible for Thompson's misguided vendetta. She had lied to her husband in order to hurt him. Sam wanted to believe she had not foreseen the collateral damage that would result. He would probably never know the truth. After all, the Thompsons were professional liars, perhaps the best he had ever encountered. Marcie was dead and he and Sidney were traumatized because of Val's lies. She could never be forgiven. He doubted he would ever be able to forgive himself for inadvertently subjecting his family to his youthful mistakes.

The voices of yesterday called only to him as if he had signed a pact with the Devil, who had wanted to collect his due. Sam would hold on. He would live with whatever unspoken guilt Sidney assigned to him, the consequences of his mistakes. They did not talk about it. Instead, they discussed the coming of winter, household chores that needed doing, and news of the world over which they had no control. Each day added a little more cheer on the surface. Privately, separately, they thought about the bond that exists between a parent and child, a bond that defies reason, an inexplicable bond that causes a son to defend the indefensible acts of a deranged father. Nick was a "good" son. He never stopped trying to gain favor with his father. Sam wondered if the same could be applied to his own relationship with Sidney.

Bridgett, Sheriff O'Malley's righthand woman, had awakened after several days. She was lucky Nick had not killed her. Her fractured skull left behind some facial paralysis, which no one seemed to notice. Upon her return to the sheriff's office, her fellow employees presented her with a football helmet featuring a gold sheriff's badge emblem on each side. She smiled and laughed and received hugs from everyone in attendance. She had cheated death.

In nearly thirty years of law enforcement, Harrison O'Malley had never discharged his weapon in the line of duty, much less taken a life. With the internal investigation and mandatory suspension over, he refused counseling. He announced he would not seek another term as sheriff. Sam gave him one of his old fly rods and promised to show him how to use it. It was the least he could do for the man who had saved his daughter's life. Sheriff O'Malley arranged for Nick to be buried at Fort Logan National Cemetery in Denver. The sheriff attended the ceremony and received the tricornered flag. Aside from the honor guard, he was the only one there.

The Denver police detective assigned to Marcie's murder wanted desperately to implicate Sam but could not refute his alibi. The police settled on a botched robbery attempt. It remained an open case with low priority and no suspects. No attempt was made to link her death with the unidentified charred remains of a man killed near Steamboat Springs.

"I'm driving the pickup to Denver this afternoon," Sidney said, bringing Sam back to the moment. "I have an appointment with Saul Katzenstein," she added, before Sam could ask why.

Sam nodded. Sidney had said nothing to him about settling her mother's estate, which he assumed was the reason for her meeting with Katzenstein.

"Did you know Mom was rich?"

He nodded again without speaking and turned his attention to L2 sprawled on the deck next to him, her white muzzle and bony hips showing her age.

Sidney stared at him, her head tilted slightly as if trying to figure out why her father, who had struggled to put her through college and did not have two nickels to rub together, had not asked her mother, a multimillionaire, for financial help. "Did you know I was the sole beneficiary of her estate?"

Sam had determined that she had already received some of her inheritance since the phone and utility bills had disappeared. One day she drove the truck to town for groceries and returned with a brand-new Ford three-quarter ton, four-wheel drive pickup.

Sam pondered her revelation for a moment. "What about Pat?" he asked with genuine concern for his ex-publisher, Marcie's husband.

"Apparently, Mom bought the publishing company a couple of years ago and promptly fired Pat so that he'd have more time to travel with her. Sort of a forced retirement, I guess. Anyway, Pat's okay. I understand he and Mom had taken out a hefty life insurance policy on her."

Sam pinched his chin between his thumb and forefinger at the realization that his daughter now owned the publishing house that had cancelled his contract six years earlier, leading to his impoverishment. "Do you want me to drive you down to Denver?"

"No, I'm fine, thanks. I promise to be back before dark," she added, sensing her father's concern for her night blindness. "Besides, you have an annual report to the County

Commissioners Association due at the end of the month. I'm anxious to see how you're going to convince them that photographing cemeteries in only two out of twenty-three counties in the past twelve months justifies contract renewal."

Sam looked upward. The buzzards were gone. He sighed with relief, smiled broadly at his daughter, and slowly shook his head. "It's been one helluva year, kiddo."

The End

ACKNOWLEDGMENTS

Birthing a book is a laborious process and usually not done alone. While the metaphor is obvious, it is still applicable to producing a book. From conception to gestation to parturition, the author is dependent upon others during the process of literary creation. Without the steadfast help of those who inspire, criticize, correct, and encourage, my books would never have been born. I am indebted to each of them.

Rachel Girt knows how to communicate. Her thoughtful recommendations allowed me to see what readers saw. Her sobering advice was honest and enlightening. Thank you, Rachel, for saving Sam.

Graphic design is often overlooked by authors and readers. Tana Stith knows how to get their attention. She reads the book from beginning to end, then creates an image that captures the attention of the potential reader. Tana, your covers and interiors jump off the shelves.

Editing is tough work. It's not for the faint at heart. Demanding is too easy of a description of the monotonous, eye-straining, brain-fatiguing work required to legitimize an author's creation. Kate Deubert does it with aplomb. She makes the unreal real with her relentless attention to detail and fact. Immersing herself in the story while surfacing to breathe helpful edits is a talent I've never achieved. You are amazing, Kate.

Daughters Tiffany, Melissa, and Amanda inspire and encourage me to keep writing. They find no fault in their father's stories even when they should. As always, they are the reason.

Wife Margaret—once a coach always a coach—never stops fine-tuning the efforts of the team and adding to the playbook. She works hard to ensure the best possible result while gently nudging me to do my best. When I resist, she tells me I'm her favorite author. What's not to love?

ABOUT THE AUTHOR

STEVEN W. HORN is the author of the award-winning novels in the Sam Dawson Mystery Series. An Iowa native and decorated Vietnam veteran, Horn earned his doctorate in Colorado. After high-ranking careers in both Colorado and Wyoming, he turned to full-time fiction writing, drawing upon his diverse educational and career experiences in crafting his stories. Horn's critically acclaimed debut stand-alone novel was *Another Man's Life. Yesterday Calling: A Sam Dawson Mystery* is Horn's fifth book in the mystery series. He lives in Wyoming.

CPSIA information can be obtained
at www.ICGtesting.com
Printed in the USA
LVHW030224210522
719225LV00004B/101

9 780999 124840